Praise for ~~Br~~
and *Two Cows* ~~for~~

"One of the most distinctive voices
in modern British fiction."
The Evening Standard

"A sharp stylist."
The Sunday Telegraph

"At a time of growing urbanism and reductive social interaction,
th delightful novel extols the simple virtues of landscape and
ove, a sentiment that is as important now as it was when
Benson first became a storyteller. Perhaps even more so."
The Independent on Sunday

"An adventure story written in Benson's distinctive,
flourish-filled style and suffused with his deep and
abiding love of the West Country."
Daily Mail

A coming-of-age novel that turns the plot of a thriller
into a lyrical celebration of the mysterious and enchanting
power of the natural world."
TLS

"A haunting tale of love, clairvoyance and cannabis."
The Guardian

Two Cows
and a
Vanful of Smoke

Peter Benson

ALMA BOOKS

ALMA BOOKS LTD
London House
243-253 Lower Mortlake Road
Richmond
Surrey TW9 2LL
United Kingdom
www.almabooks.com

Two Cows and a Vanful of Smoke first published by
Alma Books Ltd in 2011
This mass-market paperback edition first published in 2012
© Peter Benson, 2011

Cover design: nathanburtondesign.com

Printed by CPI Group (UK) Ltd, Croydon, CR0 4YY

ISBN MASS-MARKET PAPERBACK: 978-1-84688-177-0
ISBN EBOOK: 978-1-84688-216-6

Two Cows
and a
Vanful of Smoke

The author would like to thank the Royal Literary Fund for the generous support and assistance they provided during the writing of this novel.

1

I worked for a tree surgeon, fell out of an oak tree and landed on a dog. The dog bit my leg and its owner chased me down the street with her walking stick. The next day I realized I'd lost my nerve for climbing. I'd look at a branch or a ladder or a chainsaw and break into a sweat, so I told my boss I had to leave. He was a calm, good-natured man with a steel plate in his head, and on my last day he wished me luck and told me that if I ever got my nerve back I should call him. The next week I found a job on a pig farm. It was a good job, with plenty of opportunities to lean on gates and stare at fields, but I felt sorry for the pigs. They'd look at me and grunt and seemed to tell me that they needed to be free, so one evening I let six sows out and watched them disappear into a wood. They stood and blinked, did the twitchy things pigs do when they're not sure of their luck, and then they ran. Their big arses rolled and their ears flapped, and the last time I saw them they were barrelling through the undergrowth towards a stand of ash trees. I told the farmer that it wasn't my fault and I'd been busy in a barn, but he didn't believe me, gave me the sack and told me that if he ever saw me on his property again he'd shoot me. And he showed me his gun. He was serious but stupid, and that made me wonder. Wonder is stronger than stupid, so I walked and didn't go back.

At that time I was living at home, sleeping in a small bed under the eaves. There were posters of bikes on the walls, and my chest of drawers smelt of cheese. There was a worn carpet on the floor and curtains I didn't like. The window looked out over the village green, a quiet piece of grass with gardens behind and houses beyond them. The village is called Ashbrittle, but you wouldn't know it to see it. The houses are small, the hedges are tidy, the county border is up the road. It's a shy place, suspicious but knowing. It thinks for itself and has its own mind and heart and even soul, and when the night comes down and the stars shine and the weary traveller is lost in the darkened lanes that echo to their own whispers, it would be easy to think that the place was watching and waiting for the best time to do something unforgivable.

In those days Dad was a gardener and handyman. He worked for six or seven people, mowing lawns, pruning shrubs, sweeping paths, growing vegetables, painting sheds, building walls and mending fences. These six or seven people all had big houses, tidy potting sheds and fast cars, and he never did anything but a good job for them. He didn't know the Latin names of the plants he tended, but he had an instinctive and careful way of working. He drove a knackered Morris pick-up with broken suspension on the passenger side, so if you rode with him, you had to sit at a sloping angle while he compensated for the danger by leaning out of the window. He was always paid in cash, and on Friday he gave everything but twenty-five quid to Mum, who put the rest in a biscuit tin on top of the meat safe. With hands the size of plates, boots the size of small dogs and hair sprouting out of the end of his nose, and the same jacket on his back for fifteen years, he was a no-nonsense man with a no-nonsense voice. When he said something, it stayed said, like a rock in a field, or a tree.

Mum cleaned houses. Dusting, polishing, vacuuming, putting the rubbish out, sometimes doing some shopping for a posh widow in the village who couldn't walk more than five steps without falling over and breaking a bone. She rode a bicycle to work, an old bone-shaker with a basket and triangles of fabric over the back wheel so her skirt didn't get caught in the spokes. She always smelt of beeswax and dust, and wore a housecoat even when she was watching the television. She was quiet and thoughtful, and never raised her voice when Grace or I came home late.

Grace, my sister, was at college in Taunton, studying to be something to do with food and cooking. Sometimes she stayed in town, but when she stayed at home she'd try out new recipes on us. There'd be beef with Guinness and prunes, chicken with apricots, pork with nuts. I once asked her why she needed to muck around with food, and she told me that if I didn't like it I didn't have to eat it, so I never said anything about her cooking again. She's got a sharp tongue on her, and I prefer not to take a lashing.

So the week after I was sacked from the pig farm I sat in my bedroom, looked at the fields and trees, listened to the radio and stroked the cat. She was called Sooty, and could be a nervous, jumpy animal, but she was good with me. I was twenty-one years old, but that's got little to do with anything.

I could have been twenty-four. It wouldn't have made any difference to what happened. Or nineteen. Nothing would have
changed. That evening, Dad came back from work and told me
that Mr Evans was looking for help. His farm was a couple of
miles away outside a tiny village called Stawley, above a high
and narrow lane. "Labouring," he said. "Tractoring, milking,
the usual. You know how to milk?"

"You know I do."

"Then go and see him. If you don't, someone else will."

Dad is good at the obvious. Mum is good at being less than
obvious. Three hundred years ago she would have been dragged
from the house, accused of cursing a crop of cabbages, tried by
a mob, found guilty of everything bad that had ever happened
anywhere in the parish and burnt alive on the village green. Even
now there are people in the village who cross the road when they
see her or the cat. She was taught stuff by her mother, who was
taught stuff by her mother, who was taught stuff by her mother,
and so on until we don't know who taught who what. When I say
"stuff" I mean the old signs nature gives, the ones that everyone
used to know but most people have forgotten. And beyond the
old signs, sometimes she gets hunches – superstitious feelings,
some people would say. Hunches about things that are about to
happen, intuitions and insights. And beyond the insights, she
sometimes does things that other people would call spells. She
calls them charms. Mum has told me that she's seen some of the
old signs in me, and I was born with a gift I don't recognize yet.
Every now and again she gives me a hint about something, an
old story or the idea behind one of her charms. And although

she wouldn't tell me why she bought a calf's heart and speared it with thorns and hid it in the chimney, before I went to see Mr Evans she said, "Put some apple pips in your shoes." The idea is that the pips will sweat and sprout, and their sprouting will mean that your life will sprout and whatever you wish for will grow. So I did as I was told, and put the pips in my shoes and went to see Mr Evans.

He was a small man with a drooping mouth and marshed, watery eyes. His teeth were small, and he spoke slowly with a soft, slurry accent. Dad said he'd had a stroke, and that was why he was looking for a worker, but I wasn't curious. I wanted a job. The farm was eighty-five acres of pasture and copse, a herd of Friesians, a few sheep dotted at the edges, a ramshackle collection of barns and a low, squat house with small windows and a fireplace in every room. Mr Evans lived alone in the house, and after he'd written down a list of the things I'd have to do, he pointed at a caravan in the corner of the front yard and said, "You can live there. It's small, but it's got a bed and a cooker."

"Thanks."

"If you want the job…"

"Let me have a look."

"You do that."

I stood in the caravan. It was small and smelt of damp wood and old apples. The windows were dirty, and the floor was covered in dead flies. There was a sack of rotten potatoes in the place where a toilet should have been. I looked at the sack and it seeped at its corners. For no reason I thought about

Christmas and a harmonica I was given when I was six. I
blew it and frightened the cat into a musical panic. "I'll need
someone here day and night," Mr Evans said. He had a polite,
old-fashioned way about him, but I knew he could be strict. He
liked things done his way, the way his father had done them and
his grandfather before then. I thought for a couple of minutes.
I wanted to leave home, so I said, "Yes, I want the job," and
he said, "Good. You can start tomorrow," and I moved in the
next day. There was no electric in the caravan, but there were
gaslights that ran from a big blue bottle. They hissed when I
lit them and gave off a weird smell. I brushed the floor, cleaned
the windows, threw the potatoes away, and Mr Evans gave me
a chemical toilet and a hosepipe. I put my radio by the bed
and cleaned the cooker, then went to watch the herd being
milked. They were used to Mr Evans's hands, so I kept back
and watched. He called each cow by her name – "Daisy…
Florence… Jo… Fizzy…" and went through the routine with
patience and care. Feeling the back of their udders, washing
the teats, stroking the legs, whispering to the nervous ones.
Flipping the clusters onto the teats and watching the first of the
milk pulse through the line. Along the row to check the ones
that were halfway done, back to the ones that were finishing.
Off with the cluster, a dip of iodine and lanolin on the teats,
a hand up to open the exit gate and another was in.

He listened to the radio while he worked, a music programme
with old-fashioned singing, and hummed along to some of
the tunes. Once or twice he stopped to rest his hands on his
knees and take a breather, but that was the only time when he

showed his age. The rest of the time he didn't miss a trick. He loved his work, loved his cows, loved the sound of the milk as it pulsed through the lines to the tank, and he loved the smell of water and cattle cake. He'd almost finished when a cat came and walked down the parlour, rubbing itself against the stalls, tail quivering, head up. Mr Evans had been expecting it. "You're late," he said, and went to the dairy. He came back with a saucer of milk, put it on the floor by the door, and said, "Get it while it's warm…"

"That's the most important part of this job," he said.

"What's that?"

"Never forget the cat."

"OK," I said. "I won't."

When he'd finished, I washed down the stalls and the pit while he cleaned the clusters and rinsed the lines, and then he told me to follow the herd down to the pasture. Their hooves kicked up clouds of dust, and flies buzzed in their wake. The world was parched and a touch anxious, as if it were waiting for something but didn't know whether the something was sweet, shadowy or lost between the two.

I stood and watched as the cows spread out and started to graze. The sun was setting. Rooks were clattering in a hanger, cawing from their perches and collapsed nests. Rags of black feathers, grey feet and grey beaks, the bad birds of the trees. I like their calls, and I like the lazy way they fly for home, but I don't like their habits. Quarrelsome and lousy, I've heard people say that they only breed near money. If that's true, what were they were doing in those trees? But that's the trouble with what people say. One thing means one thing or it could mean another. I turned and walked back to the caravan, climbed onto my bike and rode to The Globe.

The Globe at Appley was a pub, but it was more like a house. You walked in the front door and into a corridor, and a fat woman with purple legs served the drinks from a hatch in the corridor. There was a bench you could sit on and a room with a dart board. She was a strict woman, and would have you out of there if you cursed God or said something about the Queen she didn't agree with, so I bought my beer and went to sit in the porch. I'd been there half an hour when Spike turned up. He was fresh from work at the blackcurrant farm, where he'd been spraying. He smelt of chemicals and had a bad cough. He fetched a pint, drank it in gulps and closed his eyes. I'd been to school with Spike, so we'd known each other for years. I suppose that if I'd been a hare he'd have been a fox, and we'd have met in a deserted quarry to fight. I'd have tried to box, but he'd have run rings around me, over the granite slabs and back again. He was wiry and had quick eyes, like he was always expecting something to happen. The veins stuck out in his neck, and one of his ears was a bit deformed. I think it had been caught in a door when he was a kid.

That evening he was quieter than usual, thinking, in the way he does, about something stupid. He always had a scheme going, a plan to make money, an idea that would get him away from the blackcurrant farm or wherever he was working that week. "All I need is a few grand, then I'll be out of here…" How many times have I heard that line? How many times has he decided that he could make his fortune by driving old cars to Morocco and selling them, or digging fossils out of the cliffs at Lyme, or inventing a new way to strip blackcurrants from a bush, or stealing a flock of ewes from a field on the way to Kittisford and selling them to a man he says he knows in Wales? I don't think he knows anyone in Wales, but there's always a chance. Me? I know no one in Wales, and even if I did I wouldn't sell him a ewe, a lamb, a cow or a pig. Me, I don't have any schemes. I was quite happy to do my work and go back to the caravan and stare out of the window and dream.

"What you thinking about, Spike?"

"This and that." He rolled a cigarette, lit it and watched the end glow. He blew smoke at me. I turned away and, as I did, a man and a woman on bicycles appeared. They were wearing matching jackets and had busy-looking bikes with canvas satchels, flashes and clips. They looked up at the pub sign, and the man said, "Fancy one?"

"OK," said the woman, and after they'd parked their bikes they asked to be excused as they passed us and went into the pub.

When they were inside, Spike said, "El?"

"What?" I said.

"Can you keep a secret?"

"That depends. What is it?"

"Well, I don't know if it's a real secret. Not yet, anyway. But I saw something today."

"You saw something?"

"Yes."

"What?"

"The boss and I had to go to Clayhanger. He wanted me to drive a tractor back from old Harris's. You know the place?"

"Harris at Moat Farm?"

"That's it. So we were up there, and after the boss dropped me off I drove back along this track that goes around behind Heniton Hill."

"That's just up from us."

"I know." He looked into his drink. "So as I'm driving along, the tractor stops. Stalled, it did, so I get down and I'm trying to crank it up again when I see this bloke I haven't seen before. And I know most people round here…"

"So?"

"He was walking through the trees with tools over his shoulder."

"Tools?"

"Yeah. A hoe and rake. Long-handled. Looked like he knows where he's going."

"And did he?"

"What?"

"Know where he was going?"

"I reckon he did, but it didn't bother him. I had work to do. I got the tractor going and drove back, but all afternoon, you know, I was thinking about him. Fucking beast of a bloke. And there was something odd. Like he didn't belong there, I suppose."

"And that's the secret?"

"No. There's more…" Spike finished his drink and I finished mine. "Want another?"

14

"OK." And while he went inside, I listened to the sounds of the dying day and the bleating of sheep in a field on the other side of the road. There was a heat in the evening that wouldn't let the day go. I heard the landlady scolding someone for talking about politics. I listened for a moment, then stood up, strolled into the lane and stared at the hedge. Spike came back with two pints and we climbed up the bank behind the pub and sat at a table.

"So," I said. "There you are. Under Heniton Hill…"

"Yeah. Went back, didn't I? Went back this evening. Had a little snoop."

"Nothing you like more."

He looked at me, and for a moment I thought he was going to hit me. He's not the sort of bloke who'll let you take the piss. He's got a short temper, and although he'd always come back and apologize if he did hit you, the risk isn't worth taking. He's got a punch like a whip, and he'd never leave you with just one.

"Of course…" And he said he'd parked in a lay-by and strolled down to where he'd seen the stranger in the trees. He had a story ready. Spike always has a story ready, and if anyone wanted to know what he was doing he was going to say something about a couple of ewes escaping from his boss's field and ask, "Have you seen 'em? I saw them heading this way."

So he went into the trees, found the path the stranger had followed and walked for half a mile. He crossed a small stone bridge over a stream and came to a fork in the path. One way climbed towards a distant house, the other dropped further into the woods. "It was weird down there," he said. "I didn't hear any birds, no wind, no nothing. It was as quiet as the grave, you know. All I could hear was my breathing and my footsteps. The path got narrower and narrower. It looked like it was a secret, but still it was used a lot. I was just starting to think that I should turn around and go back when I heard something."

"What?"

Spike put a finger to his lips and lowered his voice. "I crouched down and looked down the path. It finished in a clearing. The bloke I'd seen the day before was there, standing in front of a hoop house."

"A hoop house? Like a plastic greenhouse?"

"Yes."

"What's he doing with a hoop house?"

"Fuck knows," said Spike, "but that's what we've got to find out. He dived inside and I came back. I don't know. I didn't want to hang around on my own. He looked like he could be a bit useful."

"A bit useful?"

"Oh yes."

"And we've got to find out?"

"Of course."

"Why?"

"Because…"

"We've got to find out what some ape is doing in a hoop house in the middle of the woods…"

"I never said he was an ape."

"But you said he was useful."

"I can handle useful…"

There's no point in arguing with Spike when he's in one of these moods. It's best to let him go with it, so I sat back and listened while he told me that we were going to find out exactly what some bloke was doing in a hoop house in the middle of the woods.

"We?"

"You owe me, El."

This was true. Earlier in the year we'd been drinking in Wellington, and I'd told someone in the pub that he was talking crap about the beer I was drinking. He said it tasted like piss, and I said the thing about crap. Sometimes I do speak my mind, but Spike lets his fists speak his mind, which is, when it's not planning some madness, usually idling in neutral. When the someone said, "You want to say that again?" I said, "OK," and did. Spike was the other side of the bar, but he can sense trouble even if it's taking a day off in Minehead. "You OK?" he said, suddenly next to me with an empty glass in one hand and the other in his pocket. He looked very relaxed.

"Yeah," I said.

"This your mate?" he said, and the bloke who thought my beer was piss took a step back.

"We were just talking about beer…" I said.

"And you can't fight your own corner?" said the bloke.

"Did you say fight?" said Spike, and before I could stop him he'd spun the bloke around and was pushing him towards the door. I didn't see what happened next, but by the time I was outside the bloke was lying on the floor and Spike was rubbing his fist. "Want another?" he said.

The bloke shook his head.

"I'm ready."

"Forget it."

"Forget it?"

"Yeah."

This wasn't the only time Spike had stepped in for me. There was the time at Appley Fair when someone said I was looking at his woman, and the time someone's sister asked me if I liked parsnips and I said I hated them. If you asked me why he does it I suppose I'd have to say that we make some sort of partnership, like in a film about opposites walking across a desert to find hidden treasure. He's the bloke who never quite gets it, and I'm the one who thinks before he does anything. He goes, I wait. He tells, I ask. He grinds his teeth, I brush mine. I ride a Honda 250, which is half-bike, half-horse. He drives a van with a loud tape deck and a steering wheel the size of a small dish. He meets girls, spends a weekend or two with them, tells them that he's bored and finds another. I look at girls and wonder if I can open my mouth before I start dribbling. When I look at him I'm pleased he's my mate and we've managed to get this far together.

"Sometimes," he said, "when I look at you I wonder if you've got any balls at all."

"What do you mean?"

"You know what I fucking mean."

"No I don't."

"And I was thinking…"

"Thinking what?"

"When do you want to do this?"

"Do what?"

"You know what. Find out what that bloke's up to."

"I don't know."

"Tonight," he said. "I'm going up there tonight."

"Tonight?" I said, and as the word dropped, I heard a distant croak, the call of a single raven. The big bird, the black bird, the one my mother tells me to watch for. He used to have white feathers, but he stole the sun, and that's why his feathers are black. And when he flies he leaves scars in the clouds. "Beware," I whispered. "Be careful."

"Of what?"

"The raven."

"You fucking weirdo," said Spike, and then, "you coming or you going to be a chicken for the rest of your life?"

"OK," I said, "but let's be careful."

"Aren't I always?"

I said nothing.

2

The summer had been mad. It had been like a badger caught in a tarred barrel, fed on chilli and forced to listen to chanting monks. Later, when the records were examined and weathermen met to drink glasses of lemonade and talk about their business, they would say that 1976 had been Britain's longest, hottest summer ever. And they meant it. Day after day after day the sun shone in deep blue skies and baked the land dry. It was hot before it rose, and when it rose it laughed at the country. On the moors and heaths, fires broke out and frightened animals from their holes. Trees were burnt to sticks, lakes dried, bushes exploded, crops failed. In other places tarmac melted and birds failed in their flight. Hosepipes were banned, stand-pipes were used, wells and springs dried up. Politicians told us to share bath water. Ashbrittle wheezed and sweated, and in the middle of the day, dogs collapsed in the road and refused to move. The green browned and yellowed, and flowers withered. Cows lay in the shade of trees, horses panted, fish died and floated in rivers that turned to drains. Every day people would stand in their gardens and stare at their parched vegetables and search the sky for rain. Sometimes a single cloud would appear and float slowly over the village, but it was always a single cloud, white and fluffy – and nothing. And as it disappeared over the horizon, the people would shake their heads and go back inside and do whatever they had to do.

One day I was out walking and found a dead rabbit in a field below the church. I don't know why it had died, but there it was, dried to a crisp beneath a tree, flat as a postcard, lying in the cover of the exposed roots. I picked it up and held it in front of me. It didn't bend and it didn't smell, and I thought about taking it home and propping it against the wall outside the kitchen. There was a hole where one of its eyes had been, and its mouth had contorted into a manic grin. It would have confused the cat, so I didn't take it home, but the thought was there, a dry thought that walked with the weather and sun.

The days boiled, and at night the heat thickened and dripped. People lay naked under single sheets, windows open, curtains open. Sleep came in fits, and the dreams that followed the fits were filled with water and cool winds. Mr Evans's caravan, my caravan, was hotter than a threat, and when I went to bed sweat crawled over my skin. It dribbled and gnashed and left its marks in my creases, and whispered fumes in my ear. The walls and roof of the van squeaked and groaned, exhausted flies buzzed and banged against the windows, mosquitoes whined and bit.

When Spike and I left the pub, we stood in the heat of the evening and wondered if the weather would ever change. I said that I thought it had stuck and we were stuck with it, and there was nothing we could do. Spike said I was talking bollocks. I told him that my bollocks was no more bollocks than his bollocks, and we arranged to meet at half-nine in the lay-by under Heniton Hill.

I rode up to see Mum and Dad, taking the right at Appley school and into the wooded valley at Tracebridge. In the old days, a witch used to live in a wattle hut by the river bridge at Tracebridge and demand payment from passing travellers. She'd curse and rave and shake her clawed fists, and if they didn't give her a coin they'd never get up the hill. Their legs would seize and their eyes would tear, or their horses would stop and refuse to go any further, or a wheel would fall off their cart, roll over the bridge and fall into the river. When she was bored and there were no passing travellers, she'd turn herself into a weasel and steal chickens from farms. Old and cruel and vindictive, she'd eat the chicken raw and hang its sucked bones around her neck. The witch is dead now, and her hut was burnt to the ground by relieved carters, but there's the sense of something by the bridge, a waiting malevolence in the air that stops dogs and freezes rabbits. I rode by with my head down, didn't glance in the direction of the place where the hut used to stand, accelerated for the long drag up the hill to Ashbrittle, and sat back on the bike when I reached the top.

Mum was ironing shirts and Dad was dribbling washing-up water onto the lettuce in the garden. I stood at the front-room window and looked out. A hippy was standing on the green, her head tipped back, staring at the sky. She was wearing a spotted scarf on her head, baggy shorts, a tiny T-shirt and sandals. The hippies lived in the Pump Court cottages by the bakery. I call them hippies because everyone else does, but

22

that's the only reason. They could have been called something else, but they weren't. I suppose it helps to give people names and put them in groups; it means you can feel safe and know where you and they stand. Sometimes Spike and I would go up and stand behind the hedge and watch them, but we never saw them do anything very interesting. They never took all their clothes off and rolled in mud. They never sat in circles and played guitars. They never walked out in the middle of the night and sang to the stars, and they never had crazed parties that lasted all night. They were quiet people and although we wished they would do shocking things they never did, so Spike and I would go and find something else to watch or do. Not that there's a lot of something else to do in Ashbrittle. A vicar closed all the pubs down years ago, there's no shop and no bus stop. There is a phone box, and anyone can spend half an hour in there, or you can read the notices for things on the noticeboard outside the village hall. These things are usually to do with coffee mornings or jumble sales or the mobile library, and although the village is famous for a few things, you never see them mentioned on the noticeboard.

One thing Ashbrittle is famous for is the yew in the church-yard. The tree grows from a small burial mound, and some people say it's the oldest living thing in the country. It was a thousand years old when Jesus was born, and it's collected more memories and ideas than any living thing on earth. It's broad and green and split, and its trunks are cracked. It's been home to millions of insects and birds and squirrels, and the patch of ground beneath its branches is pale and soft. I know old men who bow to the yew, and women who touch the hems of their skirts as they pass. The old traditions might be dying and the old memories fade, but that's all they do. They still echo in the air, like the ghosts of flags.

Another thing the village is remembered for is the story of Professor Hunt and his skin experiments with a woman he kidnapped and kept in a run-down farmhouse beyond Marcombe Lake. The house is a ruin now, but the place has a haunted air to it, and when we were kids we'd dare each other to go down there and spend an hour alone in the shade of the broken walls. We imagined that they sighed and moaned at our passing, and held secrets we couldn't even imagine. And when we were kids, imagination was fruit to us, sweet and juicy and ripe.

If you haven't heard of the yew or Professor Hunt, you might have heard of Lord Buff-Orpington. His family used to own almost all the houses in the village and most of the land, and although the estate has now been reduced to a few fields and Belmont Hall, older people still doff their hats to him and stand back to let him pass. I don't know how old he is, maybe eighty, but he doesn't look it, and he never acts the lord. There are rumours about him, rumours that he is a man of few morals and has even committed murder, but I don't know if I believe them. Rumours are just that, and he's always seemed OK to me. I've spoken to him a few times, and he always says hello first, asks if my work is going well and tells me to give his best to Mum and Dad. I don't suppose it's his fault that he's a lord, and I think he's always done his best for the village, but maybe he hasn't. I don't know. I can't tell. That's not my job.

He once wrote a memoir, the story of his life and the story of his family. He called it a confession, and it was a best-selling book, a book of history, love, troubles and family, and when Mum borrowed it from the travelling library she finished it quickly and let me read it before she took it back. It was divided into chapters that didn't appear to be related to each other, and these were given titles like 'Gardeners' 'The Fondue' and 'The Village Fête'. There was a chapter entitled 'Mother' that stuck in my mind, and although it was tragic, it made me laugh. I suppose that might be one of the secrets of good writing; make sure it swings like a pendulum in a storm. So this chapter started like this:

My mother, Lady Patricia Buff-Orpington, was born a Stafford-Heinz. Her father was a personal friend of Edward Elgar, and believed she had made a good match, but her mother threatened to shoot my father with her cousin's revolver because he wasn't from Worcestershire. My one regret is that I never met my maternal grandmother. She was killed in a freak heron-baiting incident five weeks before my birth, but if I'd had the pleasure, my pleasure would have been to stick a fork in her ear. By all accounts she was an objectionable snob of a woman, and deserved to die impaled on the beak of an angered ardea cinerea.

So the mother the devil, the daughter the angel. My mother was a saint, a courtesan of the soul, the sort of person who made lover's lane safe for lovers. I keep her picture by my bed, and when I look at it, this is what I see: she is sitting on a gilt chair beside my father. He is standing with his right hand tucked into his waistcoat and, although he cuts a handsome and distinguished figure, he's a shadow beside her. The photograph was taken in 1932, and she stares with sharp lips and an intelligence that left half her suitors gibbering. The rest simply gave up, apart from Father, who was made of sterner stuff. He would not be put off. He determined to marry the most beautiful woman he had ever met, and after two and a half years of intense pursuit that involved both sidling and the use of landaus, he won her.

There was a time when I thought I could go to university and become the sort of person who could write like this and talk about stuff on the radio, and although the time didn't last long, it was real enough. The idea was born from reading *National Geographic* magazines, Haynes car manuals, atlases, bird-watching manuals, Grace's cook books and novels from the travelling library. And when I read Lord Buff-Orpington's memoir, I was inspired. Inspired to be more than who I was born to be, inspired to see the world, inspired to get my own place. I just never thought it would be a caravan in a farmyard.

I think Mum was sad I'd moved out, and said she couldn't believe a caravan in a farmyard would be more comfortable than my own room. And she said, "I smelt fire in the air this morning, but no one was burning anything." She rubbed her eyes. "Be careful."

"Of what?"

"I couldn't tell. But you know what smelling fire means."

"Of course," I said. In her world it means trouble, madness or danger. "And I'm always careful."

"Are you?"

"Yes Mum."

"I'll believe that when I see it," and she kissed me and ruffled my hair and went back to her cooking. I went to sit on the wall and watch Dad work, and he said that he didn't think the weather was going to break soon, and the way the birds were behaving told him they were in for a hungry autumn and a long winter. They weren't singing as loudly as they usually did, and they weren't flying as madly. He asked me if I was staying for tea, but I said I had to go back to the farm.

"Everything going OK down there?"

"Yes thanks."

"Evans treating you all right?"

"Yes. He's a good bloke. Doesn't say a lot, but then I don't suppose he has to."

"Good," he said, and after I'd watched him for a little longer I headed off to meet Spike. I waited for ten minutes, and when he turned up he parked the van in the verge, said, "Ready?" and we headed into the trees.

The path was exactly as he'd described it and, when we reached the bridge and the stream, he stopped and cocked his head at the sky. Nothing rustled, the wind was warm and still, the water tinkled like coins in a pocket. I stood behind him, listening to my breathing.

"This way..." and we headed down, further into the woods. The path was narrow, but well used. Here and there, branches had been sawn off and thrown into the undergrowth. In the old days, when Spike and I were at school, we used to go on adventures all the time, exploring derelict houses and old barns, building dens out of branches and moss, and finding new ways to make weapons out of sticks and feathers. "Remember the time..." I started to say, but he stopped suddenly, put a finger to his lips and pointed through the trees. Twenty-five yards away, I could see the edge of a hoop house. "There," he said, and we crouched down and waited. We waited and listened. A distant barking dog, another dog answering the first, the first answering the second. After five minutes, he stood up and beckoned me to follow. We placed our feet carefully, watched for dry sticks and crackling leaves and squeaky mice. When we reached the clearing, we scurried down the side of the hoop house to the far end, and waited again.

The far end of the hoop house had a roped-up opening. Spike started undoing the rope from the bottom. I stood guard, and when the opening was large enough he ducked inside. I watched his crouching shadow. Then he stood up. He stood up slowly, like weights were attached to his neck. A moment later I heard the sound of a low, quiet whistle. Silence. Another whistle. "Fuck..." he whispered. His head shook. Silence. "Oh fuck."

"Spike?" I said, and as I said his name he suddenly dropped to his knees and said nothing, and the distant dog stopped its barking. I listened once and I listened twice. I listened for another bark, but none came. I listened for anything, another curse, another whistle, the call of a raven. But nothing. Everything was quiet. I could have been standing in a place where sound was swallowed by giants and the world spun slowly like a head on a pole.

3

I once had a dream in which the world was a head on a pole and all the other planets were heads on poles, and the sun was a head of fire. Its flares and gases were hair, and its spots were eyes and mouth. It spoke to me in a language I didn't understand, and when I woke up I was hot and sweating, and felt a burning behind my eyes. I suppose someone could tell me what such a dream meant and try to persuade me that I'd read too many *National Geographic* magazines. Not that I've ever read anything in a *National Geographic* magazine about the idea that the solar system is made up of heads on poles, but I'm sure there's a tribe somewhere who believe this is so. Or maybe not. I'm not sure. I don't know. There are many tribes in the world, and some of them believe the strangest things. Anyway, at that time in the woods I felt the pole slow and the head open its mouth, and the silence thickened, turned in on itself and curdled into the ground. I could smell it there, turning the earth red in its palm, creeping against the roots of the trees and bushes and scrub. I thought about the time I sowed cress on a flannel and put it on a window sill when I was a kid, and I came home from school wanting to know if it had appeared. I needed to see, I wanted to know, and Mum said, "Be patient, Pet. It'll grow soon." Now I whispered "Spike? Spike? What's going on?" He didn't say anything and I heard a rustle from inside, beetles on a cold stone floor, claws against slate, wings against glass. "OK... I'm coming in..." and I pushed the opening to one side, ducked down and stepped into the hoop house.

It's difficult to know what was more powerful, the sight or the smell. Wait. It's easy to describe the sight, not so easy to describe the smell. The sight. Dope. Cannabis. Weed. Smoke. Twelve long rows of perfect plants, their flower heads about to burst and their leaves heavy with resin. The smell. It was heady and sickly, enough to send your head into a screw. I took a shallow breath, held it and rolled my eyes.

Spike was still on his knees, looking up at the roof of the hoop house. His lips were moving slightly, and his eyes were half closed. He could have been praying. I think he was praying. I think he'd seen his god. His fingers were touching the plant closest to him, gently stroking the leaves. He leant towards the leaves. They touched him.

"Spike?"

He murmured something.

"Hello? Spike?"

He opened his eyes and said, "Can you see what I can see?"

"Yes."

"Have you ever... have you ever seen anything like it?"

"No."

"I'm stoned just smelling them."

"I'm stoned just looking at them."

"I'm stoned."

"Stoned..."

"I'm stoned..."

He reached up and stroked one of the flower heads, licked his fingers and sucked his teeth. "Oh God…"

"Good?"

"This is fucking amazing," he said, "unbelievable." He sucked his teeth. "Have you ever seen anything like it?" He looked at me, and I saw something in his eyes I'd never seen before, a split and the look of a man who's felt the touch of a ghost in the back corridor of a tumbled house. A house with broken tiles and smashed windows, and drafts blowing down. And as the words dropped from his mouth, I heard the sound of footsteps, broken sticks and kicked leaves. I put a finger to my lips and he said, "What?" and I hushed him and he said, "What?" again.

"Someone's coming," I whispered.

He cocked his head. "Shit."

"Sshhh…"

"Na…"

"Quiet…"

"Where?"

"Spike!"

"What?"

"Quiet!"

And the footsteps got closer, the leaves flew and dropped and I heard voices. We ducked down and I scrabbled to the opening at the back of the hoop house. I pushed through the plastic and looked back towards Spike, but he wasn't moving. He was still staring at the plants, transfixed by their size and their leaves and their buds and their smell, and it was only when I picked up a stone and threw it at him that he snapped out of wherever he was and turned to leave. And the footsteps got closer and now the voices were louder.

Spike appeared with a stupid, knowing smile on his face. A smile? Now, looking back and knowing what I know and seeing what I've seen, the smile was beyond pleasure, and had moved into something wilder. I should have said something then, should have spotted the signs, but I started to fasten the opening rope and he sat on the ground and chuckled to himself. I put a finger to my lips. I shook my head. The footsteps stopped, and a low, deep voice said, "Almost ready…"

We backed into the undergrowth, ducked down and waited. Spike nudged me, smiled, opened his hand and showed me a fistful of sticky buds. He opened his mouth to say something. I put my hand up and covered his mouth and watched as the outlines of two men appeared in the hoop house. They stood together, and the deep voice said, "I reckon we'll give them another week."

The other man grunted.

"You want to take some away?"

"No."

"I've got some ready at the house. Best pick of the crop for now."

"Leave it there. I'll collect the lot next week."

The men moved slowly, stopping here and there to look at the plants and make a comment. When they reached the end, the one with the deep voice said, "What the fuck?" and stooped to look at the rope that tied the opening.

"What?"

33

"It wasn't like this."

"Wasn't like what?"

"I ribbon-tied it."

"What are you talking about?"

"The fucking rope," said the deep voice, and he started to untie it.

"Back…" I hissed at Spike, and I scrabbled backwards, further into the undergrowth, the spikes of a blackthorn ripping at my face, me tugging at Spike's shirt until he moved, and we were as far in deep shadow as we could be. "Get down…" and I lay flat, pulling him down beside me. Here, with my face pushed into the earth I could feel the curdling earth again, smell its worry and hear the sounds of ants rushing for cover and dark. A moment later the gap in the hoop house opened and a beast of a man stepped out, flexed and stood twenty-five yards from my nose.

He was six foot one or two, with thick black hair and hands the size of bricks. He was dirty, with streaks of earth on his face and arms, and his boots were scuffed and old. Jeans, check shirt, a wide leather belt, and his breathing was heavy and slow. His eyes were pushed back in his head and were the smallest thing about him. Little black slits they were, but I got the feeling that they wouldn't miss a thing. A moment later he was joined by the other man, who was as close to the opposite of the beast as could be. Dressed in a black suit, completely bald, a silver watch on his wrist, he had pale-blue eyes and thin lips. If the dirty man was a beast, then the bald man was a lizard, and he could have licked the insides of his own ears. He looked

34

uncomfortable in the woods. He didn't look at the beast and he didn't look left or right, but straight ahead. Maybe he was blind. I don't think he was blind. He had a baby face, smooth and bright, bright but closed, closed like the moon on a bad night of leaves and marshes and bitterns beaking their way through marshes. Baby face. White. Bright. Bright and closed and talced. A twitch seemed to snap at his mouth. He cocked his head to one side and, as he did, his face concentrated and took on a crazed look. The look of someone who could smell blood at two hundred paces and kill with a touch. "Listen…" he said, but the beast man put a finger to his lips and cocked his own head. He took a step towards us, placing his boot slowly and carefully, not breaking a twig or crackling a leaf at all, and whispered "Someone's been here."

He crouched down and looked towards me. I was caught between flight and stone. My heart thrashed. Spike was still. "Fucking yokels…" I felt Spike bristle. The baby-faced man shook his head and said, "Don't worry about them. You're out of here by the end of the week."

"Not a day too soon." The beast stood up and walked back. He stopped and turned and looked back towards us, and for a moment I thought he was going to point and shout, but then he followed the other man through the opening and roped it up. I looked at Spike and he looked at me. I put my fingers to my lips and we waited. We waited until they'd gone, and then we waited another half an hour. It was dark when we stood up and crept back up the path, through the trees, over the bridge and away. "Fancy a drink?"

he said, and I nodded. He freewheeled the van down the lane, and I freewheeled behind him, and our wheels slicked the road, and it was only when we reached Ashbrittle that we started our engines and flew down the hill towards Appley and the pub.

4

The next day, after I'd finished the milking, I went to have tea with Mum and Dad and Grace, and as I leant against the kitchen sink and watched Dad wrestle with a cabbage in the garden, Mum said, "Listen to me, Elliot."

When she calls me Elliot, I know she's being serious. Usually she calls me "Pet". I turned from the window, and she forced me to look into her eyes. She didn't ask me to look into them, but I had no choice. There. Fixed. Her bright blue eyes in her little round face, the thready veins on her cheeks, the nose like a brooch your grandmother gave your sister, the tiny ears, the long grey hair tied back.

"I'm listening."

"I'm smelling fire all the time. It's strong and it's getting stronger."

"Oh Mum…"

"Don't 'oh Mum' me. You know how it is." She tapped the side of her head, and her eyes dimmed like candles in a draft. They came back brighter. "I need you to stop whatever it is you're doing."

"I'm not doing anything."

"All right. You might not be doing anything, but someone you know is."

"No one's doing anything."

"Is it Spike?"

"Spike?"

"It's Spike. What's he up to?"

"Nothing."

"You know you can't lie to me, Pet. You know it makes my palms sing."

"And are they?"

"Yes. Feel."

She put her hands out and I touched them. I could feel a light vibration from them, like a choir of ants was singing beneath her skin. "He's just being his usual self, Mum. Mucking about."

"This is more than mucking about. This is stuff he doesn't want to get involved in. Believe me."

"I'll tell him," I said, as Grace came downstairs and said, "Tea ready yet?"

"Half an hour," Mum said, and she turned and went to the sink and started to peel potatoes.

Grace and I went outside, walked around the side of the house and into the road. We didn't plan to walk together, but we ended up walking across the village green towards the churchyard. She is two years younger than me, but when we were kids and old enough to play out she used to be the one with the plans and the courage. She'd tell me we were climbing a tree or building a rope swing over a river or walking down to the ruins of the house where the mad Professor kept his kidnapped woman. And she'd always climb first or swing first or say "What you scared of? There's nothing there…" and laugh when I said, "But…" Now, as we walked, she said, "Mum talk to you?"

"Yes."

"What did she say?"

I shrugged. "You know. The usual."

"And what was that?" Grace never takes no for an answer, and I knew better than to try and fob her off with nothing. "Tell me."

"She said she could smell fire and her palms were singing…"

"And you believe her?"

"I don't know."

I'd never talked properly with Grace about the things Mum thinks and feels. Whenever it came up, we always changed the subject, but now, for the first time, she said, "I think you want to listen to her. It's not that crazy."

"What's not that crazy?"

"Her gifts."

"Her gifts…"

"Yes, Elliot, her gifts. The ones she thinks you've inherited."

I laughed. "And you haven't."

She shook her head. "You know me. Miss Practical." We stopped by the yew, and I stared up at its branches. "When we were kids I used to climb up there, but you never would. You used to say it was a special tree, and that's before you knew why. I never felt anything like that."

"You sound like Dad."

"Exactly. I'm Dad's kid. You're Mum's."

"Sometimes," I said, "I wish I was you."

"And why's that?"

"With you, things are…"

"Things are what?"

"Simpler. Black and white…" I said, and now, maybe for the first time in our lives, she took my arm and we walked on, past the yew and the church porch and around and through the gate, past Pump Court and the hippies' houses.

I looked at her as we walked, her pale face that never tanned, her freckles, her little nose and her hair tied back in a bun. If you found one of those old photographs of Victorian kids sitting outside a school, you'd find her face there, a face that travels down the ages like a story. Dependable and old and untroubled by nonsense. She spoke what she was thinking, and thought carefully, and she had a plan for her life. One day, she'd told me, she was going to open a restaurant – "Nothing posh, but it'll have people driving for miles to eat my food," and I believed her. That was the essence of her, you believed the things she said, took her advice, listened. So as we walked back towards the green and home, she said, "Listen to Mum. And listen to yourself. Listen here," and she patted her chest. "When you find out what you were born for, you have to use it."

I stopped for a moment and she stopped beside me, and we looked at each other. We'd never fought, but we'd had arguments, but now I didn't think I'd ever have another argument with her. It was simple on that hot day, too simple, and I wished, for a moment, that simple could be tattooed on my heart. "OK," I said and, although I wasn't exactly sure what she'd meant, I had an idea, and an idea was better than the flight of mad wasps, or the chase of a dog in the night.

5

After the evening at the hoop house, I didn't see Spike for a couple of days. I put my head down at the farm, and when I wasn't working I sat in the caravan and listened to the radio or read a bird book. If someone asked me what my hobby was, I'd say it was bird-watching. I don't always attach the old superstitions to their flights and calls, and I'm not a twitcher. I don't keep a notebook and fill it with names of birds and the places I've seen them, and I wouldn't chase halfway across the country to see a rarity that strayed from America to Cornwall. But I do love to watch the soaring buzzards, I wait for the cuckoos of spring, and when I'm tractoring I talk to the gulls that follow my tyres as they search for the jealous worm.

Sometimes Mr Evans would bring two bottles of beer to the caravan and we'd sit on the step and drink, and he'd tell me stories about the old days. The farm had been in his family for two generations. His grandfather had rented the place from the Buff-Orpingtons, and his father had bought it when the old family's fortunes floundered and they disposed of half their estate. Mr Evans remembered the day when they became landowners. "Father set up a trestle table over there." He pointed to the middle of the front yard. "We killed a pig, bought gallons of cider, mother baked bread, and neighbours came from miles around. Father never spoke much, but that day he didn't stop. He had plans for this place, big plans. I had plans too, but the War did for them…"

You didn't ask Mr Evans personal questions. I got that straight away. You just waited for him to come out with it, but if he didn't you either waited or forgot about it. So I let what he'd said hang in the air, and when he started talking about the time they'd swapped horses for a tractor, I listened and nodded and told him that I sometimes wished I could have been alive in those days, days when things were simpler and slower.

"And harder," he said.

We talked for another half-hour, and then he said he was going to watch the news. I held up my bottle of beer and said, "Thanks for this."

"You're welcome," he said, "and I just wanted to say…" but then he stopped.

"What?"

He shook his head. "Nothing," he said, and he got up, steadied himself and shuffled across the yard to his front door. As he walked he held his hand up in parting, and left me sitting on the step.

I was watching a kestrel hovering over the farmyard when Spike turned up. The bird had its eye on a vole or mouse, and as it hung in the air it adjusted itself with little tweaks of its tail, head down and still, a bullet hanging in the place where threat meets wonder. As I've said, Spike is a wiry man, but as he loped towards the caravan I thought he was even more wiry, as if the wires had been tightened and tensed against the season. And he was wearing a stupid expression on his face, more stupid than ever. He banged on the door and let himself in, clapped me on the shoulder and said, "What about it?"

"What about what?"

He took a beer from the fridge.

"I've had a hell of a day."

"Yeah?"

"Oh yeah." He rolled a cigarette. "A hell of a day."

"You said. What's been going on?"

He lit the cigarette. "I want to show you something."

"Do you?"

"Yeah."

"And I have to tell you something, Spike."

"What?"

"My mum told me to tell you to step away from whatever you're doing."

"She did what?"

"You heard me. She'd been smelling fire and…"

He laughed. "And seeing flying cats?"

"Believe me, Spike. She's serious."

"Of course she is. But you know what they say about her in The Globe?"

"I can guess."

"You want to forget her fucking mumbo-jumbo. Real life." He tapped the table and drank some beer. "That's what it's all about. Grabbing a bit of real life."

"And what the hell does that mean?"

"I'll show you. Come with me."

"Where?"

"My place."

"Why?"

"It's a surprise."

I know about Spike's surprises, but there was nothing I could do to say no, so five minutes later I was on my bike, following him through the lanes to Greenham.

He lived in a small and draughty bungalow with a sitting room, a bedroom, a kitchen and a bathroom, and a garage to one side. It rattled in the wind, baked in the heat and wept with damp in a bad autumn. If you stood in the kitchen in September, the mould caught in your throat as the wind and rain banged on the window and laughed. It was that sort of place, and when he said, "Got to show you something in the garage," I was pleased he wasn't going to make me drink a cup of tea. His tea was shit, and always came in a dirty mug. I said, "OK," and followed him like a man in a song that echoes in my head when I'm drunk or think I can play the guitar. I've never played the guitar. I suppose I've thought that I could once or twice, but I try not to think. I remember the harmonica I was given for Christmas when I was six and how it fucked with the cat's head, but I didn't dwell. I followed Spike to the garage, and when he stopped outside the door and tapped the side of his nose, I said, "What's up?"

"This is up," and he pushed the door open and I stepped inside. I stepped inside, looked up, looked down and my blood flushed. "Oh fuck, Spike."

"I told you."

"Oh fuck…"

He laughed.

"You… you told me what?"

"That one day I'd score."

"You fucking idiot."

Smoke was hanging from the rafters of the garage.

"Spike…"

Hundreds of plants.

"You didn't…"

It must have been hundreds. Maybe it was a thousand.

"I didn't what?"

More? Two thousand? I couldn't tell. I didn't want to tell. I wanted to close my eyes, open them again and the plants wouldn't be there. I said, "You didn't do what I think you've done."

"Tell me what you think I did."

"You stole that bloke's crop."

Spike looked at me, and his stupid head nodded at me, like it was independent of the rest of his body or lost in Nepal. Mountains could have moved, climbers cried and yaks could have spoken the words of their own gods, but Spike's head would not have stopped nodding.

"Oh yes," he said. "All of it."

"Mum…" I said, and I let the word hang in the air for a moment. "My mum was right, Spike. She was fucking right."

6

Stupidity is as stupid weeps, and as weeping leaves the broken-hearted on a carousel of another's making, so stupid speaks to itself in a language it cannot spell. I stared up at the smoke, and for minutes I didn't know what to say. What could I say? Words come, words break and all they leave are shards. Broken things swallowed by the earth and dug up centuries later, brushed off, studied, valued, put in glass cases. Stared at by bored kids. Wondered at by dreamers. The things I wanted to say queued up in my head and pushed against my memory, but I couldn't let them out. It was like I knew what was going to happen already, like I could see into the future, see the ropes, the blades, the pain and the screaming in a wood, and all I could do was stand and stare and look at a garage strung with rows of plants and the smell of the plants – and the reckoning.

And the reckoning. I thought about the reckoning. I could feel it there, feel it turning and twisting in the air, and I could hear it whispering. It was certain of its place in the scheme and the story and Spike's life, and although it was impatient it could wait. It could wait as long as it wanted, as long as it took, even as long as the stars shone and tumbled in the sky.

I said, "Oh fuck, Spike."

He didn't look at me. "Brilliant, isn't it?"

"Yeah. Fucking brilliant. You're a genius."

"I know…"

"What did you do?" I said, and he laughed.

"My ship came in."

"Yeah. HMS Fuck-Up."

He didn't stop laughing. "Fuck you."

"Yeah?"

"This is what I've been waiting for. I reckon I've got twenty grand's worth here."

"Twenty grand…"

"At least. Maybe more."

"And more trouble than you can imagine, Spike."

"Trouble?"

"Yeah."

"And how's that? Only you and I know about it, and you're not going to say anything, are you?"

"Are you kidding? Any money you like you'll have a couple of pints, start bragging about it and before you know it…"

"I'm saying nothing."

"And I'm the Pope. I'm the fucking Pope and I've got a balcony the size of your house."

"Have you?"

"I'll put money on it."

He shrugged. "This time next week I won't need any of your money."

Right then I just wanted to hit him. I wanted to hit him hard, walk out of the garage and not go back, get on my bike and ride as fast as I could to some distant place where no one knew my name. Somewhere like an island in Scotland. Hole up in a rented house on the edge of a quiet village, wait for the mayhem to go away, wait for however long it took. Stare from a top-floor window at a place I didn't know, watch people who didn't know me, say hello to no one. Send a postcard to my mum telling her not to worry, and that the smell of fire would go away, find a job on a fishing boat, grow a beard. Walk along a deserted beach, feel the sand sting my face. Lick salt off my lips and watch my skin turn to leather. Sit in a pub at a corner table and drink slowly. Meet a woman with black eyes and hard hands, an honest woman who wasn't afraid to gut a fish. Grow vegetables in a hard garden, keep a rabbit in a warm hutch. But friends are friends and, whatever they do, if they remain friends you have no option but to hold your hand up and say something about standing next to them or by them or whatever.

"When," I said, "did you do this?"

"This morning. About five. It didn't take long."

He said he'd watched the place for a couple of days, and once he'd worked out the routine of the bloke who was growing the stuff, down to check the crop and water at half-eight, midday, half-three and nine in the evening, he made his move. "It only took me a couple of hours. I was going to leave a note, but then I thought that might be pushing it."

"Yes Spike. That might have been."

He walked down the garage, weaving his way around the plants, stroking them as he walked. He looked like he was in love – or, if not that, in a trance. His face shone and his lips glistened, and when he spoke there was a little catch in his voice. "Every time I think about them, I can't help laughing. I reckon I'll have them dried by the end of the week."

"Do you?"

"I know someone in Exeter who'll take them, and then it's…" he made a swooping move with his hand, a taking-off-in-an-aeroplane move and flying to Spain or Thailand or some other place where he could get jumped by gangsters and have his fingers removed as a starter.

Now, rather than just walk out of the garage, I wanted to run and never see Spike again. Forget ideas of hiding in Scotland or making a new life in a place where no one recognized my face, so I put my hands up and said, "Spike, this is mad. Either you get rid of them or I'm going."

"What the hell are you talking about? Going where?"

"Anywhere but here. I mean it, Spike."

"OK then. Fuck off." He turned away and walked back to the plants, stepping through them like they were curtains, letting them swing back and over him until all I could see of him was his legs and feet. I thought about saying something else, but it was pointless, there was nothing left to say, nothing to do, not a lot more to think, so I turned away from my friend and walked out of his garage, jumped on the bike and rode away.

I didn't know where I was going, and for ten minutes I didn't care. I wanted the illusion that I couldn't be seen by anyone. The evening had darkened, and when I reached Ashbrittle I stopped at the village green, leant on the handlebars and stared at the lights of the cottages. Tired, happy, content people eating their supper, drinking a beer, thinking about having a bath or going to bed. People dozing in armchairs in front of the television, people who didn't have the nag of collision in their heads, people whose only worry was whether they should eat some bacon or a tomato. I could have visited Mum and Dad and sat with them and pretended that I'd just called in to say hello because I was passing and hadn't seen them for a day or two, but I got back on the bike and rode to the pub at Staple Cross. I'm known in the pub at Staple Cross, but I'm not a regular. For me the place is a hideaway, somewhere I can sit in a corner and be left alone. Once, one of the walls whispered with the voices of people who had been there centuries before, and for years people thought the place was haunted. But then scientists came and looked at the walls and discovered that the ancient paint contained iron, and as the years had passed this had become magnetic and started to act like recording tape, picking up, capturing and holding snippets of conversation. Farmers arguing about the price of sheep, barmaids telling stable boys to keep their hands off, potboys laughing at gypsies, the squire remonstrating about idleness. Now the walls are quiet. Someone bought the place and stripped the old paint from the walls before anyone told them he was stripping the old voices away. He put fresh emulsion up, he hung pictures of haystacks and horses pulling ploughs, he cleaned the windows. I sat in a corner with a pint and stared at the regulars, and tried to quieten my mind. It was difficult, but by the time I was halfway through my second, I was getting there.

I was at the bar ordering a third when a couple of the Ashbrittle hippies appeared. Two women. The barman knew them, called them by name and started to pull two pints of cider. They looked at me, nodded, smiled and turned back to look at the cider. One had short red hair and freckles, the other had brown curls tied in bunches. The redhead was wearing a check shirt and jeans, the one with bunches a striped skirt and a sleeveless blouse. They looked like they'd come from the fields or a garden, their hands were rough and dirty, and their faces were flecked with earth.

Some of the people in Ashbrittle said cruel things about the hippies, said that they never did any work, that they sponged off the rest of us, that they spent all day smoking smoke, that they never used soap. Some of the people in Ashbrittle are ignorant and only see what they want to see, lost in pouring misery into complaint and back again. I liked the hippies. I liked their colourful clothes, I liked the music they listened to, and I liked the way they didn't seem to care what anyone thought about them. I suppose difference was different back then and ideals were easier to gather and hold. Or maybe not. I don't know. Years have passed since the events that stitch this story, and although the dead cannot fight their wars again, at least the hippies can appear in my dreams and smile and laugh at the memories.

I went back to my seat, and a minute later the hippies came over and the redhead said, "Anyone sitting here?"

"Help yourself," I said.

They did.

For a couple of minutes I drank and listened while they talked. One of their goats had escaped from its tethers and broken into a neighbour's garden, where it had eaten six cabbages and some plums from a plum tree. They'd chased it out of the garden, into the churchyard, over the wall at the bottom and into a field. They'd spent the next two hours trying to catch

51

it. Without thinking or excusing myself I said, "My Gran used to charm sheep…"

The hippies looked at me, and the one with bunches said, "She did what to sheep?"

"She used to charm them. Cast a spell on them, I suppose. Sheep, goats… what's the difference? I reckon she'd have got your goat back."

"So," Bunches said, moving closer to me, "How did she do that?" Her eyes were very brown, like conkers peeping from their shells, and her lips were wet. She smelt of hedges and earth.

"I don't know. She wouldn't tell anyone. I think she used to sing them a song."

"A song?"

"Yeah." I was a bit drunk. "Can you sing?"

"That depends," she said.

"On what?"

"How much I've had to drink."

"Or how stoned you are," said her friend.

I laughed, they laughed, and we spent the next ten minutes batting stuff between each other about where we lived, what we did, where we'd come from and what our names were. Bunches was called Sam, and the redhead was Ros. Before Ashbrittle they'd worked in a bar in Bristol. Now they were planning to save enough money to buy the old bakery next to their place, renovate the ovens and set up a business.

"I remember when the bakery was still working," I said. "They used to sell their stuff all over the place. Their doughnuts were amazing."

"We'll do doughnuts," said Ros, and she went to the bar to fetch some more drinks.

When we were alone, for a second I thought the old walled voices came and hang their words and laughs in the air. I don't know if Sam heard them. She didn't say, but when I caught her eye for one of those odd moments that pass between people who are prowling around each other, I saw something I wanted. I suppose I could have said that the drink was talking, spooking me, giving me ideas. I opened my mouth to say something stupid, but stopped myself. It's too easy to be stupid, and too easy to wake up in the morning with the feeling you said something that had more to do with want and despair than need. And at that time all I needed was a drink, and despair was just a word I'd heard on the radio.

7

We left the pub at half-ten. Sam and Ros asked me back to their place, but I had to work in the morning.

"You work every morning?"

"I get Sundays off."

"Then come round Saturday night. If you want."

"OK," I said, "I will," and I rode back to the caravan under a clear, warm sky. A full moon was showing, and when I got home I sat on my bed and listened to the beer in my stomach and the rustles of little beasts in the grass below the window. I suppose I'd been sitting for half an hour when I heard a distant noise, something unfamiliar and out of place. I opened the window and stuck my head out. The noise faded and then it reappeared, closer this time, weaving through the lanes, between the hedges and over the hills. A siren. The farmhouse door opened, and Mr Evans came out and stood in the yard. He cocked his head towards the sound, and then shuffled towards the caravan. He stood under the window and said, "Not a sound you hear round here."

"No."

"Sounds like they're heading towards Ashbrittle."

"It does."

"Police."

"I think it is."

"Or ambulance."

"Who knows?"

He coughed and shuffled on his feet. He was wearing slippers and a dressing gown over a shirt and long johns. His marshy eyes were cold, and his lips shone. He said something about the noise of sirens making milk curdle in the cows' udders. He asked me to go down to the grazing field and check the herd were settled. I knew they were, but the idea of a stroll in the light of the moon was a pleasant one, so I pulled on my boots and headed off. I said, "See you in the morning," and he said, "You might," and he turned and went back inside.

I carried a torch. The batteries were low, and its light was too weak to make a difference, so I switched it off and walked slowly, picking my way, the moon shadowing and failing. A cloud passed over her face, an owl called, the sirens and lights had faded into the dark. The world smelled of drought and failure, iron and dust, and the fields were crisp. The herd were in the sidling fields above the river valley, and as I approached them, they shuffled in their sleep. Some of them were standing, others were lying.

When we were at school, Spike and I used to go cow-tipping. It's a cruel game, but in those days we were both stupid and selfish, and didn't care who knew it. Although some people have said that cow-tipping is impossible because cows don't sleep standing up, and anyway they've got great hearing and are always aware of their surroundings, I can tell you that cow-tipping is something anyone can do. Though it helps if you've got a friend with you. A cow is a heavy animal. One night, drunk as goats on pig wine, we managed to sneak up on a Red

Devon slumbering in a field outside Greenham. Usually, Red Devons are more alert than the average cow, and more likely to butt you a good one in the back, but this one was slow. Slow as a tree or Spike on a good day. We were at the cow's side and had her over before she could moo, and were out of that field and back by the river bridge before you could blink. Now I wouldn't go cow-tipping and if I caught a kid tipping one of Evans's cows I'd have him and bang his face more than once, but in those days we didn't know better. Come to think of it...

I stepped carefully through the herd, counting as I went. I'd reached forty-two when my eye was caught by something in the woods below the field. A beam of torch light flashed against the trees, then another. They disappeared for a moment and then came back again, steady this time. I crouched down and watched. I saw figures in the shadows, then the figures disappeared. I heard a muffled scream. The sound of people struggling. A quick shout. A crack. Another shout, muffled, like it was coming from under a blanket.

A moment later the torches went out, and for a minute there was silence in the night and another cloud cut across the moon. Some of the cows looked towards the sound of the shouts. Easy, calm animals. They chewed, turned their heads back towards their shoulders and settled down again.

Now the torch lights came back again, and the shadows were slow and methodical. I could have stood up and made a move towards them, walked the two hundred yards to where they were, asked what they were doing, told them to move on, get off the land, you're frightening my animals. But there was danger there, menace at work, and watchfulness. I could see two people standing on the boundary of the field and the wood, sentries if you will, or watchmen. Tall figures, black against the black, with the black above and the iron smell of a broken draught in the air. I lay back and rested my head against the side of one of the cows, listened to her stomach rumble and watched the moon. She was impassive, and gave nothing away. The ground was hard, and the grass tinder. Ten minutes passed, then fifteen, then twenty. I think it was twenty, because I dozed for a while, and when I woke up the cows were still around me and the moon was still strong, and the woods were still.

I stood up. I waited. No torches shone. No voices. The sentries had gone. Suddenly, the headlights of a car swung through a lane half a mile away, shooting up the hill, around the first corner and away. I waited until I couldn't hear it any more, then started walking down to the place where the torches had been.

I didn't hurry. I was alert and on edge. I could hear my heart beating, but I didn't make any noise. I was careful. I was like the vole avoiding a lively owl. I didn't walk tall. I kept low and rolled my feet slowly over the grass like a Sioux warrior in his moccasins. I stopped. I listened. I moved on again. Stopped. Started. Listened to my breathing. I reached the edge of the wood. Stopped again.

There was a low barbed-wire fence between me and the trees. I stepped on it with my left foot, pushed it down, lifted my right leg over, stepped down, lifted my left leg, stood still. The woods rustled with bugs and leaves and birds. I flicked the torch on, saw an opening that led down to a narrow path, flicked the torch off and followed my nose.

As the moonlight cracked through the trees, it left crazed splinters on the ground, and my shadow danced and spun as I walked. Every minute or so I stopped and listened for voices or footsteps. Nothing. I shone the light for a second. I snapped it off. I walked on. I shone it again. Nothing. I looked up towards the place where I'd been sitting with the herd. They were ahead of me. I walked on. Torch on. Torch off. Stop. Listen. A smell in the air.

Can you smell fear? Is that possible? Or smell fear that's passed? Mum would say it is, and she'd be right. It was there. It was hanging in the air, musky and rank, copper and rust, fire and cotton. I could have reached out and taken a piece of that fear and broken it off, put it in my pocket, kept it for ever. I could have used it to scare someone I didn't like, someone who'd threatened me in a pub, someone who'd shown me a knife. It would have chased them away and kept them away.

I stepped on a stick. It cracked. A leaf, broken from the branch, twirled into my face. The moonlight showed something odd in the trees, something out of place, a failure in nature. I stood still, very still, like I was forgotten. The moment froze its place in the present and flattened it through time. If you could have seen it, it would have looked like a still stretch of black water, reflecting nothing, absorbing everything, willing the future into its arms. Nothing moved. Nothing moved, except... Nothing moved except something in the trees ahead of me, twenty feet ahead.

I shone the torch, swung the beam through the trees, and the swinging caught the movement of another swinging. Slow, quiet, almost gentle, maybe like the pendulum of a fine clock. A clock built by a man with the finest fingers and the keenest eye, a clock that kept perfect time and chimed the hours with an easy bell. But this was not a very fine clock, and I didn't want to see what I could see, and for a moment I forced the sight away. I pushed it towards the edge of a cliff in my head and left it waiting there, but that's as far as I went. I couldn't push any further, and I couldn't take any more steps. For here, in the lovely woods with the sweet birds and the dancing leaves, I saw a pair of feet, legs, damp-stained trousers, a check shirt, arms limp and muddy, a twisted face above a roped neck. A hung man, a fresh hung man, the man Spike and I had seen at the hoop house in the woods, the beast of a man with hands like bricks and tiny eyes, dead in these woods now, swinging like a decoration on a Christmas tree. Bad tree, bad Christmas, big boots on a very dead man. And as I stared at him, I felt the frozen moment crack and bend and snap, and all the breath rushed from my body and I reached out and grasped a tree trunk and heaved, but nothing came out, nothing at all, not a drop of anything at all.

8

Nothing can prepare you for finding a hung man in a wood. Nothing about the swinging, nothing you imagined, nothing you thought, nothing you heard or wondered about.

I stood and stared at him for five minutes. He swayed, and the rope creaked and the branch strained under his weight. Everything about the sight reeked of strain, as if the world was under this enormous pressure that could burst in a second. All I had to do was find a pin and push it at the air, and the lot would explode. Everything would go. Nothing would be left, not even the pin. I put my hands over my ears, but the pressure stayed. I looked at my feet. My legs were shaking. I looked up at the man again. I bent my neck to mirror his.

He could have been floating, but he was not. He could have been a dummy, but he was not a dummy. A trickle of blood twinkled at the corner of his mouth, and more had come from his nose. Once he had been a scary fuck with hands the size of bricks and a deep, growly voice, but now he just looked sad and lost. Lost in an unfamiliar place with an unfamiliar nothing in his legs.

And my torch light caught his fingers. They were small and delicate, too small for a big man, and there was dirt under the nails. For a moment I was held by the thought that I wanted to reach out and touch them, wash them, dry them and wrap them in clean towels. No one deserves to die in terror, and no one deserves to die so far away from his family and his friends. And no one deserves to die without a name.

I wondered what his name was, and I wondered who his mum and dad were. Did he have brothers or sisters? A wife? A child? Who were his friends, and who would miss him? Who would grieve for this body in its hung throne, and who would remember the happy times, the loving mornings and the laughing nights? Who would pick up a newspaper and read a story about him being found hanging from a sycamore tree, the leaves around his face shading him from the moonlight, the birds of the night calling after his terror? Who would say, "Oh my God, I remember him. I went to school with him..." or "I bought him a drink last week..."?

I did try to move, but my legs refused to budge. They were planted deep and fast, rooted and caught. My blood flushed, and the smell of fear knotted itself around me and held me tight. It was like it loved me and wanted me, or both, and if I didn't give in I would take a knife in my stomach. I didn't want a knife in my stomach. I wanted to go home. An owl called from a tree behind me, spooked me wet and rigid. I'd been shining the torch too long. I switched it off, and the noise made me jump. Now I could move. Now I shook some life into my fingers, and they sang at me. I took a step back, turned and started to walk. Then, suddenly, I was running, running fast, crashing through the undergrowth to the barbed-wire fence and stumbling over the fence and falling and pulling myself up, and I was away and into the field towards the herd. They saw me coming, and some of them stood quickly and lowered their heads towards me. I skirted around them, and when I reached the top of the field I stopped to get my breath, turned and stared back towards the woods.

They didn't look changed. They were still the peaceful place where the birds nested and mice hid from their troubles, safe and warm in their holes. The owl watched. The buzzard waited. The foxes prowled and stopped, moved on, stopped again, listened. All the animals' troubles would pass, and one day the blood would drain away from the ground and the trees would forget their part in the night. But now the blood was fresh and the rope was tight, and all the world was swinging. I turned, jumped the gate into the field in front of the farm house, went to the front door and banged on the door.

I waited a minute. No one answered. I yelled "Mr Evans!" and banged again, louder this time, and longer. An upstairs light came on and a window opened. Mr Evans's face appeared, and he looked down and shouted "Who's there?"

"Me," I said. "Elliot. I have to use the phone!"

"The phone? What are you talking about?"

"I found a body. I found a body in the woods."

"A what?"

"Someone hanging…"

"Are you drunk?"

"No!"

"Then what's the matter?"

"I told you!"

He started to close the window. "No! I think someone's been murdered!"

He didn't close the window. He looked down at me. He opened his mouth. His fillings twinkled in the moonlight. "Please, Mr Evans. Let me in!"

Maybe it was something in my voice, or maybe he just wanted to kick me, but two minutes later he was unbolting the front door. I didn't stop to say anything. I barged past him, grabbed the phone off the table in the hall, dialled 999 and said, "Police!"

They were there half an hour later. Two fat men in a blue-and-white car, and the first thing they said was, "What's happening round here tonight?"

"I don't know," I said.

"First it was some fracas up the road there…" he pointed to the place where we'd heard the sirens, "and now this…" He took out a notebook. "Caller reports finding a body hanging in woods. Is that you?" He looked at Mr Evans.

"Not me. Him," and he jabbed a finger at me.

"So, sonny," and they took steps towards me. "You been drinking?" He sniffed. "Been at the old apple juice?"

"That's what I thought," said Mr Evans.

"So have you?"

"No I fucking haven't!" I took a step back. "Come on. I'll show you!"

"There's no need…" said the fattest of the two policeman, "for that sort of language. No need at all." He reached into his pocket. "In fact, we could arrest you for it…"

"OK," I said. "Arrest me. But before you do that, come with me," and I headed off. "Come on!"

When I looked over my shoulder, Mr Evans was twirling his finger against his head and making drinking motions with his hands, and the policemen were nodding their heads. For a moment I thought they were going to stay where they were, but then they walked towards me and followed me through the yard gate towards the fields.

I didn't walk with them, but I didn't get too far ahead. I was fit and they were puffing and wheezing, and once, when one of them said, "Hold on, lad," I stopped to let them catch up. Fifteen minutes later we were standing beneath the swinging body, and their torches were shining in the dead man's face, and one of them whispered, "Shit..." while the other threw up into a bush.

"When did you find him?"

"An hour ago. Maybe less."

"Have you moved anything? Touched anything?"

"No."

"You sure about that?"

"Of course I'm sure."

He tried his radio. There was no signal. "OK. Stan. Clean yourself up and let's get back to the car."

Stan threw up again.

"And you," he said to me. "Don't go wandering off. We'll want to talk to you."

The rest of the night was busy. More police came, and the area around the body was cordoned off. As soon as dawn broke, an ambulance came, and police with cameras and boxes of equipment parked in a lay-by at the entrance to the wood.

I went back to the caravan and slept for an hour, then went to fetch the cows for milking. I worked in a daze, my legs felt woolly, my eyes heavy and my nose was still filled with the smell of fear. When I wasn't thinking about the man swinging in the tree I was thinking about Spike in his stupid garage, sitting beneath the drying plants with a stupid grin on his stupid fucking face and his stupid fucking hands reaching up and stroking the stupid fucking leaves. Oh why, Spike? Why don't you listen to people? Why do you have to follow your greed when all your greed does is lead you to trouble you don't even recognize? Maybe that was it. Recognize trouble and you'll protect yourself from it. Or something. I don't know. Did I care? I think I did, but that was my trouble.

As I was letting the cows out to pasture – call that pasture if you want, that scorched field, the dust rising, the faint dew making no difference, the birds still gasping on the fence – two policemen in suits came from the farmhouse, and one said, "Elliot?"

"Yes?"

"Elliot Jackson?"

"That's me."

"You're the lad who found the body?"

"I am."

"I'm DS Pollock. This is DS Brown. We'd like to ask you a few questions."

"OK."

"We'll need to take you down the station."

"Why?"

"You're our main witness, so we need to tape everything you say."

"OK. Give me a minute to get a wash."

"OK."

I stood in the caravan, stripped to the waist and washed as well as I could. As the water ran over my skin I tried to imagine it washing everything away, the sight of the man and the smell of blood, the sound of the creaking rope and the swinging torch lights. And ten minutes later, as I was driven to Taunton, the world became stranger to me. The colours of the fields and trees and sky and road and the inside of the police car and the policemen's hair and my trousers swirled and pulsed. I'd never been in a police car before, and for some reason I felt as though I'd been swallowed by a dog. A radio crackled, a bored voice said things I didn't understand, and I said, "I'm very tired…"

"I bet you are, son."

"You get any sleep last night?"

"An hour."

"Get some kip if you want."

"Thanks," I said, and I closed my eyes, and a minute later I felt myself dreaming. Big dreams of talking cows and trees that walked from one valley to another. Dreams of clouds lowering to my face and crawling into my mouth and tasting of milk. Flowing milk, boiling cream, potatoes falling like rain. I jolted awake, and we were in the car park behind the police station.

They gave me a cup of tea, sat me in a bare room, and I sat between them at a table. When they were ready, they clicked a tape recorder, spoke their names and my name and the date, and Pollock asked me to start at the beginning.

"So what were you doing in the woods at half-past midnight?"

"Mr Evans asked me to check the herd. The cows."

"Mr Evans, your boss?"

"Yes."

"And why did he do that?"

"We always check them last thing. Make sure none have got out."

"So you went to check the cows, and then what did you do?"

"I saw lights in the woods. Torches."

"How did you know they were torches?"

"There were beams of light. It was obvious," and I told them about the voices and the screams, the shadowed sentries and the deeper, wooded shadows.

Pollock asked these questions in a slow and kindly way. He was a thin man with ginger hair and a clean, close-shaved face. When I say he asked questions in a kindly way I only mean that: the rest of him bothered me. I thought he could most likely turn in a second and turn badly, switch to meanness and trouble, and use his little fists to put a bruise somewhere that wouldn't show but would hurt. His eyes were small and green, and he didn't blink, and as he listened to me he sat still and quiet, like a monk. And all the time the other policeman, Brown, sat back and watched me, until at the end he leant forwards, rubbed his chin in a thoughtful way and said, "And that's your story?"

"It is."

"And you're telling us everything?"

"Yes. Of course. Why?"

"Just a feeling, Elliot. You know. Sometimes I get a feeling. In my waters."

"I told it like it was."

"And you didn't recognize the body when you found it? You'd never seen the man before?"

"I don't think so."

"You don't think so? That's not what you said half an hour ago." Brown leant forwards again. He was less disguised than Pollock, more upfront and obvious. He hadn't looked after himself as well as his friend, and was starting to pork out. His face was jowly and his lips were fat, and his eyes were beginning to do that thing that eyes do when they get old. They were watery and distracted, maybe like they'd seen too much for one life and wanted to go home.

"Well you know…" I said.

"No, I don't know. You'll have to explain."

"Maybe I saw him in the pub or something."

"Maybe you saw him in the pub or something?"

"Yes. Or the shop."

"Or the shop?"

"Yes."

"Which shop?"

"The post office. In Greenham."

"Well which was it – the pub or the shop?"

I was very tired, and felt the words drop from my mouth. There was nothing I could do to stop them. "The pub," I said, without thinking.

"So now you had seen him before?"

"Maybe."

Brown leant towards me. He rubbed his eyes, but it didn't make them any better. He smelt of coffee and cigarettes and damp wool. "Elliot, Elliot. Maybe... maybe not. Definitely, definitely not. You need to tell me the truth."

"I'm tired."

"So are we."

"Would you like a coffee?" said Pollock. I wasn't sure if he meant it, but I said, "Yes please."

"Sugar?"

"One big one."

"Coming up..."

Brown leant forwards and said, "Interview suspended 11:16, 17th August 1976," and clicked the tape recorder off. Pollock came back with the coffee, put it on the table and said, "Smoke?" I shook my head. "Mind if we do?" I shook my head again, and for the next ten minutes we sat in silence in a growing cloud of smoke, and I felt the world lighten and haze and fade. A buzzing started in my ears, and my eyes watered. When they finished their cigarettes and turned the recorder on again, I was swimming in a world of half-remembered stuff that swirled between the first site of the plants in the hoop house, the sound of the dead man's voice, the sight of the dead man's eyes, the hanging plants in the garage, the hanging man in the wood, the creak of the rope, the sleeping cows, my sleeping eyes, the smell of my caravan, the hippies in the pub, Mr Evans in his vest. "Elliot?"

"Elliot?"

"Elliot?"

I snapped back. "Sorry. I was gone."

"Interview resumed 11:31, 17th August 1976," said Brown.

"All you have to do is tell us the truth and you'll be gone," said Pollock, and for a moment his smile slipped and I saw his teeth. They were small and polished-white, like mints.

"I have," I said.

"But you maybe saw the victim in the pub. Which pub?"

"The Globe. The Globe in Appley."

"And was he with anyone?"

"I don't remember."

"Try to."

"I can't."

"Try!" The smile was gone now. He leant forwards and Brown leant forwards and I didn't feel like drinking my coffee.

"I think he was with a man in a suit."

"A man in a suit? Anything else?"

"He was bald."

"A bald man in a suit…"

"Yes. He was small…"

"A small bald man in a suit."

"Yes."

"Well that narrows it down. What were they talking about?"

"I don't know. I couldn't hear."

"Anyone else with them?"

"No," I said, and I slumped forwards until my head was touching the table.

"OK. OK."

"I'm tired."

"Of course you are. Maybe we'll let you go home and get some sleep, Elliot, but we'll need to speak to you again," and now they stood up, and Pollock went to the door while Brown said something into the tape recorder and I stood up and felt my legs wobble like fuck in a breeze. "Thanks," I said.

"No, thank you," said Pollock, and now the smile was back and he reached out and touched me on the shoulder. "Next time we see you, try and remember everything. OK?"

"OK," I said, and Brown opened the door and they showed me to the front desk. "We'll get someone to drive you home," said Pollock. "Wait over there," and he pointed to a chair. I sat down. I did as I was told. I waited. And as I waited, I dozed. Five minutes? Ten minutes? Who knows how many minutes? Then I felt someone shaking my shoulder.

"Mr Jackson?"

I sat up. A policewoman was looking down at me.

"Yes."

"I'm your lift."

"Oh. Thanks," I said, and I followed her out of the station.

"Over here," she said, and as we crossed the car park, I stopped as a white car passed in front of us. It slowed, parked in a corner, and a moment later two men got out. The driver was in uniform, the passenger was not. The driver took his hat off. The passenger wasn't wearing a hat. The driver had brown hair. The passenger was bald, completely bald, and had blue eyes and thin lips. He looked comfortable in the car park,

71

but he wasn't smiling. If he could have smoked from the top of his head he would have. His face was a picture of fury, as if a storm was raging beneath his skin and in his mouth and behind his eyes and ringing in his ears. He had a policeman's badge clipped to the top pocket of his suit jacket, and as he walked to the station someone in a uniform said, "Morning, sir," to him. He growled something, shook his head and looked at me. We snagged for a moment. His pale eyes narrowed, and I saw demons in them, real demons with their own red eyes and twitching tails and snorting nostrils, and I heard them flail and yell. The mad twitch flicked the corner of his mouth, another twitch caught his arms, and then the brown-haired man opened the door for him, and he was gone.

9

On the way back to the farm, I felt the first twang of panic, like I had strings in my stomach and something was playing a bad tune on them – a tune that made no sense or music, a frightening tune that would have dogs running for cover. For a second I thought about telling the driver to turn around and take me back to the station, but I stopped myself. She was a happy woman, proud of her uniform and her car and her work, and all she wanted to do was talk about the weather. All I wanted to do was sit in silence and think about what I could do. The bald man's face, the way his lips twitched and his fingers fidgeted, and the threat in his eyes. I didn't know if he knew who I was or why I was there or what I knew, but I thought his demons would tell him. They knew. They had all the knowledge he needed, and he would listen to them.

"When's the weather going to break?"

I shook my head.

"It must be bad for you farmers."

I nodded.

"How's the hosepipe ban affect you?"

I shrugged. "It's difficult."

"I bet it is."

When we got to Stawley I asked her to drop me at the bottom of the track and I walked the rest of the way to the farm. I walked slowly, picking my way carefully over the stones and ruts, and when I got back I found Mr Evans in the hay barn. He climbed down from the bales, slapped his hands together and said, "Sorry I didn't believe you lad. That must have been a shock."

"It's OK," I said.

"What did the police say?"

"They asked me questions. Too many questions. They didn't stop. Gave me a headache."

"They know who it was?"

"I think so."

"Or who did it?"

I shrugged. "You been down there?" I nodded towards the woods and the river valley.

"They told me to keep away for a couple of days. I think they've got more investigating to do."

"I suppose they have."

"You look like you need some sleep."

"I do."

"Get all you need. I'll do the milking later."

"Thanks."

"You need anything? Tea bags? A sandwich?"

I shook my head. "I think I've got everything," I said, and I went to the caravan. I stood in the doorway and felt the heat, poured myself a glass of water, drank, lay down, closed my eyes and tried to sleep. I don't know how long I waited for it to come, but when it did I think I slept long and hard, and when I woke up I'd been out for six hours. When I opened my eyes I had one of those moments when you're disconnected from life, surroundings, feelings, memories and thought. Everything came back in a flash, and I sat up with a jolt. And the first thing I thought of was the bald man with the pale eyes, the policeman who'd come to look at the hoop house and the smoke. The policeman who knew the hanged man and looked straight ahead, neither left nor right. The one with the twitchy mouth and the slow way of talking.

This was getting too mad. Too mad by about a million times. Steal a plant from a hippy's window sill and you might get a spanking, steal hundreds of plants from a bent policeman and a bent policeman's friends who'll hang someone they think has fucked them over and you'll get a spanking, a kicking, a hammering and then you'll be executed. It was simple.

I washed. I changed my clothes. I went to see Mr Evans. He was letting the last of the cows out of the parlour. "Did you sleep?"

"Yes thanks."

"Feel better?"

"A bit." I grabbed a broom and started to wash the floor.

"Don't worry about that," he said.

"It's OK. I need to do something," and as I brushed, the work lifted my mood. I felt the dread and panic drift away for a few moments and park itself away from my mind. The relief was sweet, like someone had put cool towels on me. But the moments passed and I was back. The world seemed closer to me than it had ever been, tighter and black. I finished sweeping, walked with Mr Evans and the herd down to the pasture, and after we'd seen them safe, I got on the bike and rode out to look for Spike.

I stopped at The Globe, but no one had seen him. I tried to make a quick exit, but the word was out and people wanted to hear about the hanging man. They wanted me to tell them what I'd seen, how his face had looked, was his neck broken, was he blindfolded, were his hands tied? The rumours were wild; someone said he'd been a heroin smuggler from Bristol, someone else had heard he was a London gangster who owed his boss a million pounds. The landlady said it didn't matter who he was, the world was well rid of people like him, and it was a shame that people like me got caught up in things like that. "Here," she said, and she poured me a glass of cider. "On the house, Elliot. You get that down and put all this nastiness behind you."

So I stayed in the pub for half an hour, sipped my drink and listened to the rumours expand. By the time I left, the hanging man had been sacrificed to a blood god by a family of devil worshippers who lived in the woods. They'd been seen dancing naked around a fire, they'd been stealing sheep for months, they chanted songs in a language no one understood, everyone agreed that murder had been coming. As I left, someone suggested the regulars should pile into a Land Rover and hunt these bastards to the ground and dish out the sort of treatment they'd dished out to the hanging man. "String 'em up," said a farmer from Kittisford, and his wife agreed.

It was getting dark as I climbed onto the bike and rode away from the pub. The drink had calmed me, smoothed the knots and ties, and as I headed towards Appley Cross and the turning to Spike's place, I knew what I was going to tell him.

I was going to sit him down in his kitchen. I was going to put my panic in a box and be steady and reasoned. I was going to tell him to clear the smoke out of his garage, dump it, take a few weeks off in a place where no one knew him. Forget it had ever existed. Explain what was likely to happen to him if he didn't. Explain what was definitely going to happen to him if he didn't. And if he didn't listen, then I'd describe the look on the hanged man's face. Easy.

He was sitting in his front room, drinking beer and smoking a spliff. He had the look of someone who'd been smoking for days. His eyes were watery, and his lips cracked, and a sick haze hung in the room.

"Yeah..." he said when he saw me.

"Spike..."

"Yeah. What's happening?"

"Don't you know?"

He shrugged. "No. You going to tell me?"

"Where have you been?"

"Here. I've been relaxing."

"You seen anyone?"

"Not a soul."

"So you don't know about the guy in the woods?"

"What guy in the woods?"

"Shit, Spike. I found that bloke we saw up at the hoop house. He was dead. Someone hung him from a fucking tree."

"Someone what?"

"Someone killed him, Spike. He was murdered."

He dropped the spliff. "He was what?"

"Murdered, Spike."

"You're kidding. You're fucking kidding…"

"I went to check the cows last night. Saw torches in the woods. There was screaming. I waited for them to go, and when they did I found him."

He bent down and picked the spliff up, blew on the lit end and took a drag. "Shit."

"Yes," I said, "It is. He was growing a load of smoke for someone, and now he's dead because you stole it…"

He took a long draw on the spliff, blew smoke at the ceiling and said, "You sure about that? You sure someone would kill him? Kill him for a few plants?"

"A few plants? It's more than that. And this is probably about more than plants. That's what I think, anyway."

"Do you?"

"Yes, Spike. I do."

"That's a lot of shit to lay on me, El."

"You laid it on yourself. You went out, took your stupid head with you and did what you always do."

"Right…"

"Right? Is that all you can say?"

"No…"

"I told you, didn't I? What did I tell you?"

He shrugged.

"When you said your ship had come in?"

"Dunno…"

"HMS Fuck-Up?"

"What are you talking about?"

"You know exactly what I'm talking about."

He yawned and closed his eyes.

"You can't avoid it, Spike. You have to face it."

He shook his head.

"For the first time in your life, you have to face the consequences."

He closed his eyes.

"Spike?"

Nothing.

"Hello?"

His head dropped to one side.

I looked at him. He was my friend. He was my oldest friend, the friend I'd been through things with. Small things, big things, things with spikes and things with feathers, things weighed down with lead, things that drowned in deep ponds. We'd climbed trees, fished rivers, swum lakes, chased girls, learnt to drink together, removed engines from old cars and put them back again. But now I didn't know what to do. Whack him over the head, lock him in a shed, take the smoke myself and dump it in the river? That was the only thing I could think of doing, so I went to the kitchen and looked for something heavy.

The place was a mess. Dirty plates and saucepans filled the sink, half-eaten cans of beans and a spilt packet of cereal cluttered the table. Empty cans and bottles littered the floor, a smell of sour milk filled the place. A torn poster of somewhere tropical hung on the wall. I opened a cupboard and a broom fell out and smacked me in the face. I pushed the broom back in, closed the cupboard and went to the back door. I stepped outside and stood in Spike's yard, looked around and found a spade. I carried it inside. It was heavy and crusted with earth. I went to the living room. Spike had fallen asleep. The spliff had dropped out of his hand and was smouldering in the ashtray. I stubbed it out. I looked at his head. I looked at the spade. It could do a lot of damage. It was impossible to predict how much damage. I could just wake him up. I could give him a bruise and a headache. I could leave him with a fractured skull. Or I could kill him. So many options and so little time, and so many mistakes that I could or could not make.

10

Three hours later I lay on my bed in the caravan. The night was close and heavy, and I lay in a pool of sweat and filth. I needed a bath, but I didn't have the strength. I'd tried to read a book, but it was impossible to concentrate. The words wouldn't keep still on the page, and the story made no sense, so I turned on the radio and listened to a woman talk about a holiday she'd spent in Italy. I thought I'd like to go to Italy. I'd like to see the beautiful buildings and drink the cold beer and learn about the way Romans lived. To have a peaceful week with happy people who smiled at simple things and ate good food. To sit at a pavement café and drink a glass of beer and watch the world slip by. Peace in a crowd. Scooters and women with brown legs. Olives. Tomatoes. Not havoc in noise, or the constant feeling of threat around the corner or over the ridge of a shadowed hill.

It was good to have the burble of a stranger's voice in the dark. Comforting. Comfort is too easy to take for granted. Comfort is important. The woman was talking about Rome, and how the ancient buildings weep with blood and sorrow. Sometimes, she said, you can even hear them laugh, but mostly they scream. And when you walk the old pavements, the memories of the buried bones can amplify your own grief or pleasure or whatever emotion you might be experiencing. Yes, I thought, I understand that.

When the programme about Italy finished, it was midnight, and the news came on. I leant out of bed, turned the radio off, listened to the rustling silence and peeped through the curtains at the farmyard. Everything was still. Except for the shadows of moonlit branches in the breeze, nothing moved. And when I looked away from the shadows I could have been looking at a picture from a story book. Elves could have been hiding in the yard, plotting cruel deeds and bad tricks. Or a slavering dog could have been sitting behind the farmhouse wall, its tongue lolling and its head full of the idea of meat. It was the sort of night when anything could have been out there, but nothing was. I lay back down and closed my eyes.

I'd stood over Spike with the spade in my hand. I'd looked at the flat steel blade and I'd looked at his head. I have never been a violent man. I have never raised my fist in anger and never hit another person. But for a second I didn't see any way out. Fright was confusing me, I saw that, but what else could I do? And then I thought I'd been infected. Infected by Spike's disease. Lost in Spike's madness. You could steal the smoke, I could find a hung man, he could fall asleep, I could kill him, I could try and disappear. Stupid Elliot. Stupid, stupid Elliot. Spend the rest of your life in regret? Or stand up to panic, tell it to get lost, sort yourself, move on? Wise boy. Good, wise boy. Almost. I took a deep breath, lowered the spade and put it back where I'd found it, then went inside and put my mouth to his ear, whispered, "Get rid of the smoke, Spike," and left him where he was. There was no point trying to argue with him or reason with him, and as I rode back to the farm I rode slowly and carefully, as if the road was glass and I was a skater.

It was Saturday night. The hippy girls had asked me back to theirs for a drink. When I reached Appley crossroads I had a choice – right and home or straight on to Ashbrittle. I went straight on, and ten minutes later I was standing outside their cottage, knocking on the door.

Sam answered. She was holding a bottle of cider and smiled such a wide smile when she saw me. "If it isn't Elliot!" she said. "Come in!" and she led me inside. "Cider?"

"Yes please."

"Won't be a sec," she said, and we went through to the kitchen.

I sat at a plain wooden table. There were flower-filled jam jars on the window sill, and empty bottles with arrangements of leaves. Pretty pictures of the seaside hung on the wall, and the smell of baking filled the air. Now my fear was swept away and overwhelmed with a feeling of ease. Life could be like this. It didn't have to twist so madly. Quiet. Relaxed times. Slow motions. The room felt like a sanctuary, and after the days I'd had, I felt as though I was being washed and looked after. Sam passed me a cider, we chinked bottles and she sat opposite me.

"So what you been up to?" Her voice was light and careful, as though it was stepping on slippery stones across a river.

I shook my head. "It's been hell."

"Hell? What's happened?" She leant forwards and gently touched my knee. I felt her fingers. They were soft, like a cat's paw.

I ran my hands through my hair. I really needed a bath. "Well…" I said, but I couldn't go on.

"Tell me. Please. I'm a good listener…"

I looked at her. I believed her. I believed her, but I wondered. I didn't want to get her involved, but maybe she already was. I didn't know. Who could I trust? Could I trust anyone? I didn't know. Maybe I was just paranoid. Maybe I was as stupid as Spike. Oh fuck it, I thought, and I said, "I found a body hanging in the woods…"

"Oh God, it was you who found him?"

"Yes."

"Jesus…"

"It was a nightmare."

"I'll bet. Mind you, so was he."

"You knew him?"

"Not very well, but we saw him a couple of times up the pub."

"What was his name?"

"Fred."

"Fred?"

"Though some people called him Ox."

"Ox?"

"Yes."

"Know anything else about him?"

"Only that he was from Bristol. He came down in the spring, moved into a farm under Heniton Hill. I think it was his brother's place, though I'm not sure. I didn't take much notice. All I know is it was a bit heavy."

"Heavy?"

84

"You can't be growing that amount of smoke without it being heavy."

"I suppose not. You know what happened?"

"What do you mean?"

"You know… with the smoke…"

"I just heard some idiot nicked it." She put her cider to her lips and sipped. "I wouldn't like to be in their shoes. OK, so it wasn't much, but people like that like to make examples of people. It's the principle. I suppose they thought Fred had nicked it himself."

"They?"

"Whoever he was growing it for."

"And who are they?"

She shrugged. "I don't know, and I don't want to think about it. Do you?"

"Not really."

"Good."

"But it's hard. I keep seeing his body…"

"That must be awful."

"It is."

"And when the police took me to the station, they talked to me like I had something to do with it."

"That's the police for you."

"Like it was my fault the man was dead," and then for a moment I thought about telling her. Telling her about Spike and telling her about the bald man and his eyes and how I couldn't get the feeling of panic out of my bones. My thumping heart, my sweating skin, my dry mouth. I took a swig of cider, swilled it around and swallowed.

"Try and think about something else."

"Like what?"

"I don't know. What do you like?"

"What do I like?"

"What do you do when you're not working?"

I thought. I thought carefully. "I read books sometimes."

"So what are you reading at the moment?"

"It's a bird book."

"You like birds?"

"Yes."

"Me too. I saw three buzzards the other day, all circling around each other…"

"That'll be the parents teaching a chick," I said, and for the next twenty minutes we talked about the birds we'd seen and how the drought had been so tough for them, but maybe next year would be different. God, we hoped so. And I told her stories I heard about buzzards, about how they carried the souls of dead farmers to a field in the sky, and sowed their souls in furrows of cloud. About how the way they held their wings in their soaring could be interpreted by people who knew the secret signs.

"Do you know the secret signs?" she said.

"I might do."

"Tell me."

"I said I might do."

"You do, don't you?"

"One or two…"

"Then tell me one."

"If two buzzards circle in opposite directions, there'll be a fire in the parish. That's one of the signs. And you know what?"

"What?"

"It's true," I said, and she said, "I'm sure it is," and I said, "Sometimes I think there are things going on that we know absolutely nothing about," and she said, "I know there are," and as we talked I felt a lightness come down and finger itself into my head and take away some of the madness. It pushed this madness into a basket of its own making, covered it with a cloth and let it lie in the dark, and I sat back and listened to Sam. She had a quiet, easy way of talking, and when she started telling me stories about how she'd ended up in Ashbrittle, a long route of working in one place and then another, of living in one place and then another, of drifting and finding, losing and stopping, starting and settling, I lost myself in her voice and her face.

She'd been born in Portsmouth. Her father had been in the navy, and she'd spent half her childhood moving around the country. "Plymouth, Chatham, back to Portsmouth, Faslane. When I left school I was going to be a nurse. I trained for a couple of years, but then I gave it up."

"Why?"

"I'm not sure. I think I just got bored. And then other things happened. I went on holiday to Greece, spent most of the time drinking in a bar or lazing on the beach in the sun. I had a brilliant time. It was the first time I'd been on holiday on my own, and I just loved the place, the people, the whole Mediterranean thing. A couple of days before I was due to fly back, the owner of the bar asked me if I wanted a job. I didn't have to think twice. The thought of going back to a dingy bedsit in Swindon, the wards, the boring lectures, the rain, sick people… you get the idea."

"Oh yes."

"I stayed in Greece for a couple of years, met some brilliant people, but then the bar changed hands and I didn't have a job any more. When I got back, I didn't have any idea what I was going to do next. I found a job in a bar in Bristol, but the place was a dive. One day, a friend told me she was going to visit some mates in this place in Somerset; turned out to be Ashbrittle. I stayed a couple of days, the couple of days turned into a week, the week into a month. That was last year."

"I remember the first time I noticed you."

"When was that?"

"Last autumn. You cycled past our place."

"And what did you think?"

"I thought… I thought you looked very happy. Happy and free."

She laughed. "I think I am. At least as happy and free as I can be."

Her voice and her laugh and her face took me and held me quietly, and I was getting lost in cider and her eyes. I'd never seen eyes like them, not as brown and deep and knowing, as if they understood the things I said before I said them. They were old eyes, but they were fresh and instinctive, maybe like a cat's eyes. Or a hawk's. Waiting. Patient. Wanting. And I was thinking about telling her this, thinking about embarrassing myself and maybe leaning towards her and telling her something that I shouldn't, when the other girl I'd met at the pub came back with three hippy blokes. They'd been at the Staple Cross pub and had ridden back on bicycles.

Sam said, "You remember Ros?"

"Of course," I said, and Ros leant forwards and kissed my cheeks. She smelt of apples and fish.

"And these are the three Ds – Dave, Don and Danny," she said. Hairy blokes with rough hands and watery eyes, they shook my hand and fetched some more cider from the kitchen. We went out and sat on the lawn outside the cottage.

Pump Court was made up of four cottages. They were called Milton's, Parson's, Galilee and Venture. The hippies rented them from a naval commander who lived in the Old Parsonage. There was a cobbled path that ran along the front of the houses, and everything – garden, cooking, shopping, cider, bicycles – was shared. When Dave wanted some peanuts, he fetched them from the kitchen in Parson's even though he lived in Venture, and when Ros needed to use the loo she went to Galilee even though she lived in Milton's with Sam. There was no running water in the cottages – they used outside taps and chemical toilets, and washed in zinc baths in front of open fires – but they didn't care about that sort of thing. They cared about what was happening to the world, the way we were pouring shit into the sea and pumping crap into the air. I don't think they'd worked out how we could make things better in a big way, but they were doing things in their own small way. Ros had written to the local MP and suggested the government give everyone in the country a bicycle, and Danny was working on a plan to supply everyone with free lettuce seeds. "You don't need a garden," he said. "All you need is a window box."

"You've got to think," said Dave.

"Think, plan, do," said Don.

I couldn't disagree, and I wanted to say something that made sense to them, but before anyone had the chance to ask me anything I said, "I've got to be up at six."

"Six?" Don said.

"Milking," I said.

"Oh, right. Yeah…"

"That's early," said Danny.

"That's farming," I said.

"Sure," said Ros.

I went to the door, and Sam followed me, and as I was saying goodnight she leant forwards, put her arms around me and hugged me. She smelt of hay, and her body was warm and tight. Tight as a promise, warm as a toy in a child's hand. "Good night, Elliot," she said, and as we pulled away she kissed me once on the lips, a quick, light kiss. It felt like a bird had landed on my lips and left dust there. A house martin or a swallow or a swift. Something darty and quick. I said, "You want to see me again?"

"Of course," she said.

"Good," I said, and I almost asked her if she was sleeping with Dave, Don or Danny, or Dave and Don, or Danny and Dave, or Don, Dave and Danny, but I didn't have to. I knew she wasn't. Even I could see that. It was in her eyes, like a cat holds a bird in its mouth, plain and obvious and quiet, and as I turned and walked to my bike, I left her smiling and standing at the door to Milton's cottage with her hand waving above her head.

I rode back to the farm, and fifteen minutes later I was lying on my bed in the caravan. I thought about Sam's voice and the feel of her fingers on my knee, and I thought about how the simplest things can calm terror. I turned onto my side, switched on the radio and listened to some music. It was classical music, sad and slow, and when it was finished someone talked about Russia and how romantic it was to walk in the snow and watch a frozen river as it cracked. I thought about snow and ice. I wished for snow and ice. Then some different music started. This was faster and came from Germany. I tapped my fingers to it, and as I did I heard the sound of something moving underneath the caravan, a rat or a mouse, and the distant bark of a dog. The normal things. The easy things that leave no traces.

When the programme about music finished it was midnight, and the news came on. I leant out of bed, turned the radio off, listened to my beating heart and closed my eyes. I saw things in the dark and heard things there, but I let them pass. They weren't going to spook me. I was stronger than imagination, stronger than fright and stronger than the idea that trouble was permanent. It wasn't. Not even life was permanent. And as the comfort of that thought found a warm place to settle, I began to drift away like a bird on a thermal, and watched myself dip and swoop towards the west.

11

Sunday. I milked, mucked out, swept the yard and left the farm for the day. I didn't milk on Sunday evening, Mr Evans got a relief in, so I told him I'd see him in the morning and went to see Mum, Dad and Grace. We always have Sunday lunch together, and as I sat in the kitchen and told them about the hung man and the police they listened with their mouths open and their heads nodding.

"The world's gone mad," said Dad.

"I know," I said.

"And are you all right?"

"Not really. I'm having nightmares."

"Maybe you should see the doctor."

"Why?"

"He'll give you something to help you sleep."

"I don't want that. I wouldn't be able to get up in the morning."

Grace had learnt a new way to cook a chicken, and after she'd sat and listened for five minutes, she went to fuss in the kitchen and make some gravy. When I'd finished the story, Mum said she wanted to talk to me in the garden, so we walked down to the shed where Dad keeps his tools, stood by the door and she said, "That poor man in the woods; it's got something to do with whatever Spike's up to. Hasn't it?"

"Yes. But I don't know how."

"I knew it. Have you seen him?"

"Yes."

"So tell me. What's going on? What, exactly, is going on?"

"Mum…"

"You'd better tell me."

"I can't. I promised. And I'm afraid that if I tell you, you'll get caught up in it."

"I'm already caught up in it. I wake up every morning with the stench of it in my nose and the taste of it in my mouth. Everywhere I go I can smell it, and I can feel it in the wind. And every time I think of you, I see shadows where there shouldn't be any, and they follow me around until I stop thinking about you."

"What does it mean?"

"It means danger, Pet. More danger than you can imagine."

I didn't know what to say. What could I say? Sometimes I think Mum makes this stuff up to scare me, and that she hasn't the powers she thinks she has. Sometimes I think Spike is right and it is all mumbo-jumbo, but then I stop because however hard I try to turn away from the things she says, her words won't let me. They pull me in, suck me in, they make me believe.

"I think," she said, "that it's time you started listening to your heart. Really listen to what it says. And recognize the signs."

"What signs?"

"You know what I mean, Pet. My signs, your signs. Our signs. The old signs. They're everywhere, and you know it."

I looked at her face. Lines were appearing where lines hadn't been before, and her hair was turning white around its grey edges. She was smaller than me, but didn't feel it. Sometimes

I thought she was taller and sometimes when she talked I thought she might be able to stop a train with her voice. Most of the time it was like a moth in flight, a flutter, a touch of powder against a night window, but then it could turn. Now it turned, and her face hardened. "Do what you're told," she said. "Because if you don't, you'll meet more than trouble."

I opened my mouth to say something, anything, but was saved by Grace, who opened the kitchen window and called us into lunch, but as we walked to the house Mum said, "If you don't do it for yourself, do it for me."

"Do what?"

"You know," she said, and there was no doubting it.

When we sat down to eat, Mum said she didn't want any talk of "bad things", so Dad told us about a job he'd been doing for a retired army Major in Kittisford. The man had fought in the War, and once captured a German tank armed with only a pistol and a hand grenade. His family had been the biggest landowners in the area, hundreds of acres of the best land, farmhouses, cottages and barns, flocks of sheep, herds of cows and fast horses. Over the years the estate had dwindled, a pocket sold here, another there, and now he lived in a coach house with his library and his war pistol beside his bed. He smoked a pipe that bubbled with spit and moist tobacco, and although he had an appalling back and put up with constant pain, he was a keen trout fisherman. Which is where Dad's story began.

"He's got a small lake – more of a pond really. Lots of nice goldfish swimming about, minding their own business. So what does he do? Buys a dozen trout, sticks them in the pond and tells me he's going to fish them out in a couple of months. Good practice for when he's fishing properly, he says."

"Is that the pond you can see from the road?" said Mum.

"Yes. So the trout have been in for a couple of days, and he sends me down there to clear some smoke from the bank. Filthy job, stinking mud, and I've been working for a couple of minutes when I see these fat, bloated fish floating on the surface. It's the trout. I put the tools down and go up to find the Major. He fetches a net and we go down there and started collecting them. Twelve fish, they're all dead, and when we walk round the pond to look for the goldfish, we only see a couple. It's a mystery."

"Lovely chicken..." said Mum.

"So when we get back to the house, the Major goes to the kitchen, pulls out his sharpest knife and starts gutting the trout. And guess what?"

"Tell us, father," said Mum.

"Every single trout is stuffed full of goldfish. They've eaten themselves to death."

"What a way to go."

"That's exactly what I said. And when he'd finished gutting, he put them in a bag and told me to bury them at the bottom of the garden. It was disgusting."

"Sounds like it," said Grace.

A typical Sunday lunch at Mum and Dad's, and as I cleared the plates away and Grace took a trifle from the fridge, I glanced out of the window.

Ashbrittle is a small place. Everybody knows everybody, and everybody knows everybody's dogs, cats and cars. If you take a letter to the letter box someone will ask you if you're going to post a letter, and if you don't peg out your washing on the day you usually peg out your washing, someone will tell everyone else that you've had a heart attack while listening to the news. Every now and again, someone will come and visit the old yew tree, but other than that the place isn't visited by many strangers. So when a car no one knows appears, it's an event. It might not be mentioned in the parish magazine, but people will probably talk about it over their tea, and wonder who the people were and what they were doing.

As I was staring out of the window I saw a car I hadn't seen before driven by a bald man I had seen before. He was sitting there, staring straight ahead, his hands out of sight, still as a corpse. The moment I saw him I felt a wash of ice flow through my blood, and I froze. And as I looked at him, he turned his head very slowly towards me. Deliberate and knowing, and his eyes fixed on mine. His mouth twitched. His teeth were clean and white, and he flicked his tongue. He flicked his tongue again. I tried to look away, but I could not. The car window was open, and his eyes were as pale as clouds reflected on snow, and as cold. He stared on and on, and then he did something inside the car, reached up and his hand dropped a lit match onto the road. He wasn't smoking, and he looked like the sort of person who had never smoked. He looked like he kept himself very fit. A fanatic. A maniac in the gym with the weights and the heavy bag and the rowing machine. In the corner, pumping and swearing and pumping and swearing and pumping some more, towel around his neck, arms glistening, sweat on his face, dripping down, dripping in pools, blood under his fingernails. A tough man, wiry, sprung and ready. Swift. Planned. Silent even when he screamed. A screech owl. All these things. And then, as slowly as he had turned to look at me, he turned away again, ran his tongue over his lips, started the car and pulled away, and I was left standing with my dirty plate and a black feeling in my stomach that twisted and turned and fed on its own dark bile.

12

I didn't feel like eating trifle, and made up an excuse to leave early. Something about a cow ready to drop a calf and Mr Evans wanting me back at the farm. But they knew I was lying. They could tell. They could see it in my face and the way I thanked Grace for the food and told Dad he told a good story. Mum came with me to the door. She put her hand on my shoulder and stared into my eyes, but she didn't say anything. She just nodded, touched the middle of my forehead with her middle finger and let me go. When I got on the bike, I didn't go back to the farm. I took the road to Spike's.

I smelt it before I reached it – the dark, acrid smell of burning filled the air around Greenham. For a moment I thought that everything Mum had said was true. I was listening to my heart and recognizing the signs, and I was smelling the fire she smelt. But when I was fifty yards from his place the lane was blocked by a fire engine. Smoke was billowing over the trees, and the sound of cracking and spitting filled the air. I dropped the bike in the hedge and walked past the engine until a fireman stopped me. Hoses were snaking up the road and filthy water was running in the verge.

"Sorry mate. You can't go up there."

"What's happened?"

"House fire."

"The little bungalow?"

"Yeah."

"Is he OK?"

"Who?"

"Spike. The bloke who lives there."

"There was no one home. The neighbours called..."

"OK..."

"When can I get up there?"

The fireman shrugged. "Not sure, mate. It'll be a while. The state of the place, I reckon they'll be pulling it down."

"OK. Thanks," I said, and stood for a moment and watched as the smoke blew, then went back to my bike, picked it out of the hedge and rode back to the farm.

I rode fast and I rode badly, and all the time my mind was chasing. A voice was yelling in my head "Enough! Stop! Enough! Stop!", and when I took the junction at Appley Cross I almost came off the bike. It slewed towards the bank and I caught my foot in the hedge, took my hand off the throttle, slipped sideways and stopped. I stopped for half a minute, took deep breaths and started up again.

When I got to the farm I found a note tucked under the caravan door.

EL. I HAVE GONE BECOSE SOMEONE COME
TO MINE LAST NIGHT. I WAS OUT AND WHEN
I GOT BACK I SAW THEM ROUND THE BACK. I
GOT THE WEED SO I'LL CALL YOU WHEN I NO
WHERE I AM. SPIKE.

As I was reading the note, Mr Evans came from the farmhouse. "You missed him," he said. "Came round just after you'd gone for your lunch."

"Know where he went?"

"No. Looked in a hurry though."

"Thanks," I said, and now, in a rush of anger and flame, I thought that this was it. I was tired. Tired of living with stupidity and panic and fear and death, and I wanted to go back to how it was when I first moved into Mr Evan's caravan and I could watch birds without worrying. I wanted to be able to make a cup of tea and drink it slowly. I wanted to be able to jump on my bike and ride for no reason. I was going to talk to someone, and I was going to talk to them now. Maybe they wouldn't be there or maybe they would, but what the fuck. You do what you have to do even if you don't know if it's the only thing to do.

I rode to the phone box in Appley. I was going to take a risk, the biggest risk I could take without jumping off a bridge with a stone tied around my neck. I'd thought about it, but I didn't have any choice. I was trapped, and the trap was bolted to the floor of a cave. I could hear things in the cave, scrapes and whispers, and all the things imagination barks in the night.

I dropped the bike in a hedge, stood outside the phone box and listened. The sky was quiet, but the trees tweeked with birds. An owl here, a crow there, a family of blackbirds watching for a cat. Something rustled in the field beyond the hedge, a fox or a badger, and beyond them, sheep. They were standing in quiet groups, staring at each other as if they were having deep conversations. When sheep look like they're talking you can be sure that something bad is going to happen. I didn't doubt that, I didn't doubt it at all. There are people who say that superstition is a blanket the poor use to keep their minds warm with, but don't believe it. Superstition isn't a blanket at all. It's more than that. It's not even superstition. It's a bridge we use to cross to the place where meaning is wearing a feathered hat, an embroidered shirt, velvet trousers and big leather boots. And this meaning doesn't run. It walks and jangles the change in its pocket. I felt in my pocket for some change, jangled it, listened again. Now everything was quiet and still.

The phone box smelt of sick and beer and fags, and the floor was covered in crisp packets and something sticky. I picked up the receiver and called Taunton police station. When someone answered I dropped a coin and said, "Can I speak to DS Pollock?"

"Hang on a minute."

"Thanks."

A minute later I heard "Pollock speaking".

"DS Pollock?"

"Yes."

"This is Elliot."

"Who?"

"Elliot Jackson."

"Elliot Jackson?"

"Yes. I found the man, the man hanging in the woods."

"Oh yes. Elliot. Hello. How are you?"

"Fucked."

The man laughed. "So you've got something you want to tell me?"

"Maybe."

"OK."

"I know it's Sunday, but can I come and see you?"

"Sunday, Monday, Tuesday – it's all the same to us."

"Can I just talk to you please? In a pub or something. Somewhere quiet…"

"Well…"

"Please?"

I could hear him thinking. "Is this important?"

"Very."

"OK. You know The Black Horse? It's on Bridge Street."

"I'll find it."

"Meet you there in an hour?"

"OK."

I was there in three quarters, ordered a half and found a quiet corner table. The place was busy, but I was ignored. People played darts, stared at the juke box and chose their music, men eyed women, and a bored dog lay by the bar hatch and snoozed. Pollock appeared on time, bought a bottle of Coke, sat down opposite me and said, "This isn't how we like to do things, Elliot…"

"It's the only way I can," I said. "I'm scared."

"You're scared? Now why would that be?"

"Well…" I said, "it's difficult."

"Start at the beginning."

"Can I trust you?" I said, knowing that even if he said that I could I was taking a chance.

"Of course you can trust me, Elliot. I'm a policeman."

I laughed.

"Why the laugh? And why the question?"

"Can I fucking trust you?"

"Yes," he said. "You can trust me."

I looked into his eyes. I watched his mouth. He gave nothing away, but there was nothing I could do. Nothing at all. I had to ignore whoever he was and whatever he knew. I had no choice. "OK," I said. "I'll tell you," and I did.

I started at the beginning, told him about the time Spike came to me and said he'd seen someone in the woods below Heniton Hill, and how we'd found the smoke in the hoop house, and how he'd stolen it. And how the hanging man had been the someone we'd seen, and now Spike's house had been burned to the ground, and then I said, "We saw someone else with the man who died."

"You said."

"But I saw him again."

"Where?"

"In the car park behind the police station."

"What?"

"I think he's a policeman."

Now Pollock narrowed his eyes, leant towards me and lowered his voice. "You think he's a policeman? And why would you think that?"

"He was in a suit, but he had a police badge sticking out of his top pocket. And someone called him 'sir'. And I saw him again. He was sitting in a car outside my mum and dad's house. And I think he burned my mate's house down."

"And why do you think that?"

"Because he dropped a lit match out of the car window."

"Not a lot of evidence to go on, Elliot."

"I know. But he has a twitchy mouth. And a look in his eyes."

"A look in his eyes? Don't we all?"

"Not like they want to kill you."

"OK." He sipped some Coke.

"Now you see why I asked if I could trust you?"

He nodded. "I do."

"And can I?"

"I told you. Yes. And can I tell you why?"

"Please."

"Because you're talking about DI Dickens."

"DI Dickens?"

"Detective Inspector Dickens, Elliot. We call him Twitchy."

"Because of his mouth?"

"Exactly. He's not a man to fuck with. He's got more decorations than a Christmas tree, and he's twice as prickly. And he's as mad as…"

"So you think I'm kidding you?"

"Not at all." He moved even closer to me. "Far from it. There are people out there who've been trying to nail him for years."

"Why? What else has he done?"

"Lots, Elliot. He's got his fingers in a lot of pies. He's a vicious bastard. But there's nothing anyone can prove. Not yet, anyway."

"And who are these people?"

He tapped the side of his nose. "Look," he said, and he fished in his pocket, pulled out a card and put it on the table. "First of all, you're a lucky bloke. When you decided to call me, you called the right man."

"You've got an honest face." I sipped my drink. "I think."

"That's what my missus says." He pushed the card towards me and tapped it. "This is my direct line. If you call it and someone else answers, don't say a word. Just hang up. In the meantime, I'm going to speak to someone I know in Bristol."

"Who?"

"Don't worry. But they might be the best friend you ever had."

"OK."

"You know where your mate is?"

"No. But I've got an idea."

"OK. Because if I'm thinking right, we might need him."

"Why?"

"And we'll need the smoke."

"I think he's got it."

"Good."

"So go and find him. Try and talk some sense into him."

"That won't be easy."

"The difficult is never easy, Elliot. Maybe you're beginning to learn that."

"I think I am," I said, and I leant back and for a moment I caught a look in Pollock's face that spun at the edge of deceit. Either he was honest or he was a genius liar. "Fuck…"

I said, and he smiled. At least I think it was a smile, though it could have been a grimace or a response to the Coke he was drinking, or the news he was taking back to the police station.

13

I'm a good worker. I put my head down. I do what I'm told.
If I'm asked to do something I don't want to do, I'll still do
it, usually. I don't mind getting dirty. I don't complain if my
shirt is torn. I sweat. And when I sweat I take my shirt off and
tuck it in my belt and work on. I whistle and I sing, and if I
have the time I'll stop for five minutes and listen to the world
in its turning and ripping. But then I'll go back to work and
sweat some more.

I used to sweat when I worked for the tree surgeon, and I
used to sweat at the pig farm. And before those jobs I sweated
for a man called Albert who made ornamental blocks. We'd
work in a shed at the bottom of his garden, mix cement in a
knackered mixer and pour the stuff into patterned moulds.
When the cement had set, we'd knock the blocks out, stack
them in a corner and wait until they were dry. Then we'd load
samples into a van, visit garden centres and landscapers and
try and sell them. Albert was an optimist, but his optimism
took a beating as everyone we tried to sell the blocks to shook
their heads and said that they bought their ornamental blocks
from someone else. "But ours are handmade," Albert would say,
scratching the palms of his hands and making weird clicking
sounds with his tongue. "I can see that," the customer would
say, shaking his head and pointing at some flaw on the block.
I worked for Albert for a couple of months, but when the

ornamental-block business went tits up he told me it would be best if I looked for work somewhere else. He didn't have the heart to tell me that he'd have to let me go, but I could see it in his eyes and the way his lips shivered. He was down, but he wasn't beaten – the last time I saw him he told me he was buying one of those old-fashioned bicycles with an ice-cream box in the front. He was going to take it to Torquay and cycle up and down the sea front selling lollies and cones. "I'm going to make a killing," he said, and I believed him. I'm like that. I believe people and I try to believe myself. So if I haven't felt sweat roll off my neck and down my back I'll think I've had a dishonest day, and I'll have a word with myself. Maybe I'm old-fashioned like that, or maybe it's in my blood. I don't know.

In the morning I used work and sweat to block the fright and panic. I could have asked Mr Evans for the day off, could have made up some excuse, but there were jobs to do. So when I'd finished the milking and he asked me to go to the copse beyond the top fields and cut some wood for his winter fires, I did as I was told.

The copse was long and thin, untidy with hazel coppice and ash, and it slipped down a frightened slope like a skirt off a thigh. I took an axe, a bow saw and some sacks, and when I found a good stand, I started chopping. A robin came to watch me work and wait for the likely worm, and hopped from branch to branch with a cheep and a twitch. I remembered a story I'd heard about how robins were only brave in England: if they live in any other country they're furtive and shy, and hide behind leaves in the densest bushes. I said, "You're a brave bird," to him, and he tweeted back at me, flitted towards the place where I'd piled the sacks, sat on one and stared at me. "But you're not to follow me home and come indoors," I said. A robin in the house means a death in the family. "You hear me?" The bird looked at me, hopped to a closer branch, sang a little song and carried on watching me. I went back to work, and when I had a stack of wood as high as a bale, I found a crook and started sawing.

The work was hard and hot, but the shade of the copse kept the worst of the heat away. And for a while I did force the trouble away. If it had been a mouse it would have hidden itself in a hole in the ground, curled itself up and tucked its tail to its nose. It would have breathed so quietly not even a beetle would have heard the noise, or an ant. And as the logs piled up, so the trouble faded to a whisper and all my mind did was think about how Mr Evans would keep warm and cosy through the long dark nights of winter.

I love the smell of fresh sawn wood. It's the smell of promise, like the smell of a cut tomato or baking bread. If it could be a person, it would be a good listener, someone with kind eyes, a smile and a glass of cold lemonade. It wouldn't have travelled much, but it would be wise. And when it spoke it would speak slowly and quietly, short sentences, simple words, nothing complicated. It wouldn't threaten, wouldn't understand violence, wouldn't welcome trouble. And as I started to fill the sacks with wood, I thought, for a moment, that the smell of the wood did speak to me, did say, "One day, all this will pass. One day, you will be able to sleep again."

The robin got bored with watching me and flew off to find something more interesting to do, and an hour later I was back at the farm. I stacked the sacks of logs in a lean-to behind the house, then fetched the cows in for milking. They were waiting at the gate, dusty and swishing their tails at the flies. As I followed them to the backyard, Mr Evans came and stood at the kitchen door and said, "Don't forget the cat."

"I never do."

"Good lad," and he went to make a cup of tea.

After milking, I ate a sandwich and went to look for Spike. There were two places he could have run to. The first was his sister's. She lived in Wellington. It didn't seem likely: the last time I heard they weren't talking, but I called in anyway.

She answered the door with a kid on her hip. She had her brother's wiry look, but this was doubled by her tired mouth, the rings around her eyes and her thin, spidery hands. As she looked at me she was joined by a huge dog. It had a bandage on its head and weird, crossed eyes. It looked at me, showed its teeth and growled. "You're kidding," she said, when I asked if he was there. "I wouldn't have that bastard here if you paid me."

"Have you heard from him?"

"No. Not for months."

"OK."

"So what's he done now?"

"Oh you know…"

"No I fucking don't. If I did I wouldn't be asking, would I?"

"No, I suppose you wouldn't," I said. "He… he said he'd meet me for a drink, but didn't show."

110

"Really?"

"Yes. Really."

She shook her head at me, the kid started to whine, and I could see she didn't believe me, but I didn't care. "Look," she said, "I've got stuff to do. You run along, and if you find him, don't say hello from me..." The dog took a step towards me. It looked hungry, and for a moment its eyes glazed over.

"OK. Thanks."

She looked at me in amazement. Maybe no one had said "Thanks" to her for years. Or maybe they had. But whatever. She said nothing in reply, and slammed the door in my face. I stood for a moment and listened as she disappeared into the house, and then went back to the bike.

I rode on, out of Wellington towards Milverton. The road was quiet and twisty, the shadows were long in the parched fields, and there was a corner near the turning to Langford Budville where a little whirlwind of dust suddenly appeared, spinning over the hedge. The dust was curling and rising like a ghost, a thin woman in a yellowed dress, her features blanked by trouble and loss and death. Spinning towards whatever hell she thought she was due, lost at the edge of what I could see and what I didn't want to know. I slowed down to look, but as quickly as it had appeared it – or she – disappeared behind the hedge, leaving clear air, blue sky and the outline of a pear orchard. I heard a dog bark, I accelerated, I leant into the corner and headed down the hill.

Milverton was a smart little village with rich houses, tidy gardens, roses growing on honeystone walls, a trimmed churchyard and neatly parked cars. The place smelt of money, but here and there were places where money and tidiness couldn't get a grip. One of these places was behind a raised terrace on the Taunton road, a filthy cottage with rotting windows, holes in the roof and the sound of bad music booming from an upstairs room. Rubbish was piled in the garden, and a broken bed was leaning against the front wall. This was home to some of Spike's smoking friends, a crowd of crusties who rented the place and didn't do a lot else. I knocked on the door, but there was no reply. I yelled towards the upstairs window but it didn't open, so I went to the pub in the main street and found one of the crusties sitting at the bar. He was as drunk as fuck, and when I asked him if he'd seen Spike, he said, "Who wants to know?"

"I do."

"And who are you?"

"His mate."

"Spike's got a mate?"

"Yeah."

"You could have fooled me."

"I don't want to fool anyone."

The crusty looked at me, tried to sit up straight, slumped back, stuck a finger in his ear, pulled it out, stared at the crud he'd found and said, "Are you fucking with me? Cos if you are I'll fuck you." He belched. "And when I fuck you you'll stay fucked. Got it?"

"Hey…"

"And don't fucking 'hey' me!"

"OK." I took a step back and said, "Thanks. If you see him, tell him Elliot was looking for him."

"Tell him your fucking self."

I took another step back, then turned and made a swift exit, jumped on the bike and was out of Milverton before anyone had a chance to spot me, chase me and whack me on the back of the head with a mallet.

I rode without knowing what I was going to do next. I headed towards Bathealton, slowed to look in pull-ins and green lanes and copses and hidden gateways, and when I reached the top of the hill on the road to Stawley, stopped and stood and scanned the fields below. I wasn't expecting to see him, but I thought it was better to look than not.

The sun was setting, and it coloured the land green and gold. A flock of crows was heading to its roost, and cows, fresh from milking, were fanning through the meadows. The woods looked cool, the single trees looked right, the farms and houses were safe. It was easy to feel fooled by the scene, the peace and quiet and beauty and dying heat. Easy to think that here was the secret of calm, here you could find the end of some rainbow. Some place where leaves drifted and water lapped, and the earth folded like sheets over sleepers. Quiet guitars could strum, a flute could warble, rabbits could skip and jump from their holes. A paradise of colour and quiet, a place where worried people could meet and leave their worries behind.

And people did leave their worries behind in this place. They walked footpaths through the fields and over the hills. They held hands, they talked in low, quiet voices, they laughed. They had picnics in the shade of green trees. They leant with their backs against gates and shared bottles of beer. And when they'd finished eating and drinking and talking, they closed their eyes and let warmth and comfort bathe them.

I sat and stared and smelt the air for half an hour. A couple of cars drove by, and a tractor, and in the distant lanes I saw other cars and other tractors, but no white van. I heard a motorbike, another motorbike, a buzzard high over my head. A bee. A squad of pigeons. Another bee. Some walkers crossed the field below me and disappeared into a copse. I waited for them to appear again, but they didn't. They were probably bird watchers or maybe they were looking for a quiet place to fuck. It's impossible to tell what people are planning or thinking when all you can see is their backs from half a mile away, so I got back on the bike, rode on and stopped at The Globe for a pint. All the talk was about the fire at Spike's place, and how he was an accident waiting to happen. Someone said, "I went down there one day, and the place was a pit. Shit everywhere. You wouldn't sit on the sofa. He had a gas fire that looked like it had come out of the ark, and his cooker... I don't want to think about it."

"He wouldn't be told," someone else said.

"Wouldn't be told what?" I said.

"To tidy himself up."

"All he has to do is make an effort."

"Not a bad worker though. Always puts his back into it. He doesn't look it, but he's as strong as an ox."

"True."

"But that's not everything, is it?"

"No."

"You've got to have some discipline, a sense of responsibility."

"True."

"Talk of the Devil…"

I looked out of the window as Spike's van slowed down outside and pulled into the car park. I left my pint and went outside to see him. He parked and sat with his hands on the wheel. He was pale, and his lips were cracked, and had a mad, hunted look in his eyes. He was shaking and sweating, and biting his nails. I'd never seen him like it before. He looked like some sort of mirror of the friend I used to know. Life had been sucked out of him and something blank had been put in its place. I got in the van and sat in the passenger seat. The smoke was stacked in bags in the back. It was sweating and it stank. I said, "What the fuck are you doing here?"

"I didn't know where else to go. I went up to your place, but you weren't there. I've just been driving around. I'm scared…"

"You're scared?" I thought I'd never hear him say such a thing, but there it was, the words bare and out. "I'm not surprised."

"Fucking scared, El."

"I got your note. There are some heavy guys looking for you, Spike."

"I know."

"And they're pissed off."

"More than pissed off, El. They burned my fucking house down. I've lost everything. All my clothes. My records, the telly, the stuffed badger."

"The stuffed badger?"

"Yeah."

"Fuck. You've had that for ages."

"I know. And my pictures."

I put my hand on his arm. He looked at it as if it was a surprise. "But you've got your van…" I said.

"Sure."

"And the smoke. How did you manage that?"

"I'd put it in the van last night. I was going to see my man in Exeter."

"You were going to see your man in Exeter…" I said the words slowly, like I couldn't believe I was saying them.

"But I got paranoid."

I shook my head. "You know what you've got to do, Spike."

"What?"

"Get away. Disappear."

"Disappear?"

"Yes."

"And how the fuck am I going to do that? Whatever I do, wherever I go, they'll find me. They'll hunt me like a fucking dog." He put his hand on mine. It was hot. "I should have listened to you…"

"You should have what?"

"Listened to you."

I didn't believe what he'd just said. "That would have been a first."

"But I didn't realize, I didn't think it would end up like this."

"You never do think, Spike."

He shook his head. "OK, El. Tell me. Tell me what I've got to do."

"Only if you listen. And only if you do as I say. No arguments. Can you manage that?"

"I'll try."

"You'll have to do better than that, Spike. A lot better."

"I'll try."

"Try?"

"I'll do whatever you say."

"Good. And you'll have to trust me."

"Trust you?" He scrabbled in his pocket, pulled out a packet of fags, put one in his mouth and took half a shaking minute to light it. He inhaled deeply, blew the smoke at the windscreen and said, "OK."

"And do everything I say."

"OK."

"Promise?"

"I promise."

"Good."

"To start with, we have to hide the smoke. OK?"

"OK."

"So get this fucking van started and follow me."

"Where are we going?"

"My place."

"But…"

"I said no arguments, Spike…"

"But…"

"Spike!"

117

He put his hands up. "OK."

He followed me. It only took ten minutes to get to the farm, but it was a long ten minutes. They could have been anywhere, waiting in a gateway, behind a wall, in a barn or at a crossroads. They didn't take a day off. It was obvious. They could be spying from a hedge or the top of a tall tree. They could be in that car or that van, or waiting on bikes in a lay-by. Behind the curtains of a rented cottage, through a crack in a fence, or watching from a shepherd's hut in the middle of a small field. Hiding like a vole in a hole, whiskers twitching and nose going, tongue licking its little lips at the thought of a fat worm. So when we reached the farmyard we parked by the caravan and I told him to stay in the van. He nodded and sat with his hands on the steering wheel, looking this way and that, licking his lips. Mr Evans was in the house, watching the television. I knocked on the front door, and when he answered I told him that a mate had turned up. I thumbed towards the van. Spike nodded and tried a smile. I knew Mr Evans didn't like strangers on his land, so I said, "I didn't want you to worry."

"Worry? Me?" he said. "What have I got to worry about?" and he went back to his programme.

We stepped into the caravan, sat down for half an hour and drank a beer. We tried to talk about things that wouldn't panic us, things we'd done when we were kids, places we'd been, scrapes we'd avoided, but whenever there was a silence I knew what he was thinking, and he knew what I was thinking, and we'd lock eyes and I'd shake my head and I'd think he was about to cry. I opened another couple of beers, another half-hour passed, and then I saw Mr Evans's downstairs light go out. I checked the time. It was ten. He was going to bed. "Give him twenty minutes," I said, "and then we'll get going."

Another beer, a couple of cigarettes for Spike, an upstairs light went out and then the house was dark. When I thought it was safe, I said, "OK. Do exactly as I say."

I went back to the yard, sat in the driver's seat with the handbrake off and the gears in neutral and told Spike to push. Once we had it out of the front yard, it was easy freewheeling past the hay barn and into the sunken lane that skirted the top meadows and the field where Mr Evans grew winter kale. An old barn stood in the bottom corner of this field, a place where we kept an old trailer, a set of harrows and some other broken bits of machinery. It was hidden by a high hedge and surrounded by clumps of old coppice. I got Spike to open the field gate, started the van, gunned it up the track, swung it round and stopped by the barn doors.

We spent half an hour making a space for the van, pushing the trailer to one side and pulling the harrows into the field. Then we pushed the van inside, covered it with an old tarpaulin, and rolled the trailer back inside. The harrows stacked beside the trailer, and we tossed a few old hay bales on top of the tarp. When we stood back, the van was invisible. I closed the doors, slid the bolt, and while Spike wasn't looking I tucked a stick of straw behind the bolt.

"Job done," I said.

"Thanks El…"

I faced him. "You've got to promise me something, Spike."

"What?"

"You won't come up here. If I see you snooping around, this is the last help you get from me."

"I promise."

"Swear. Swear you'll keep away."

"I swear, El. I don't want to see that stuff again."

I stared into his eyes, and I thought he was telling the truth. He had to be, otherwise he was lost to me. "OK," I said, "where are you going to stay?"

"Well, I was wondering, seeing like you've got a spare bed and…"

I put my hand up. "Not a chance. I'll drop you somewhere, but after that you're on your own…"

"OK. Maybe my sister's."

"I don't think so. I went to see her when I was looking for you. She said she wouldn't have you there if you paid her. What did you do to piss her off?"

"Nothing."

"You're such a fucking liar, Spike. And your mates in Milverton weren't that pleased to hear your name either."

"You saw them too?"

"Yeah."

"Fuck."

"I suppose I could try someone in Wiveliscombe. I'm owed a favour."

"OK. Wivey it is," and when we got back to the farm, I got him on the back of the bike and we left. I rode carefully and slowly, let the panic settle in my stomach, and avoided a fox in the road at Bathealton. I felt his heart thumping against my back, and for a few minutes I thought that this was how friends should be: joined, attached, travelling through a night for a reason that had something to do with anything but running away from fright. We should have been able to ride slowly and not have to look around every corner, and we should have been able to laugh. The lanes should have held no threat, the fields should have been gold and hedged and voled. But we didn't laugh, and we didn't talk, and when we reached Wivey he directed me to a place on Golden Hill. It was a quiet street. No people, no dogs, no cats. A few pieces of paper blown in air, but that was all. I said, "What are you going to do?"

"Keep my head down."

"I think that's a good plan."

"I might read a book."

I couldn't remember Spike ever reading a book, but the idea that he was going to try was a good one. I said, "Have you got one?"

"Jim's got plenty."

"Jim?"

"My mate. He lives here." He thumbed at the front door of a cottage.

"OK. Well, choose a long one."

"I might do that."

He held out his hand. Another thing I couldn't remember Spike doing before. Shaking hands. We shook. "OK," I said. "You take care. I'll come and see you in a day or two."

"Will you?"

"Of course."

"Thanks," he said.

"Take care, Spike," I said, and I watched him until he was in the house and I thought he was safe, and then I turned back the way we'd come, home to some sort of peace and shelter.

14

In the morning I milked, did my chores, and after breakfast I walked down the sunken lane to the kale field, and checked the barn. The stick of straw was still tucked behind the bolt, and when I put my eye to the crack between the doors I could see the trailer, the harrows, the tarpaulin and the hay bales, but the van was hidden well. I couldn't see any part of it, or smell the smoke. I tapped the doors for luck. Back at the farm, Mr Evans fetched some creosote from the store, and I helped him to paint the yard fence.

He was in a talkative mood, and when I told him where I'd been with Spike he told me that in the old days he used to walk to Wivey to go to the Saturday dances. "Those were the days…" He'd meet up with friends along the way, and by the time they reached the town there'd be five or six of them. "We could be terrors," he said, "but the girls liked us."

"I bet they did."

"Oh yes," he said, and he let the words kindle something in his head, something stronger than a quiet and simple memory. Sometimes he could look smaller than he was, and weaker. His eyes went misty and he wiped his nose with his sleeve, and he said, "Oh yes," again.

I knew what I wanted to ask him. Maybe he sensed the question, because he said, "I met a lovely girl. Mary. She worked in the school. I don't think her parents approved of me, rough farm-hand, dirt in his turn-ups, all that. Not that they made any difference…"

"What do you mean?"

"The War did for it."

"The War?"

"Yes lad, the War."

"Why?"

"I was called up. 1941. I'd never been further than Taunton, but suddenly I was on a train to God knows where. Spent the next year and a half square-bashing, rifle-training, cleaning kit. They used to move us from camp to camp, and we never knew if the next day we'd be off to do some proper fighting. I'd write to her, but I don't know if she ever got my letters. Maybe the censors got hold of them. Or her parents. I don't know."

"Did you fight?"

"Did I fight?"

"Yes."

He was holding a paint brush. Creosote dripped off its end. "Oh I fought. I fought like a demon."

"Where?"

The creosote dripped on, black tears into the dust.

"Sicily," he said. "Sicily. That's where it started. Then the mainland. Italy. The Germans, they were tough. The Italians usually ran."

"Did you kill anyone?" I said, but as the words came out I knew it was a question too far.

He looked at me and shook his head. "Why would you want to know that?"

"I don't know. I just wondered."

He snapped at me. "Well you can keep wondering, Elliot. You can keep wondering and not ask me those sort of questions again." He was getting angry, but then I couldn't be sure. I hadn't seen him angry, so didn't know what to look for. Maybe he was just irritated. "There are some questions you don't ask."

I wanted to say I was sorry, that I hadn't meant to ask the question, but the way he looked at me told me that I should shut up. Not say another word. His face had hardened, and his eyes were distant, and when he slapped the creosote on the fence now he did it quickly, carelessly. We had work to do, and there would always be work to do. Work was more important than bad memories, more important than questions or answers. Get on with it. So I did.

When it was time for lunch, he dropped his brush in the pot and went inside without a word. I rode to the phone box at Appley. It was time to call Pollock again. Someone else answered, so I did as I'd been told and hung up. I walked down the lane to The Globe, sat outside and ate a sandwich with a glass of Coke. I was edgy, I jumped every time a car pulled up at the turning beside the pub, but the sandwich was fresh and filled me up.

Before I went back to work, I tried Pollock again. This time he answered. I told him I'd found the smoke and hidden it where no one could find it, and Spike was staying somewhere which was as safe as it could be.

"Good man," he said, and he cleared his throat. "We've been thinking."

"We?"

"Yes, Elliot, we. You know the expression 'it takes a thief to catch a thief'?"

"Yes."

"Well…" and he lowered his voice to a whisper, "it takes more than one copper to catch another copper."

"OK."

"So you and I have to meet again. I've got a few loose ends to tidy up here, but I'll be out by seven."

"Seven it is," I said. "Same place?"

"Never the same place twice, Elliot. I'll come to Wellington. You know The Dolphin?"

"Yes."

"Be there," he said, and he hung up.

I was mechanical for the rest of day. I painted the rest of the yard fence, stacked a delivery of cattle cake in the store beside the parlour, dug some potatoes from the vegetable garden and milked the herd. A couple of times my brain even forgot about the smoke and Spike and the hung man, and when my head came back to thinking about these things, for a moment they felt like part of a dream I'd had, or a dream I was having.

I got to The Dolphin early, and settled in a corner with a pint and a packet of crisps. A few regulars were sitting at the bar, men who looked as though they lived there and had been drinking since breakfast. When Pollock arrived, he walked straight to where I was sitting, bent down, said, "Finish your drink and then come and find me in the car park," and he left before I could reply.

What could I do? One second I thought this might be a normal thing to do, the sort of way policemen worked. The next second

I thought this is a trap, this is what was always going to happen, this is the last pint I'll ever drink. But what could I do? What else could I think? Where else could I go? I drained the glass, took it to the bar, thanked the barman and left.

As I turned into the car park, Pollock was waiting for me. "OK?" he said.

"I think so."

"Good. Then follow me."

I followed, and when we reached the car, he opened the back door and said, "In you go." I climbed in and found myself sitting next to another man, a plain-looking man with cropped hair and small ears. He was wearing a suit and tie and sat with his hands on his knees. He looked calm and quiet, like a priest at an altar. Pollock said, "This is Inspector Smith."

I said, "Hello."

Inspector Smith nodded, but didn't say anything to me. He carried on looking straight ahead. "OK Pollock. Drive."

"Sir."

We drove, and as we headed out of Wellington I said, "Where are we going?", but when neither of them answered I sat back and stared out of the window at the houses and the people and the cars. And when we crossed the bypass and started to climb the road towards the Blackdown hills, I counted sheep and cows.

The Blackdowns are hidden and secret, a place where lanes disappear into ancient hill forts and don't come out again, and where women on bicycles smile gappy smiles and leave the smell of chicken shit in the air. Broken machinery stands in hidden fields, cars rock with illicit lovers, kestrels hover over knowing rabbits. The wind whistles across damp marshes, and the ghosts of pilots and soldiers stalk the remains of World War Two airfields. Cows are thin and sheep look nervous, more nervous than sheep usually do, though I wouldn't know why. It's difficult to know what's going on in a sheep's head, or to understand why they do the things they do. Like leap four feet vertically for no reason, or follow each other over cliffs. There were no cliffs on the Blackdowns, just tiny fields and dark woods, deep ditches and high hedges.

We drove for twenty minutes, and when we reached the top road we turned onto a bumpy track that led through beech woods. The trees were tall and full, and when we stopped and the engine settled, I wound the window down and listened to the leaves in the breeze. Birds sang for a moment, stopped singing, started again, watched us. I knew they were watching us, because I could feel their beaky little heads pointing in my direction, and sense their black little eyes boring into me. Maybe they thought I had some seeds for them, or bread, or maybe they didn't think at all. I suppose the average bird has a brain the size of a peanut, so thought might not have anything to do with what birds do, and instinct is the only thing that makes them do what they do. We sat in silence, and for a moment I thought about asking Pollock if he had any idea how a bird's brain works, but then Smith turned to me and said, "So. Elliot."

"Yes?"

"I work in Bristol."

"Do you?" I said. I'd been to Bristol a few times. I'd driven across the suspension bridge and looked down at the river, and

I'd walked across the downs and wondered why people throw rubbish in bushes.

"Yes. I work for a team that investigates corruption. Police corruption. You understand what I mean?"

"I'm not stupid."

"Of course you're not."

"And you're investigating Dickens."

"Very good."

"Has he been a bad policeman?"

Smith's expression didn't change. He had eyes and a nose and a mouth, but his face was a blank and featureless nothing. It was a wall and there was nothing behind it. No garden, no sea, no road, no milling crowds. I suppose it was the ideal face for his type of work. "Yes," he said. "He's been a very bad policeman. And he's been a very bad policeman for a long time now, and we want to do something about it."

"Why haven't you done anything before?"

"You ask a lot of questions, Elliot."

"Do I?"

"Yes. Too many. I think you should think about asking less and doing more."

"Maybe I could say the same thing to you," I said.

For a moment, Smith's expression did change. A hint of annoyance crept onto the corner of his mouth, and he blinked. But then the blankness was back. It slapped his forehead. "You'll say nothing of the sort," he said. He clicked his tongue against the roof of his mouth.

"OK," I said. There was no point arguing and no point fucking around. "So what do you want from me?"

"The truth. From the beginning."

"I already told Pollock. He knows everything."

"And he tells me that every time you do, the story changes a bit. So this time I'd like you to be careful. Think before you say anything."

"OK," I said, and I started at the beginning again. Spike. The Globe. Meeting Spike at The Globe. Listening to Spike at The Globe. Following Spike to the hoop house. Hiding in the undergrowth. Seeing the men. Seeing Dickens. Going round to Spike's and seeing the plants hanging in his garage. And on and on, the hung man, the bald man, Spike's house burning down. Hiding the van and the smoke.

"And where have you hidden it?"

"Somewhere safe," I said.

"How safe?"

"Very," I said.

"You can tell us."

"I'd rather not."

"We'd rather you did, Elliot. We really would."

I shook my head.

"Elliot?"

"Yes?"

"When I say we'd rather you did, I mean it. If we're going to help you, you've got to help us."

"But I thought it was the other way round. I thought I was helping you."

"We're helping each other, Elliot."

"Good," I said.

There was silence in the car for a moment and then Smith said, "Sergeant Pollock and I are going for a little walk and talk. We won't be long, and we'll keep you in sight, so don't think about doing anything silly."

"What do you mean, 'silly'?"

"We don't want you doing a runner."

"Would I?"

"No. I don't think you would. But if the thought occurred, you wouldn't be doing yourself any favours. You know that, don't you?"

"You think I want to walk back to Wellington?"

"No."

"I'll be here."

"Good lad," he said, and they climbed out of the car.

They didn't go far. I watched them walk and heard their feet crunching on the dry leaves of the forest floor, and I heard them talking – low voices mixing with the rustling trees and the calling birds. I sat still and quiet. I was starting to get a faint buzz in my ears. I tried to distract myself by counting. I reached fifty, but got bored, so I started to think about what I was going to do when I was out of this. A holiday would be good. Two weeks in a place where no one knows who I am. Somewhere warm where I could wear shorts and sandals and drink without getting drunk. Somewhere quiet where I could sit on a wall and learn to play a musical instrument. I was listing the places I'd like to visit – Italy, Spain, Greece, Turkey – when they came back to the car. "OK," said Pollock, "We've had a little chat, and we're going to trust you, Elliot."

"You're going to trust me?" I snorted.

"Yes."

"But can I trust you?"

"Why ask?"

"If one of your lot is bent, then why can't all of you be bent?"

"Good question. Not one I can answer."

"I can," said Smith. "Some of us believe in truth. Decency. Serving the public. Keeping the world safe for good people. And some of us know that if those ideas are lost, then the world is lost. Then we might as well close up the shop, go home and wait for the balloon to go up."

"What balloon?" I said.

"*The* balloon," said Smith. "The one with the skull and crossbones on it," and then he sat back, folded his arms and said, "Drive."

Pollock started the car. "We're going to take you back to The Dolphin now, but when we're ready to move, we're going to ask you to do something for us. It might be a bit dangerous, but I think you're up for it."

"How dangerous?"

"Well, put it this way," he said, and he pulled off, bumping down the track towards the road, "we won't be asking you to fight a badger's dad."

"Thanks."

"And we might even pay you for your trouble. A little something out of petty cash…"

"Pay me?"

"You never know."

"And what about Spike?"

"What about him?"

"Are you going to need him?"

"Need him? For what?"

"To help?"

"Well, if what you say about him is true, he's not that reliable. Is that true?"

"Probably."

"The sort of person you couldn't trust in a crisis."

"Well, I don't know about that."

"No," said Smith. "We'll leave him out. Let him stew in his own juice."

I didn't like to think of Spike stewing in any sort of juice, lying on a mattress in a room in a house in Wivey with no work and no money, scared to go out, playing his idiocy over and over in his head, wondering when he was going to get out of this mess. But what could I do? Nothing more, and there was probably nothing more he could do either, so I said, "OK," and when we reached the end of the bumpy track, Pollock turned onto the road and the long hill towards Wellington. When we reached the pub, Smith said, "You've been very helpful, Elliot. We've been trying to nail Dickens for years, and you're the break we've been waiting for. And you're not to worry. We'll keep you safe."

"That makes me feel a lot better."

"Good."

"I didn't mean it."

"I know."

"Do I call you?"

"Yes. Give us a couple of days."

"OK."

"Keep safe, Elliot."

"I'll try."

He reached across me, opened the door and said, "You're free to go."

"Thanks," I said, and I stepped out of the car and walked to my bike.

15

Stawley church sits like an ark in its own green sea, a drop of warm stone, somewhere to stop and hope for balm or help. It's a peaceful place, and when I was at primary school the teacher took my class there for a history lesson, and we learnt about the Normans and a man called Henry Howe. He was a rich and powerful man in the parish, and when he died the words "Pray for the soule" were carved backwards over one of the doors. I suppose I was about nine or ten, but I remember how it was on that day: it was spring, and buttercups were growing around the graves, and Spike was laughing instead of listening to what the teacher had to say. I was never a swot, but I listened and thought that if I'd been born in the olden days I would have liked to have met Sir Francis Drake and travelled with him to the Spanish Main. I would have stood next to the man while he navigated and fought and stole, and when he returned to show the Queen his treasure, I would have told her that yes, I was as brave as he was, and as bold.

I stopped at the church on my way back to the farm, stood in the graveyard, stared at the dying flowers in their vases, and then went inside. It was cool and quiet, and I sat in one of the pews and let the place calm me. I've never believed in gods, never thought that anything could have a greater power than a wood or a field, so I didn't say a prayer or hope that someone would lay a kind hand on me, but I did dip my head, fold my hands and listen.

A bee was trapped against one of the windows, and as it banged against the glass its buzz rose and dipped. It was too high for me to cup and carry outside, so I let it do what it had to do. Maybe it would find some pollen in the flowers by the altar, and maybe it would find its way home through a crack in the door. I wondered – do bees recognize the problems they face? Do they worry? Do they ever stop for a moment and wonder? Or are they, as I read in a *National Geographic* magazine, simple machines, useless without their queen, as their queen is useless without them? Tiny cogs turning until they die, with no chance to make a choice or take an unexpected opportunity? Maybe, I thought, and probably. And when I left the pew and the cool and stepped into the evening, I left the bee against the glass, and the buzz of its futility echoing around the old church like, I supposed, my own.

It was half-nine by the time I got back to the farm. As I dropped the bike in the front yard, Mr Evans came from the house and said, "Someone came looking for you. I told her you'd be back later, but she wanted to wait, so I let her into the caravan."

"Her?"

"Yes," he said.

"Thanks," I said.

"And I wanted to say," he said, and he cleared his throat, a loud crack of a noise, "that I didn't mean to be short with you this morning. But there are some things it's difficult to talk about."

"No," I said. "I'm sorry."

He reached out and put his hand on my shoulder. I waited for him to say something else, something about the War or the woman he left behind and the letters he wrote. "She looks like a nice girl. So don't make my mistake."

"What do you mean?"

"Don't lose her." He turned and hobbled up the steps to his front door. He stood at the door and said, "And don't be late for milking."

"Am I ever?"

"There's always a first time, Elliot."

"I'll be getting them in before you're up."

"Just make sure you are," he said, and he turned and went back inside for a cup of tea in front of the television, and a snoozy climb up the stairs to his bed.

Sam was sitting on the cushions at the front of the caravan, her legs tucked up, reading a book by the light of a candle. She was wearing shorts and a T-shirt, and her hair was hanging loose.

"Hope you don't mind," she said.

"No," I said. I wasn't sure whether to stay where I was or kiss her. I felt stuck.

"I couldn't work the lights."

"Here," I said, and I got the matches, dropped them, picked them up again, lit one of the lamps and said, "Want something to drink?"

"What have you got?"

"Beer?"

"Great."

I took two bottles from the fridge, passed her one, sat on the opposite cushion, took a long swig and stretched.

"You look like you needed that," she said.

"I did. I've had a hell of a day. Sometimes… sometimes I feel like a bee against a window."

"What do you mean? What's been going on?"

I looked at her little eyes and her red mouth, and the way her neck curved to her shoulders. Her neck curved to her shoulders in the same way as any other woman's neck would curve, but hers had a ridge that caught the gaslight and the candlelight, and made the shadows dance. Even if the shadows hadn't wanted to dance they would have danced, they would have loved to see her skin and feel the tiny hairs that grew there.

I suppose I could have explained, could have told her about my day, but I didn't want to spoil her mood or remind myself. I didn't want questions and I didn't want to give answers. All I wanted was to listen to her breathe and talk, so I said, "Tell me about your day, and maybe I'll tell you about mine."

"Well," she said, and she took a little sip of beer, rested the bottle on her knee and dabbed her lips with her fingers. Even the way she drank beer made me feel good. "I went to work…"

"Work? I didn't think you worked."

"Of course I work. We all work."

"Where?"

"In Bampton. Some friends have got a little shop. I work behind the counter."

"What sort of shop?

"Food. A few craft things for the tourists. It's nice. I got back and had some tea with the others, then thought I'd come over and see where you live. Had a bit of an accident down the lane though…" she leant forwards and showed me a bruise on her forehead.

"Ouch," I said. "What happened?"

"I slipped in a cow pat."

I laughed. I couldn't help it. "I'm sorry," I said. I put my hand over my mouth. "I didn't mean to."

"No. It's fine. It is funny," and she took my hand and rubbed between my fingers. "Kiss it better if you like."

I looked into her eyes and I looked at her cheeks. I reached out my other hand, crooked the little finger and rubbed her nose. I leant forwards and kissed the bruise.

As my lips touched her she closed her eyes and I closed mine, and I felt her breath on my neck. She gave a little sigh and moved her head up, and she brushed her lips against mine. Then we were kissing, and behind the taste of beer I tasted cake mix, the sort of mix my mum would leave in the bowl and let me scrape out. Vanilla and sugar and the old flavour of a wooden spoon. I pulled away and said, "Yes," and then we kissed again, harder this time and deeper.

And it was as if a door had opened in a wall, a wall I knew was there, but a door I hadn't seen, a low door that led into a wet garden lit by washed sunlight. Sunlight that laddered through the trees and made the leaves dance in their twisting and tumbling. A place where puddles coined in the undergrowth, and paths led from one hollow to the next. And the hollows were made of whispered words and careful thoughts, and the paths carried bad memories away. They carried them to a burning ground beyond the garden, a place where ash was swallowed by kind beasts and smoke was taken and woven into ribbon.

And the door opened wider and I stepped into the garden and walked beneath the trees and touched their trunks with my fingers. They were smooth and cool, and leaves tinkled above me. A bird, a bright tame bird came and brushed its wings against my face, and the dust of its feathers became the air. And the air was scented with hay.

Music was playing in the garden, the sort of music monks make with bells and bowls of water and wooden sticks. Music recognized by mountains and glaciers. Music that can fold in on itself and make pictures out of its own notes. And the pictures are more than pictures. They smell of skin and hair.

Rain began to fall in the garden, soft and light, and more birds came, and small animals. Hares and voles, lambs and cats. At a place where the path met another path, the ground sloped away, the trees thinned and the sea shone in the eye of the horizon. I saw a little fishing boat with a red cabin and a yellow hull. It had a brown sail over its stern and was moving slowly, lumbering through the glassy swell like a cow in heat. Seagulls were following its wake, and a man was standing on the deck, staring at something. He was wearing a check shirt and blue jeans. He shaded his eyes. I opened mine and said, "I can smell a garden."

"Me too."

I closed my eyes. "And I can see the sea."

"Me too."

I wouldn't say that I experienced an overwhelming wave of something that I can only describe by talking about something else, but I had never felt what I felt with Sam in the caravan that night, not with any of the girlfriends I'd had before, or with anyone else. Maybe the things I was going through gave Sam in the caravan that night an edge, and made me see things in a different way. A clean café on a busy street, a raft floating at sea, a wooden bench in an evening park. So when she said, "Can I stay?" it was the only question left to ask, and the answer was simple.

I dropped the table between the two couches at the front of the caravan, spread the cushions and made a double bed. I made it comfortable with sheets and pillows. She asked for a biscuit. I gave her a biscuit. She ate it in front of me, slowly. She caught some crumbs in the palm of her hand and gave them to me. I poured them into my mouth. We washed. I found a clean towel. I leant her a toothbrush. I gave her a glass of water. We stood in front of each other and listened as gravity held onto us. We stood in front of each other and tasted the failing season. We stood in front of each other and I touched her face. It was that easy.

She went to bed first. When I joined her she was face down, propped up on her elbows, looking out of the window at the fields, the moon and the flights of stars. Sheep moved through the half-dark like nervous lights. The tower of Stawley church shone. The caravan smelt of something I hadn't smelt before. Primrose and the removal of dust. She'd pulled the sheet up to

141

her waist. Her back shone. The gaslight flared. I reached up and turned it low. I lay down next to her. She turned towards me and rested her right hand on my shoulder. She traced a circle with her finger. She said, "This must be the best view from the best bed."

"I think it might be," I said.

"Make it better," she said.

"Make me better."

16

In the morning, Sam helped me fetch the herd in. The day was bright and clear, no threat of rain, just more heat. We walked down to the bottom fields, and while she strolled around to fetch the stragglers, I stood and looked down at the place where the hung man had died. The woods didn't give me any sign, no clue, just darkness and silence.

On the way back, Sam opened gates, closed gates and said kind things to the cows as they passed by. I stood back, leant on my stick and watched her. I loved the way her bunches of hair flipped across her face, the way she reached out and stroked the flanks of the slowest beasts, the sound of her quiet voice, the line of her back as it curved into her waist, her deep brown eyes. I remembered the first time I'd seen her eyes and how I'd thought they were like conkers peeped out of their autumn shells, jewels in the dying season.

When the cows were in, she leant against the parlour wall, watched me milk, asked me questions – "What's that for?" "What are you doing that for?" "Do the cows like it?" – and fetched a saucer for the cat. Then she helped me wash the floor, watched the herd go back to pasture and followed me back to the caravan. As we were eating breakfast, Mr Evans knocked on the door. He had a rifle tucked under his arm. He pointed at the yard fence and said, "When you've finished that, make a start on the parlour. There's whitewash in the store."

Sam appeared behind me. She was eating a slice of toast and holding a cup of tea. Mr Evans smiled, blushed a little and said, "Good morning, missy."

"Morning, Mr Evans."

"Sleep well?"

"I did, thanks. Very well."

He looked at me, took the rifle out from under his arm and tapped the stock. "I'm off to the top-field copse. Some of those rabbits have been doing what rabbits like to do…" He winked at me. "And they've been doing it a bit too often."

"Nice gun," I said.

"Rifle," he said. ".22. Perfect balance, fits me like a glove…" He held it up to me. "Have a feel."

I took it, and he was right. It felt almost light, hardly lethal. It could have been made of wood and feathers, the bullets wax, the stock rubber. I put it up to my shoulder and aimed at a hedge. "Careful," said Mr Evans. "We don't want any accidents." I passed it back to him. "No," I said. "We don't." And he tucked it back under his arm and headed off for his shooting.

As he disappeared, Sam said, "I don't like guns."

"Nor do I," I said. "Too much to go wrong," and we went back inside the caravan, took our clothes off and went to bed.

A couple of hours later I gave her a lift to Ashbrittle. I dropped her at her place, put my arms around her, kissed her and said, "I like you."

"As much as biscuits?"

"More than biscuits."

"Good," she said, and she blew in my ear.

"See you tomorrow?"

"I'm counting on it."

I left her at the door and freewheeled down the road to home. Mum was in the kitchen, listening to the radio and baking a cake. When I appeared, she threw her arms around me and said, "Pet!"

"Hi."

"I've been worried about you."

"Mum…"

"I heard about Spike's fire…"

"It's been a nightmare…"

"How did it start? Is he OK?"

"I don't know what happened," I said, "but he lost just about everything. Not that he had a lot in the first place. He's staying with a friend in Wivey."

"He could stay here if he wants."

"No, Mum. You wouldn't want that."

"Why not?"

"You just wouldn't."

She opened the oven, took the cake out, stuck it with a knife, put it back in the oven and wiped her hands on her apron. "He's in trouble, isn't he?"

"Yes Mum. He is."

"Are you going to tell me about it?"

"He's been an idiot."

"Wasn't he always?"

"Yes. But he is my mate."

She patted my hand and said, "You're just like your father." She was warm.

"What do you mean?"

"You're loyal. You stick by your friends."

"What else am I supposed to do?"

"I think you're already doing it."

There is nothing like the smell of a baking cake. The comfort, the memory, the touch and promise. I stayed with Mum until it was ready, and although she said it wouldn't be ready or proper to eat for a couple of hours, I persuaded her to cut me a slice. She made a pot of tea, and we sat and drank and ate, and she said, "Have you got anything else to tell me?"

"I've met a girl."

"Anyone we know?"

"She lives in Milton's Cottage. At Pump Court. Her name's Sam. She works in Bampton…"

"One of the hippies?"

"Some people call them that."

"You and Spike do."

"Yes," I said, "but they're more than that."

"I'm sure they are. They seem very nice to me. Those boys always say good morning. And I think they work hard."

"They do. They're just getting on with their lives. Just like everyone else. They don't do anyone any harm."

"Of course they don't. And she's a nice girl?"

"She's lovely."

"I'm glad. And when you say you've met her, does that mean you're courting?"

The cake was warm and moist, sponge with raspberry jam in the middle. "We've only been out a couple of times, but I suppose so, yes."

She reached across the table and took my hand in her right hand, put the left over the top, closed her eyes and took a deep breath. As she let the breath out I felt a tingling beneath my skin, and a buzzing behind my eyes. "Maybe it's the start of good things for you."

"I hope so."

"Don't forget to listen to the signs."

"Sometimes I wonder, Mum…"

"You wonder what?"

"Spike says it's all mumbo-jumbo. He says real life is what it's all about."

"Well, you can tell him from me that if his life is anything to go by, maybe he should get a bit of mumbo-jumbo. And when it comes to you, Pet, you can wonder all you like. In fact, the more wondering the better. I know what I know, and even though you might not know it yet, you'll come round. You'll understand soon enough. Probably sooner than you think."

I knew it was best not to argue with her when she was in this sort of mood, so I said, "I expect you're right," and pulled my hand away from hers. As I did I heard a little click in the air, a sound like a bird would make as it guards its territory. Mum smiled and said, "Your father understands. And if he does, then anyone can."

I laughed at that, finished my cake and said, "I'd better get back to work."

"I think you'd better."

"Mr Evans will be wondering where I am."

I left her sitting at the kitchen table, put my plate and mug in the sink and kissed the top of her head. "Ride careful," she said.

"Don't I always?"

"No."

"I will," I said, and I went out by the back door, round the front, climbed onto the bike, kicked it over first time and gunned off through the village and back to the farm. I fetched the can of creosote from the store and carried on painting the yard fence.

It was easy, satisfying work, and I'd been at it for ten minutes when I heard the crack of a gunshot. Mr Evans had got a rabbit. As the sound echoed across the lands, I said, "One for the pot," to myself, and waited for the next shot. It came. Maybe another rabbit. I reached the last rail, put the top on the can, carried it back to the store and went to the parlour to get ready for milking.

The smell of creosote was strong, but I could smell Sam through it, Sam and Mum's cake and hay. This, I thought, is how it should be. It should be easy and simple and quiet, and all our senses should chat to each other. But how it should be didn't remain how it should or could or would be. As I was checking the clusters it turned. It turned with the sound of a car I didn't recognize. I went to a window that looked out to the front. A white car was parking in the yard. I felt my blood do that thing blood does when you're scared: it didn't chill, but it seemed to flush and rearrange itself in my veins. And my eyesight sharpened, and I heard a vague whistling in my ears, like the sound of a distant alarm.

Two men were sitting in the car. I didn't recognize the driver, but I recognized the passenger. He was bald and had pale-blue eyes, and his baby face glistened with sweat. He lifted up his hand and scratched his face. His silver watch twinkled. He turned his head and said something to the passenger, who got out of the car and walked towards my caravan. He knocked on the door. He waited for a moment, then kicked the door. It didn't budge. He tried the handle. It swung open. He stepped inside, and I heard him banging around for a minute before he came out again, went to the car and said something to Dickens. Dickens stepped out of the car, looked at his shoes and spat. I saw him mouth the words "Fucking hell". He pointed one way and then pointed in the other, and the driver walked the first way and then he walked the other. I got down from the window, crept along the parlour and left it by the side door. I crossed the backyard and stepped into a half-ruined barn where we kept hand tools, baler twine, tins of paint and forgotten old stuff. I picked up a long-handled hook, the sort we use for trimming hedges, and climbed a ladder at the back of the barn. This led to a loft, a place where broken bales of straw were scattered around. The floorboards were rotten in places, and holes and broken joints were hidden by scattered straw. I stepped carefully and found a place where I could hide behind the bales. I had a good view of the yard, the back of the house and some of the fields. I lay down, put the hook at my side and waited.

I didn't have to wait long. The driver appeared in the yard below me. He was slightly crouched, walking slowly and deliberately, eyes swivelling. A nondescript, ordinary man with brown hair and two days' stubble on his chin. The sort of man you wouldn't notice if you sat down next to him on a bus. He was carrying a stick. He opened the door to the parlour and went inside, and I watched his reflection pass the windows. When he reached the far end, he stepped out and walked towards the barn below me. He put his head inside and, as he did, Dickens appeared in the yard and shouted "Found him?"

"No," said the ordinary man.

"Keep looking."

"OK."

The ordinary man stepped into the yard below me and started poking around the tools. I heard some fall over, and I heard him curse. He reached the bottom of the ladder. He started climbing the ladder. The rungs creaked, and as he reached the top I could hear his breathing. It was slow and heavy, like wind rolling through a narrow valley. Or a bull. Or a chicken sighing as it roosts. I kept absolutely still. I was a stone. He stopped climbing. He waited. I could sense his waiting, sense that he could sense something. Ten seconds passed, then twenty, and then I heard the rungs creak again and a thud as he put his shoe down. Then another shoe. He took a step towards me, stopped, took another. Now I could smell him, and he smelt of burgers. He started poking at the straw with his stick, flicking it up and tapping the floor beneath. He sneezed. He took another step, and for a moment there was silence, the silence of waiting and promise. A crack split the air, the board gave way beneath him and his foot fell through. As he went down he yelled, "Fuck!" and tried to grab something. I don't know what he tried to grab, but it made no difference. I didn't sit up, didn't show myself, but I could imagine what he looked like. I could see him with one leg through the floor and the other at a crazy angle behind him or to the side, and his fingernails splintered by the boards. He cursed again and scrabbled and thrashed, and as he tried to haul himself up, another board cracked. Now I stood up, slowly, carefully, picked up the hook and looked down at him. It took him a second. He looked at my boots, and then he raised his head and looked up at me. He was splayed at a crazy angle, his left leg in a gaping hole, the other bent and twisted behind him, his right arm in another hole. The boards beneath his chest were sagging, and the splintered pieces around him were riddled with worm and mould. He opened his mouth, and as he did there was the loudest crack and the floor shuddered beneath him. He reached his free hand towards me and said, "Help me…" I say "he said", but it was half question, half plea, knowing he was half doomed.

"Why?" I said.

"I'll say I never…" he said, but before he could finish what he was about to say the floor gave way completely and he fell the twenty feet into the barn below. I took a step back, but saw his eyes widen and his legs flail. He hit the tools below and yelled as something pierced his leg. I jumped into the hole, hopped onto the ladder and skipped down. I stood next to him. He was out cold. A pitchfork was sticking in his thigh and he had a huge reddening bruise on his head. I stepped out of the barn, crossed the yard and ducked into the parlour. A moment later I heard running feet. I watched from a crack in the door as Dickens went to the barn door, looked inside and said, "Hello?"

No reply.

"You there?"

Nothing. He stepped inside.

"Shit…"

Half a minute later he pulled the ordinary man out of the barn by the shoulders, and started dragging him across the yard. "Fuck…" he said, "Fuck, fuck, fuck…" Across the yard, through the gate, around the corner and down to the front of the farmhouse. I crossed the parlour so I could look out of the windows, and I watched as he dragged him to the white car, propped him against the door and stood up straight. He put his hands to the small of his back. He stretched. He looked down at his bleeding friend. He shook his head. And then, as if he'd been waiting for his moment, Mr Evans appeared, gun held at his waist and his face red with fury.

"And what the hell are you doing?" he yelled.

Dickens's hands shot up in the air. "I…"

"Yes? You what?"

"We're old friends… friends of Elliot's."

"Are you now?"

"Yes."

Mr Evans looked towards the caravan. "And you just popped in to say hello?"

"Yes."

"And what happened to him?"

"We were looking over there. In the man… he tripped."

"Must have been a hell of a trip."

"It was…"

"And did you find Elliot?"

"No…" Dickens said, and as he did, the ordinary man moaned and opened his eyes. He winced and put his hand to the wound in his thigh. "That bastard is…" he started, and then he looked up and saw Mr Evans and his gun.

"Which bastard?" said Mr Evans.

The ordinary man looked up at Dickens, then back at the gun. He looked totally confused, as if he'd woken from one bad dream only to discover he was in another. "Hurts…" he said. "That bastard is killing me."

"I think," Mr Evans said, and he lifted the gun and pointed with it as he spoke, "that you need to get in your car and go back to wherever you came from. I'll let Elliot know you came calling, and if he wants to see you I'm sure he'll get in touch."

"Yes," said Dickens. "That's a good idea."

"I'm full of them," said Mr Evans.

"We'll be off then." And Dickens opened the passenger door, put his hands under the other man's armpits and helped him into the car. Then he went to the driver's side and slowly drove away. I watched until the car was out of sight, then stepped out of the parlour and went to see Mr Evans.

He was in his kitchen, washing at the sink. Three rabbits lay on the table. As I walked in he turned on me, wiped his hands on a towel, threw the towel at me and yelled, "What the bloody hell is going on?" His face was red with fury and his hair was sticking up like corn stubble. He picked up a gutting knife and planted it in the table. It made a twanging sound. I stared at it and shuddered.

"It's complicated."

"I don't care how bloody complicated it is! This is my farm! My land! When I come back from an afternoon's shooting I don't expect to have to use my gun on a couple of thugs!"

"But you didn't…"

He stepped towards me. His anger was growing. His eyes were flashing and spit flew from his mouth. I'd never thought he could get like this, so mad with rage. I'd always thought he was the calmest man in the parish. "I was ready to! The safety was off, my finger was on the trigger! If I'd have squeezed it you'd have had your answer!"

"What answer?"

"To the question you asked me the other day, Elliot. About the War. Remember?"

"Oh…"

"Yes. Oh."

"So you'd better tell me what's going on. Before I throw you off the farm and tell everyone else round here that you're the worst damn worker I ever had!"

"But Mr Evans…"

He gripped the table. His knuckles turned white and the gutting knife wobbled on its tip. "No 'but Mr Evans', Elliot! Just bloody well tell me!"

What could I do? Where could I go? I couldn't back out, couldn't not tell him something, so I explained as much as I could. I told him that Spike had found the smoke and stolen it from the man I found hung in the woods, and that the men who'd just turned up had something to do with the smoke. I didn't say that I'd hidden it in the kale field barn, and I didn't say that one of the men was a bent policeman. I let those things go. I let them lie for later, or maybe not at all. And when I finished the story I let Mr Evans shout at me. "You idiot!" he yelled. "You and that Spike, you're as bad as each other!"

"No we're not. I…"

"Shut up! If I say you're as bad as each other, then that's what you are."

"But…"

He put a finger to his lips, and when he did that it meant more than anything he could have said. There was threat in the action, even menace. "How long have you been working here?"

"A few weeks."

"And you want to carry on working here?"

"Yes. Of course I do."

"Well, I'm not sure I want you to stay."

"Shit."

"You could say that. You could say it louder."

"I've been trying to clear the mess up. I warned Spike. I told him…"

"Did you? Maybe you should have done more than just tell him. Maybe you should have shouted."

"I think I did."

"You think you did?"

"Yes."

"I don't know." He shook his head and turned away from me. "I just don't know…"

"I'm sorry."

"Sorry?"

"Yes."

"You probably will be. I'm going into the other room now, and while you're fetching the cows in I'm going to phone the relief. You can take a couple of days off – no pay mind you – and she'll do the milking. While you're away you can sort this mess out, and when you get back we'll decide whether you're going to stay here."

"Thanks, Mr Evans."

"I don't know what you're thanking me for."

"For giving me a second chance."

"I haven't yet." He took a step towards me and for a moment I thought he was going to hit me. He clenched his fists and wheezed, narrowed his eyes and tapped the side of his head. Then he said, "You want to think about what you're doing, Elliot," and he stepped around me, left the kitchen, walked down the corridor, went into his front room and slammed the door. I stood and stared at the gutting knife in the table, reached out, touched its handle and closed my eyes. I saw spits of light in the dark, and heard the sound of distant birds calling from trees. At least I think they were birds, but they could have been the sounds my brain makes when it's tired and wants to go somewhere else.

17

Milking was tough. I sweated, and my mouth was dry, and every time I let a cow out and a gate slammed shut I jumped. I didn't know what Dickens would do next, but I did know he could do anything he wanted. As he'd left the farm he'd looked at Mr Evans's gun, but there hadn't been fear in his eye, just the look of someone who'd recognized a friend in a pub and wanted to say hello. "This is a gun; it can kill me, but it won't. I could have it off the old man, but I won't. I could come back any time, but I won't. I'll wait. I might be mad, but I'm patient. I'm as patient as the fucking hills and as patient as a fucking river. I'll wait. I'll wait some more. I've got all the time I need, and I love time…" These were the sort of things I imagined he thought as he drove away, but maybe he didn't. Only he knew. And when Mr Evans suddenly appeared in the parlour and shouted, "Don't forget the cat!" I almost pissed myself.

"I never forget the cat!"

The cat was sitting on a window sill.

"Good for you."

He left me to it, and as I carried on, the fright and worry stayed with me like a itch in my eye. However hard I tried to push it away, it came back, tweaking my mind and whispering stuff I didn't want to hear. "You're dead… feel the pain… die in a heap… lose your head… the dogs will catch you… the dogs are mad… we've sharpened the dogs' teeth… we'll push you through a window… you'll fall off a bridge… you'll eat your own heart…"

"Shut up!" I yelled to the ceiling.

"We'll snap your fingers one by one… we'll stick pins in your eyes… we'll stick pins in your tongue…"

"Quiet!" I yelled to the ceiling.

"We'll have you swallow glass… you'll bleed from the inside out… you'll split like a plum…"

"No!"

The whispers didn't quieten so I turned the radio on, loud music with a loud DJ, and I talked to the cows as I let them into the parlour. That almost did the trick and, by the time I'd finished, my head had almost returned to normal. When I say "normal" I don't mean normal like it used to be, like it was before Spike stole the smoke, but the panic was nothing more than a light ache, and the whispers had stopped.

I packed some stuff into my rucksack, and as I was tying it onto the back of the bike Mr Evans came out. He'd calmed down, his face had lost its redness and he almost smiled. He said, "When you've sorted this mess out, give me a ring. You're a good lad, and I don't think you need to be this stupid."

"I'm not stupid."

"I never said you were."

In all the excitement I think he had. But maybe he hadn't. I wasn't sure, so I didn't contradict him. I just said, "Thanks, Mr Evans," and rode to Ashbrittle. When I got to the top of the hill, I stopped and rested for a few minutes, and took some deep breaths. My hands were shaking and my heart was beating hard, and for a moment fright swam back to the surface and bared its teeth. "Oh fuck off," I said to it, and I went home.

Mum was in the yard, collecting some washing from the line. When she'd unpegged everything, I carried her basket, followed her into the house, told her I'd been given a couple of days off and asked if I could stay in my room. She said, "Are you in trouble?"

"No."

"You're in trouble. Did you get the sack?"

"No."

She took my chin in her hand and held it tight, and said, "When's it going to end, Pet?"

"I don't know. Soon."

"That won't be soon enough."

"You can say that again," I said, and I went to see Sam. She was on her knees in Pump Court's kitchen garden, staring at some onions. She jumped up when she saw me, hopped across the vegetables and kissed me.

"The future is ripe," she said.

"What do you mean?"

"Gardening."

I nodded but I didn't know what she was on about. "What have you and your mates been talking about?"

"Gardening's the future," she said.

"Yes," I said, "I suppose it is." I didn't want to say that gardening was also the past and the present, and saying it was the future was the sort of thing I'd expect a hippy to say, but I didn't want to upset her. Not that I think I could have upset her.

She wasn't the type. She took my hand and pulled me towards the onions. She knelt down and said, "I don't know whether to leave them in the ground or pull them up. But I don't suppose they'll grow any more."

"No," I said. "I don't think they will," so we started to pull them up.

It was satisfying work, and although the onions were small there were lots of them. The earth was grey and thirsty, and as we worked Sam hummed a little tune. I don't know what it was, but it sounded like it had come from far away, maybe a country where farmers live in felt tents and herd goats and ponies across steppes. I've read about these people in *National Geographic* magazines and other books, and seen films about them on the telly. Their tents are called yurts, and their fields stretch for hundreds of miles. Their grass is coarse and brown, and when it sways it sounds like the ghosts of dead children have gathered and are whispering down a chimney. And as we worked and the tune swam around us, I had a moment of foresight, a clear thought that made me stop and take a breath. I don't know if it was the sort of foresight Mum has, but I think it was. My body felt light and my fingers tingled, and I saw myself as an old man. A happy man, a contented man, a man with a wife and children and grandchildren, someone who could charm birds out of their nests and colour their feathers with stories about yurts and goats. When I say I saw myself, I didn't have a vision – an apparition didn't appear, clouds didn't part or faces loom. I just felt something deep inside my body, a pinprick of warmth that started deep and swelled like a cake in an oven, and the flavour of this cake was the sight of myself in the future. I don't think I'm explaining myself very well, but then it's difficult to explain something so strange. I'd never expect Mum to explain the things she feels, and I know that if I asked her she'd tell me not to be so foolish.

I let the feeling fill me, I listened to Sam's humming, I felt the sun on my back. And when we'd finished, we piled the onions into boxes and sat down with our backs against a wall and listened to the evening.

A wasp, drunk on flight or anger or both, surprised us, and an exhausted cockerel crowed in a garden beyond the green. A couple of crows flapped towards their roost, and somewhere out of sight a buzzard mewed its hunger at the sky. A dog barked. A car passed. My heart beat.

Sam took my hand, traced a circle on the back of it and said, "Happy?"

I nodded. I wanted to tell her about the afternoon, but I didn't want to spoil the moment. There was plenty of time to spoil plenty of moments, and there was plenty of time to tell as many stories as I wanted. For now I was happy, and I didn't want the feeling to go away. "You?" I said.

"Very."

"Good."

"Fancy a drink later?"

"Yes," I said, "but I've got to see someone first."

"Someone?"

"Yes."

"Who's someone?"

161

"A friend."

"Are you being mysterious with me, Elliot?"

"No," I said. "My best mate. Spike."

"Where is he?"

"Wiveliscombe." I stood up and brushed the backs of my trousers. "I won't be long. He's been having a bit of trouble. I just want to check he's all right."

"OK then."

"I'll see you in a couple of hours."

"Here?"

"Yes," I said, and I kissed her. I kissed her on the lips and I kissed her cheek, and I smelt the onions on her fingers. I told her she smelt lovely, and I told her that when the drought broke we'd go swimming in the river. She asked me which river, and I said, "The Tone. I know a place. We can take a picnic." And then I went back to the bike and rode away.

I love riding a bike through a warm summer's evening. The brass glow of the land, the gathered smells of the dying day, the feeling of a night's promise, the offering of that promise, the promise of the offering, the twist of words, the words that mean whatever you choose them to mean. And even though I carried the constant nagging of threat, it couldn't kill my pleasure. Maybe threat was just a word, and what could a word do to me? I remember reading somewhere about how water was soft and rock was hard, but water was stronger than rock. It always found a way through it, always crumbled it, always left it mud. Maybe I read it in a *National Geographic* magazine, or maybe I heard it on the radio, but wherever it was I thought it made sense. And when I got to Wiveliscombe and knocked on the door of the house where Spike was staying, I was thinking "rock, water, water, rock, pebbles, sand, mud…" – and when the door was answered by a bloke with red eyes and a plaster on his face I looked straight at him, didn't flinch, didn't take a deep breath, didn't do anything at all except say, "Is Spike in?"

"No."

"Know where he is?"

"Try the pub."

"Which one?"

"Dunno. Do I look like a mind reader?"

I stared at the bloke. He was stoned and drunk, and wearing a huge woolly hat. I don't know what the plaster covered, but he needed to change it. It was curling at the edges and crusted blood was there. He put a spliff to his mouth and took a long drag. He was smoking ragged stuff, and when he stared at me I thought, for a moment, that his eyelids were going to fall off. But they didn't, and when I told him that no, he didn't look like a mind reader, he narrowed his eyes as he tried to make sense of what I had just said. Was I playing with him? Was I serious? He couldn't tell, and I wasn't going to get any sense out of him, so I said, "Thanks," and rode back up the hill, parked the bike in the square and went to the first pub I found. As I walked in the door, ten heads turned towards me, stared for five seconds and turned back to their drinks. Owls, I thought. Or sheep. There was old, bad music playing, and someone in a leather jacket standing over a juke box. A waiting air of menace hung in the air, like the time was almost come to give someone a good kicking, and I might be that someone. I looked around, but didn't see Spike, so I nodded to the barman, ducked out of the door and went to the second pub. This time six heads turned towards me. More owls. Or sheep. There was less of an air in this place, more of something that approached a welcome, so I walked down the bar, nodded to someone I didn't know and saw him. He was sitting at a table in the corner with a pint in one hand and a cigarette in the other. The smoke was curling like hair around him, drifting in the air and settling in clots around the pictures of old Wiveliscombe that hung on the walls. He had a local paper opened in front of him. He was reading about the hung man. I fetched a pint, sat down and said, "Spike."

He looked up and said, "El…"

"How you doing?"

He shook his head. "Fucking awful. You?"

"You wouldn't believe it if I told you."

"Are you going to?"

"What?"

"Tell me."

"No."

"Why not?"

"Because you wouldn't believe me."

"Oh," he said, and he took a drag on his cigarette and pointed at the paper. There was a picture of a corner of the wood where I'd found the hung man, and some stuff about who he was and what he might have been doing. His name was Fred Baxter, and a local was quoted as saying "He kept himself to himself.

He moved into the area about six months ago, but we hardly saw him. There were rumours about what he was up to, but we never thought it would come to this."

"I never thought it would come to this either," said Spike, and he stared into his pint. He looked like he was trying to see something in it, the future maybe, or a way out of his mess. "I don't know what to do. But I did have an idea," he said. He didn't look me in the eye, and I knew what that meant. It meant he knew it was a bad idea, and he was about to prove that he was a twat.

"What is it?"

"My mate down the road knows some people in London."

"Good for him. He certainly looks like he's got his wits about him."

"What do you mean?"

"I just met him."

"Right," said Spike, and he squinted at me. "Anyway. He called them last night. They'll buy the smoke. Reckons they'll take everything I've got."

"He told some people in London that you've got half a ton of smoke?"

"It's not half a ton…"

"That's not the point."

"Then what is?"

"You just don't get it, do you, Spike?"

"Get what?"

"It's over. Finished. It's not your smoke. You can't sell it. All you have to do now is keep your head down, forget everything about what you did, take a deep breath and think about what you're going to do next. This whole thing has gone way beyond you."

"What do you mean?"

"You think I'm going to tell you?"

"You're my mate," he said. He looked into my eyes, and his eyes were wide and pleading and watery, like he knew chances had slipped by and he was hanging on by his fingernails. "Please, El."

"Please what?"

"Tell me you're still my mate."

"I wouldn't have come out to see you if you weren't," I said, and I put my hand on his arm for a second, took it away, picked up my pint and drank. "I was worried about you."

"Why?"

"Because the heavies are still out there, Spike."

"Still?"

"They came to the farm. Mr Evans had to chase them off with his gun. And they're not going away in a hurry."

"No," he said. "I don't suppose they are."

"So forget all about thinking you're going to sell the smoke. I'm going to sort it out. I'll make everything go away."

"How?"

"I'm not going to tell you. You'll just have to trust me."

He looked at me again. "I'm sorry," he said.

"Forget it, Spike. You just did what you always do."

"I did, didn't I?"

"Yes," I said, "but you're still my friend. My best friend."

He took another drink and whispered, "Thanks."

Friends are rare, I thought, but didn't say it, friends you can stick with and who stick with you whatever happens. But what makes friendship? How does it work? What makes one person know that another person is a person you can rely on, call on, talk to? Is it understanding that whatever you say will be understood, or is it wanting for your friend what you want for yourself? I wanted Spike to have what I had, I wanted him to have a job he liked, a girlfriend with a beautiful back and beautiful eyes, and I wanted him to be free of stupid ideas. Being able to say anything to a friend is another good sign of having a real friend, and I suppose if that's the truth then Spike wasn't as real a friend as he could be. Because there were things I couldn't say to him, deep things you might hear people say to each other in a book or a film. But I don't think you should ever think that something you hear in a book or a film has anything to do with real life. Books and films are false things. They come from imagination, the air of a different planet. And once Spike had said, "Thanks…" there wasn't much more to say. So we sat for ten minutes, talked about how The Globe was as good a pub as you could visit and how when we thought about it, school wasn't as bad as we thought it was when we were there. Things we could agree about, things that could remind us that there was a good world out there, things that were straight and easy, and when we'd finished talking about these things, I stood up, put my hand on his shoulder, reminded him that I was going to make everything go away and he was to do nothing, left him at his table and rode back to Ashbrittle.

I don't like to think that I spend all my time in pubs. I don't. But some pubs are easy places to relax, places where it's easy to feel safe, easy places to hide. So when I met Sam and she asked if I fancied going up to Staple Cross, I said, "Let's go," and she slipped on the spare helmet, hopped on the bike, threaded her arms around my waist, held her face against my back and we headed off.

We sat at the same table we sat at when we first met, and we talked about that night, and how we'd talked about baking and my Gran's talent for charming sheep. And the same feelings were there, and we talked about them too, how when I was with her I felt as though I was walking in a safe place where no one could touch me. And she agreed.

Other people came and went, some people I knew and some I didn't, but we hardly noticed them. We were in our own world. I thought about how I'd sat with Spike earlier and how there was something similar about how I felt then and how I was feeling now, and I tied the feeling down. It was about feeling complete. Spike completes part of me, and Sam completed another part – and that, I supposed, was another thing about friendship. And it was something about love. Until you meet these people you are only part of a person. You need others to make you. So when we left and she climbed onto the back of my bike again and held me tight again, I imagined that she was melting into me, and adding the last bits that made me whole.

I pulled away from the pub and rode slowly, loving the feeling. I slowed down at a crossroads, turned the corner and stopped, turned and looked at her. She smiled, and I reached back and touched her lips with my fingers. She kissed my fingers and I stroked her cheek, and as I did this, headlights appeared in a gateway. They came on like day had suddenly broken for a second, and a car pulled out, skidded into the lane and accelerated towards us.

I turned left, and for a hundred yards I didn't think about the car, but then it was right behind us, too fast, swerving into the middle of the road, pulling back at a bend, swerving out again. A white car. A growing engine. The driver looking straight ahead, his bald head shining and his mad mouth twitching. Dickens. When we reached a short straight, I gunned the bike, took a couple of bends, settled into another straight and Sam yelled, "What the hell's he doing?"

"Hang on!" I shouted.

I'd given myself a couple of hundred yards on the car. It was easy. I was quick and I was slick and I had a choice. The car pulled up behind me. Dickens flashed his lights. At the next junction I could head up towards a fast empty main road or I could ride into the lanes – lanes I knew, narrow lanes, lanes I could lose the car in. I slowed, made as if I was turning towards the main road, watched as the car turned with me, then turned the other way and throttled up.

The night was falling fast now, a scarf of cloud slow and high across the moon, the high hedges looming and black. For a moment the noise and headlights disappeared, and we were alone and quick. Maybe I'd been imagining and maybe we weren't being followed or chased or both. Maybe nothing was wrong. Maybe everything was a dream, and things were simply a fake. Maybe not. The car was back in my mirrors, coming at us again.

I felt like a hunted animal, adrenalined and head down, eyes wide and feet quick. But nothing was going to catch me. I knew the land. I knew the places to hide, the turnings and dips, and the shadows in the hedges. And I was brave, braver than Dickens and his idiot head.

A crossroads. A quick left. A house. A farm. I could turn into the yard. I didn't. Just past the farm I hit a patch of gravel, and as my back wheel spun out from behind me, I eased off, turned into the skid, steadied, kept upright and pulled away again. Headlights cut and flew, the car gunned up close again, howling against the night. Another farm, and then a long straight that led towards darkening woods. Sam held me tighter, and I turned towards her and yelled, "We'll lose him up here."

We didn't. For a minute we were away, but he caught up again and as we rode under the trees he started blaring his horn and flashing his lights. "What does he want?" Sam yelled, as we flew out from the trees and dipped into a nasty series of bends. "Fuck knows!" I said as the bike caught another patch of gravel and sprayed the car's windscreen. I heard the stones splatter against the glass, and this slowed him for a moment, a moment to gun the bike again and head down to a place where the road widened and a tractor and trailer were parked in a lay-by. There was a place here where I could turn, and if I hadn't had Sam on the back I would have, but I couldn't. The balance was wrong. And suddenly the car was next to me and I was gunning the bike, but it wouldn't pull away. The road narrowed again, and climbed. The hill was gentle at first, but then it got steep, and as we reached the top I couldn't see beyond the brow. The car kept coming, and as we reached the top, I saw the brush of the lights of another car coming towards us. They disappeared for a second, and then they were in front of us, fifty yards away. I swerved towards the hedge, the lights flashed in front and the lights flashed behind, and I squeezed the bike through the gap between the hedge and the oncoming car, and as I did, I clipped its wing mirror. Then the bike hit something in the road – a branch, I think – and we were skidding sideways towards a field gate.

We hit the field gate at sixty and, at the time, I thought we were lucky. The gate splintered and smashed, and we stayed upright, rolling into the field. The grass swished beneath the tyres. I braked. I held it together. We were going to be OK. I started to lose the back wheel. I pulled it back. But then we hit a ridge, Sam screamed, and I felt her arms slip away from my waist. The bike lifted into the air, turned on its side, twisted and crashed into a pile of corrugated iron. For a moment the engine revved, but then it coughed and died, and the only sounds were the spinning of the back wheel and an engine in the lane. The moon shone. The moon shone on like a wish. And the moon took my wishes, broke them in pieces and scattered them across a pool of spreading oil.

A car door opened. It slammed shut. I tried to stand up. The bike was lying on my leg. I said, "Sam?" She didn't reply. I couldn't see her. "Sam?" Nothing. For a moment my mind failed me, and I lost focus. It came back as a figure walked towards me. I heard the sound of bleating sheep. I looked up. A man looked at me. He had a big face and was wearing a bright white shirt. His eyes were grey, and his lips were wet. He crouched down and said, "You all right, mate?"

I nodded. "I think so…"

"What was that bloke doing?"

"Which bloke?"

"The one that was following you. He was driving like a crazy…"

"I don't know," I said, and the man reached down, pulled the bike upright, and I tried to stand up.

My trousers were ripped, I'd taken skin off my leg, bruised my ribs and twisted my wrist, but I hadn't broken anything. I pulled off my helmet, tossed it at the bike and looked around. I saw Sam. She was lying twenty feet away. She wasn't moving.

I ran to her and the man followed. I bent over her. "Don't move her," the man said. "And don't take the helmet off…"

I reached down and touched her shoulder. I leant towards her head and listened. She was breathing – small, shallow breaths like a cat would make in its sleep. A little trickle of blood was running from her nose. "Oh God," I said, and the man said, "I'll get help," and turned and ran back to his car.

I sat with Sam for half an hour. I sat and listened to her, and every five minutes I said her name, but she didn't say anything. I held her hand and squeezed it gently, and I cursed under my breath. I cursed Spike and I cursed friendship. I cursed smoke and I cursed greed. I cursed my thoughts and myself, and I cursed fate. And when I heard a siren in the lane, I stood up, ran to the gate and stood in the middle of the lane.

The ambulance men followed me to where Sam was lying. They had bright torches and a stretcher, and a big bag of equipment. They asked me if I was all right. I said I was. They said, "You sure?" and looked at my legs. I shouted at them to look at Sam. They told me to be calm and stand back while they looked at her, and they went to work. I don't know what they did, but after ten minutes they gently picked her up and laid her on the stretcher. They carried her to the ambulance, and they spent another ten minutes doing things to make her comfortable. Then they told me to get in beside her and we drove away.

I don't know about the rest of that night. When the ambulance man who sat in the back with me looked at my leg, he gave me an injection of something and put a dressing on the skin, and something in the injection made me sleepy. So when I looked at Sam with a mask on her face and a drip in her arm, she looked well one minute and dead the next, and her skin switched between different colours. One minute it was white, the next it was grey, then it was blue, and then it was white again. Or maybe this was real, maybe she was turning into something from a bad film. I closed my eyes and saw her flying through the air and cracking against the pile of corrugated iron, and I saw her bleeding from a deep cut in her head. Her hair was matted with blood, and her skull was showing. And I think I slept for ten minutes. And then I woke up. The ambulance doors opened. People came running from a hospital. They pulled Sam out, laid her on a trolley and wheeled her away.

The ambulance men followed. Nurses asked them questions. I stood and tipped my head back. The sky was orange and black. The air smelt of diesel. Someone said, "You hurt too?"

"I'm OK."

"You're not."

"I am…" I said, and then I felt something sweep through my body, feathers and damp wool, and sharp filings of steel. I tried to stay upright, but my legs had decided they didn't want anything to do with me. I reached out and grabbed someone's shoulder, and then everything failed, dark came down and I was gone.

18

When I was a kid I used to rush home from school, grab a piece of cake, stuff it in my mouth, swill it down with orange squash and go out on my bicycle with Grace. Sometimes I'd go first, and sometimes she'd go first, and sometimes we'd go together, and sometimes we went to the river at Stawley Mill, walk as far as a place where the river widened to a pool, and play on a rope swing we'd tied to an overhanging branch. You'd take a running jump from a slope on the bank, swing out over the water and scare the ducks. There was a log tied to the bottom of the rope, so you had a choice: you could sit down or stand up. If you stood you could push back and become almost horizontal as you swung, but if you sat down you could lean over and look up and imagine yourself as a bird. In the spring the breeze would tinkle through the branches and play on your face, and in the summer the sun would coin on the water like treasure. When the leaves fell in autumn, they'd drift past your face as you swung, and if you were lucky you could catch one in your mouth. Then they'd float away on the river, down towards Tracebridge and the memory of the witch who lived there, and on and on through the valleys and woods towards Taunton. We had happy days on the rope swing. We were never afraid of anything. We never fought. We were good children.

If we were feeling more adventurous, we'd forget the swing and dare ourselves to ride down to the ruins of the house at

Marcombe Lake. This was the place where Professor Hunt kept his kidnapped woman and did his terrible experiments. He'd turned her skin into snake's skin by injecting her with a special chemical he'd made, but she was rescued by a man who'd come to value a collection of books for the old Lord Buff-Orpington. I think Professor Hunt went mad when he discovered the woman had been stolen from him, and before he left the place and went back to wherever he'd come from, he set fire to the house. All this happened years ago: there were no firemen to come and put the blaze out, so it burned until there was nothing more than walls and gables and chimneys in the place where a decent house had been. And as the years went by, the walls and gables and chimneys crumbled, and ivy and elder grew in the places where the Professor had cursed and spat, and the woman had screamed.

One day we went down there even though we hadn't planned to. I think we started by going for a walk in the woods below Belmont Hall to look for dormice nests, but before we knew it we were standing in the field above the ruins, and then we were running down the field, laughing and chasing each other. "Dare you!" yelled Grace, and I didn't need daring twice.

The walls still had scorch marks, and when I stepped through the place where the front door had been, I tripped over a blackened plank of wood, part of the old collapsed roof. I turned around, waited for Grace, but she didn't appear.

"Grace?"

No answer.

I laughed. "Please yourself," I said, and I started to explore.

I think I would have liked to have been an explorer. I don't know how people become explorers, what they need to do at school or who they need to know, but if I'd been a bit more adventurous and brave I'd have taken myself off to places like Mongolia or Patagonia, and searched for something that no one had seen for centuries. Treasure buried by dead monks or a dead king, jars filled with coins, tablets with secret writing on them, an odd-shaped object hidden in a cave. Then I'd have bought my finds back to England and written about it for the *National Geographic* magazine, and had my photograph on the cover, me smiling with a beard, bright eyes and a big scarf.

"Grace?"

Still no answer, so I started exploring the ruins. There were some people in the village who said that Professor Hunt had never done evil experiments on a woman, so maybe I'd find proof. Maybe I'd find a bottle of the stuff he injected her with buried in the floor, and I'd be able to take it back and show it around and tell everyone that the stories were true. I picked up a stick and started digging at the floor in front of the hole in a wall where the fireplace used to be. I found stones and a piece of broken china, more stones and some cinders, but no bottle. I picked the piece of china up, licked my finger and rubbed it. It was blue and white, with half a little flower painted on it. I heard a footstep on the other side of the wall, then another and another, light steps like you'd make if you didn't want anyone to hear. I said, "I'm here, Grace."

"I know," she said, from behind me. I stood up.

"How long have you been there?"

"A couple of minutes."

"Liar."

"I am not," she said.

"Yes you…" I started to say, when I heard the footsteps again.

I froze and Grace froze, and I dropped the piece of china. "Who's that?" she whispered.

"I don't know…"

We stared at each other. I didn't know what time it was, but the sun was starting to sink, and long shadows were gathering around the ruins. I heard a scratching in the wall. A mouse. Grace said, "It's getting late…"

One more footstep.

I said, "I don't like this…"

"Nor do I."

"Let's go."

Grace went first. We went the way we'd come. She looked around the corner of the wall, looked back at me and nodded. "It's OK," she said. Then she disappeared around the corner. A moment later I heard stones crashing over each other, the scrabble of feet, Grace's scream. I ran after her and, as I did, a sheep shot past me, leapt over the remains of a fence that used to go round the old garden, and disappeared into a ditch.

Grace was sitting on the ground. She looked up at me. "Bloody hell," she said. I think that was the first time I'd ever heard her swear, but it didn't bother me. All I wanted to do was run home, sit in the front room and watch something nice on the telly. "Bloody sheep. Half-frightened me to death."

"Come on," I said.

"Give me a minute."

"OK."

So she sat for a minute and I stood next to her, and I watched the sun. It turned orange as it sank, and crows smudged its face with their filthy wings. They called their dirty caws, they flapped and they dropped, and they disappeared into the tops of some old trees. I suppose they sat in their nests and rearranged the sticks of their nests, scrapped with each other for a while and then settled down for the evening. I don't know if they slept and I don't know if they tucked their beaks beneath their wings; maybe they did, and maybe they pecked for fleas and ticks in their feathers. Something to eat before the night came, something to keep them occupied, something to keep for their dreams.

I dreamt about crows. Big birds with ragged wings and long beaks. They bothered me in my sleep, and when I woke up I was lying in a bed, and a doctor was shining a light in my eyes. I tried to sit up, managed to get halfway and flopped back onto the pillow. I said, "Where am I?"

"Hospital, Elliot. In Taunton. You had an accident. You were on your bike…"

"An accident?" And it came back. It came back like a punch. A winding punch from a big man with a fist like a hill. I remembered. It wasn't a dream. The car in the lane, the other car, the gate, the bike twisting in the air. The ambulance. Sam. Beautiful Sam. Sam with the free eyes and the sweet voice and the fingers that smelt of onions. "Sam," I said. "Where is she?"

"Who's Sam?"

"The girl I was with. She came in the ambulance."

"Ah…" said the doctor. "She's being looked after now."

"What do you mean?" I didn't like the way he said, "Ah…" It was like he'd invited me to die. "I want to see her."

"You can't. Not at the moment. Not for a while."

"Why not?"

"She's quite poorly. We're operating on her now."

"Operating on her? Why? What do you mean?"

"I think you should try and get some sleep now, Elliot. Do you want us to call anyone?"

"No, why? Why are you operating on her?"

He looked at the floor and looked back at me and shook his head. "She took a knock on the head."

"But she was wearing a crash helmet."

"I know."

"And that didn't help?"

"I'm afraid not."

"But she's going to be all right?"

"We'll know in a few hours."

"A few hours?"

"Yes," said the doctor, and I slumped back in the bed, looked up at him and said, "Could you call my mum?"

"Of course. Where is she?"

I told him and then I closed my eyes, turned on my side and watched the lights in the dark as they twisted and faded. Some of them were shaped like snowflakes, others looked like cows, others made sounds like bells chiming underwater. And then I let the lights disappear, and I dozed.

I dozed for a while. I think I dreamt, but it was difficult to know what was happening in my head; was a dream a dream or was it really happening? When I saw door after door opening and faces swimming from the walls, were they the faces of people I knew, or people I hadn't met yet? And when I joined these people on a flying bus, did they feed me food or dust? So when I heard a voice calling my name I couldn't decide if it was coming from the room or my mind, or even if my mind was in the room.

"Elliot?"

I opened my eyes.

"Elliot?"

My mum and dad were standing by the bed. She was holding my hand and he was standing to one side. They both looked grey and old, older than I'd ever seen them before. I had one of those odd thoughts where you think nothing is real. Maybe I was looking into the future, and they really were old. I tried to hold my hand up and look at it. I wanted to see if it was lined and wrinkled and covered in liver spots. I opened my mouth to say something, but I was dry. Blank. Empty. Nothing came out.

"You want some water, Pet?"

I nodded.

Dad picked up a cup, gave it to Mum, and she put it to my lips. The water tasted sweet, and as it trickled over my lips and down my throat, my body lightened and the pain in my leg faded. I wasn't looking into the future at all. I was there. Real was the thing.

"Thank you," I said.

"What happened?" said Dad.

I shook my head. "I got into a skid. Smashed through a gate, ended up in a field."

"I always worried about you and that bike," said Mum.

"My girlfriend... she was on the back."

"The doctor said something about her."

"What did he say?"

"That she'd been hurt."

"I know that..."

"She's in intensive care."

"Intensive care?"

"That's what he said, but he wouldn't say anything else. But he did say you're going to be as good as new."

"But Sam..."

"I know, Pet..."

"I have to see her."

"I don't think you can. Not yet, anyway. All you can do at the moment is be quiet and rest."

"Rest?"

"Yes."

Rest? I couldn't rest. I felt hot and fevered, and my head was raging. I had to get up. I had to move. I had to see her. I had to see her and help her and tell her I was sorry and hold her hand in the day and the night. I had to, and that was all I had to do.

Mum and Dad stayed for a while and tried to cheer me up with stories about home and when I was a kid and the ways I used to wind Grace up, and how she used to get back at me, but nothing they said made me feel better. I asked Dad to go and see

Mr Evans, and tell him what had happened, and I asked Mum to give Grace a kiss from me, and when they'd gone I stared at the ceiling and listened to beeping machines and snoring patients and burbling nurses. Half an hour of this began to drive me mad, so I sat up, swung out of bed and looked at my leg. It had been cleaned and bandaged, and when I put weight on it, it hurt, but was strong enough. A nurse came to me and said, "What are you doing?"

"I need the toilet."

"I'll fetch a pan."

"I don't want a pan. I want to get up. I want to do it myself."

She picked up a board hooked to the end of my bed, looked at it, looked at me and said, "OK. You know where it is?"

"No."

"End of the ward on the right."

"Thanks."

It felt good to walk. It felt good to go to the toilet. And when I'd finished, I splashed my face with cold water, and that felt even better. Then I thought it would be good to take a longer walk. I couldn't lie in bed. I couldn't rest. I wandered down to a long corridor, and stood at a window.

Dawn was breaking, streaks of pink and orange and blue filled the sky, birds were singing from bushes and trees and roofs. I thought about the cows. They'd be coming in for milking. I thought about all the people who were sleeping in their beds. They'd be dreaming. I thought about Sam. I thought about her beautiful face and her hair tied in bunches, and I thought about her head. I went to look for her.

183

I walked down the corridor until I found a map of the hospital. Intensive care was on the floor below me. I followed the signs. It was easy to follow the signs.

When I pushed the door open, a nurse looked up from her desk and said, "Can I help?"

"Sam. My girlfriend. She's here."

She stood up. "And who are you?"

"Elliot. I was with her on the bike."

"Well, Elliot, you shouldn't be here, and you can't see her. She's asleep."

"But…"

"No buts, Elliot. It's the rules."

"Can't I just…" – I felt a bit faint, reached out and held onto the edge of the desk – "…just look. Look at her. Please?"

The nurse stood up, took my arm and said, "Listen, it's against the rules. But I suppose… I suppose you could have a minute. Just one, mind you. No more…" and she led me to a window. "She's in there," and she pointed.

Sam was lying on a high bed. Her head was wrapped in bandages, and she had tubes up her nose. Drips were stuck in her arms, and a frame kept the sheets and blankets off her body. Machines beeped, lines danced, a nurse in a mask came and stood by her, checked her pulse, ticked a chart and walked away. I said, "Oh God…"

"We'll know in twenty-four hours…"

"You'll know what?"

"If she's going to make it."

I felt my blood ice.

"Are you her next of kin?"

I shook my head. "No."

"Do you know where we can find them?"

I shook my head. "I know where she lives. Her other friends will know."

"Good. I'll leave you for a minute, but give me an address before you go."

I nodded, and when the nurse left me I pressed my face and hands against the glass and watched her sleeping.

What was going on in her head? Did she still have a brain? Was she dreaming or was her mind a blank, a place where nothing would do nothing for the rest of her life? The bits of her I could see, her arms and her face, were white and shiny under the lights, almost transparent, almost lost. And as I looked at her, the last week began to collapse inside me, all the stupidity and blood tumbling through my body like stones and wire. I felt heavy and lost and smoky, and all I wanted to do was break through the glass and bleed to death on her dying body. Too much dying, too much endlessness, and all the world did was carry on its selfish way.

19

I'd visited hospitals before, but I'd never been a patient. I didn't like it. The food was watery and the air smelt sick, and the other patients snored and moaned. I wanted to leave, but I didn't want to leave Sam, didn't want to leave her lying so alone and drifted, like a piece of wood at sea.

I lay in my bed and stared out of the window at the tops of the buildings on the other side of a car park, and I watched the nurses as they did their work. And I slept a dozy sleep, one that slipped in and out of vague dreams and thoughts and fears. One minute I was imagining Dickens appearing in a doctor's coat, leaning over me with poison in a syringe, the next I was seeing Spike in a dream, struggling in the waves of a sea storm, lifted up and dropped down again, always just out of my reach. Then I'd see Sam's smiling face, blood trickling from a wound in the top of her head, her mouth opening and closing, and her eyes black. And slowly, as the hours went by and the thoughts curdled in my head, I began to hate myself, the things I'd done and the weakness I'd shown. I tried to think of a way out of the mess, but couldn't, and every time I tried to think of something else in an attempt to chase away the bad thoughts, I failed. I was cursed and haunted.

The next time I went down to see Sam, a man and a woman were sitting by her bed. The nurse told me they were her parents, and I could wait to talk to them if I wanted. I stood for a moment and looked at them as they sat and stared at their daughter. Her mother was holding a handkerchief in her hand, screwing it slowly this way and that. Her father was leaning forwards and resting his hand on hers. He had a grey face, hers was wet, Sam's was white. I couldn't look for very long, and I couldn't stare. I was a coward. I didn't know what they'd say to me, but I knew they'd blame me and want me to answer questions I couldn't face, so I said to the nurse, "I think I'll come back later."

"You want me to tell them you were here?"

"No. Don't do that. I haven't met them before. I don't think this would be the right time."

"No," she said. "I don't suppose it would be."

"I'll come down later." And after a last look at Sam I went back to my ward and the smell and my thoughts.

A doctor came to see me in the afternoon, looked at my leg, read some notes and said, "How are you feeling?"

"Not bad. I'd feel better at home."

"Well," he said, and he scribbled something on the notes, "I think we can let you go in the morning."

"Thanks."

"And you ride a bit slower next time."

I didn't bother to tell him that riding slower had nothing to do with why I was there. I just nodded and watched him walk down the ward to the nurses' station, and then turned my face away and stared at curtains that hung around my bed. They were yellow and gave me no comfort at all.

I got no comfort when I went to see Sam again. When I asked how she was, a nurse said, "She's in a coma, but we think she can hear us. So sit with her for a bit and talk to her. She'll be able to feel you too…"

"A coma?"

"Yes."

"What does that mean?"

"It's like she's sleeping, but she's not…"

"I don't understand."

"She could wake up in a minute or she might…"

"Might what?"

"Not wake up for weeks."

"Or months?"

She nodded.

"Or ever?"

"I don't know about that."

I didn't want to get angry, but it was difficult to bite my tongue. I was going to ask if the nurse knew anything, but then I told myself to stop it, leave it, just be quiet. If Sam could hear me, I didn't want her to hear me shout or swear, so I nodded, sat down, touched the top of her hand and said, "Hello Sam. It's Elliot…"

I looked at the nurse. She nodded and smiled and went back to her desk.

I didn't know what to say. I felt awkward and guilty, so I just let the words hang in the air and stroked her hand and stared at her for half an hour. That, I thought, was enough. If she could hear me, she'd know I was there, and if she could feel, then she'd know my hand was warm. And if she could see something in the dark, then maybe she could see a field of flowers and birds in the singing sky, and a river running through the woods, and a place where we could sit and dangle our feet in the water. And maybe all these things could take her pain away and make her better, and form themselves into a promise she could hold in her coma, and in finding her way back to real life.

I tried to sleep. Maybe I did, maybe I didn't. I had one of those nights where nothing seems or feels right for the night. When I woke up, I went back to intensive care, sat with Sam for half an hour, said goodbye and told her I'd be back soon. I collected my stuff from the ward, signed a form, and a man drove me back to Ashbrittle. He tried to talk to me as he drove, but I didn't have anything to say. I just stared at the streets and houses, and when the streets and houses turned to hedges and fields I stared at the hedges and fields. I still felt heavy and lost and smoky, but other things had added themselves to these feelings. Here was fury and here was rage, and they were walking with grief and the nagging idea that none of this was real, that I was simply drowning in a dream of my own making. A stupid idea, and I chased it out of my head with a stick, beat it to death in a corner and turned my back on it.

Mum had my old room ready for me. For a moment I thought I was going to get a lecture. I waited for her to tell me that the signs had been in the clouds or the song of birds or the tracks of rabbits, but she said nothing except that I should go to bed and she'd bring me a cup of tea. I did as I was told for half an hour, but I couldn't rest or keep still. When she came up, she asked me about Sam, and I told her everything I knew. She tried to reassure me, and told me about someone she'd read about in the newspaper who fell out of a window and banged her head and the doctors thought she'd never recover, but she did, and now she was a concert pianist. "They do miracles these days," she said.

"I know."

"And I'll think of something that might help."

"What sort of thing?"

She tapped the side of her nose. "I'll tell you when I've thought of it. But in the meantime you're not to worry."

Not to worry? I drank the tea and stared out of the window at the village green and the familiar cars, but I did nothing but worry. It was impossible not to. It took chunks out of me, chewed me, spat me out and took another chunk. I got up and went downstairs. I stood in the kitchen, and the cat came and rubbed itself against my good leg, then went to look for a patch of sunshine. My bike had been collected from the field, and was leaning against Dad's shed. I went outside and stood over it. The front wheel was buckled, the tank was dented and the wing mirrors were smashed. I didn't know where to start, but I thought that I should try and mend it. I went inside the shed to look for some tools.

Dad's gardening tools hung on the back wall, flower pots and a bag of compost were stacked behind the door, and a work bench stood by the window. Random jam jars were filled with nuts and bolts, nails and screws, cup hooks and washers, and some hand tools were arranged in a rack. I didn't know what I was looking for, so I picked up a wooden box, opened it and looked at a small collection of metal brackets, coils of wire and string. For some reason I was suddenly overwhelmed by a feeling of sadness, a sadness that took me by the hand and begged me to weep. I suppose it was the way Dad had saved and collected stuff he'd never use, and the idea that one day it would be my job to come to this shed and gather the same stuff up and throw it away. Why had he saved a rusted water tap, two cork tiles and a bicycle bell that didn't work? Or a single boot with a hole in the sole, a small bag of bottle tops and a hardened paint brush with a piece of twine wrapped around its cracked handle? The force of nostalgia or the promise of potential? I didn't know, but I did care. Everything in the shed was part of Dad, like his eyes or hands or his voice. I could smell him in everything I touched, feel his wishes and dreams.

The shed was his place, and he didn't like other people rummaging through his stuff, so when I saw him coming down the garden path I stepped outside. And before he could have a go at me, I said, "Sorry Dad. I was looking for a spanner."

"What for?"

"That." I pointed at the bike.

"Oh don't worry about that. I'll fix it for you. It'll be as good as new."

"You sure?"

"Of course. It'll be a project for me."

"Thanks, Dad."

"Oh, and Mr Evans called. He said you're to take all the time you need."

"He's a good old boy," I said.

"And you're to listen to your mother," he said. "I know sometimes she says things you might not understand, but there's a lot going on up there." He tapped the side of his head.

"I know," I said, "and I do listen to her." And when he went back to his lettuces I left the garden and walked up to the churchyard and the yew.

The yew. I've heard it whisper and cry, and I've heard it hum and sing. There are stories about it, stories about the old religions and the roots of the tree drinking blood while its branches made patterns in the air. Once, the warm guts of living men were nailed to its trunks, and the men forced to walk around the tree, unravelling their entrails, bees humming, women laughing and yelling to their mad gods, children in lines singing pretty songs and waving ribbons in the air. Gods looking on, laughing back and nodding satisfaction and waiting for the next man to be brought for slaughter. The blood running, dogs howling and waiting to eat, sick smells in the air. Music played on instruments people smashed and burned a long time ago. Purple. I believe it was purple in those days, but now the colour was green, and it was cool in its shade like a still draught, and birds chirped in the branches. Someone had put a posy in a crack in the bark, little yellow and blue flowers that had faded now. I touched them: petals dropped away, and the church clock began to chime the hour.

The yew's trunk is hollow and split into six smaller trunks, and even now people bring sick babies to its shade and pass them through the trunks, and the babies are healed. I sat in its hollow, rested my head and looked up at the branches. The bark was flaked and pale and running with ants. I suppose I was thinking that the tree gives itself to anyone who believes, and maybe it could help me. That if Sam's head died, but her body lived, I could bring her here and thread her through these trunks. That Spike could be made to change if he slept beneath these branches. That violent men could be calmed by its sight. Or maybe not.

I sat for an hour, and when I stood up I did feel stronger, my leg felt better and my thoughts were running straight and easy. I walked to the far end of the churchyard, left by the top gate and stood outside Pump Court. I was going to knock on the door, but I couldn't. I was trapped between guilt and fear. Sam's parents would have called her friends, they'd have told them the news. I couldn't tell them anything more. I walked down the road towards the green and the telephone box.

I stood in the box for a couple of minutes, holding the receiver in my hand, listening to the buzz. It started beeping. I put the receiver down, picked it up again and called Pollock.

"Where have you been?" he said. "I've been waiting for you. What's been going on?"

"I had an accident."

"What sort of accident?"

I explained. I told him about the chasing car and the crash and the hospital and Sam, and as I talked I heard him light a cigarette and take a long, deep drag. When I'd finished, he said, "You're all right?"

"I'm OK. I can walk."

"You sure about that?"

"Yes."

"Good. Because we're ready to move."

"When?"

"We have to meet."

"You'll have to pick me up. My bike's fucked."

"All right. I'll be over. This afternoon?"

"OK."

"Tell me where."

"I'll walk to Tracebridge, at the bottom of Ashbrittle Hill, and wait on the bridge. You can't miss it. You'll feel the place before you see it."

"What?"

"Never mind…"

"I'll feel the place?"

"Forget it…" I said, and I could hear Pollock's silence. He was wondering something. Eventually he said, "Half-two?"

"I'll be there."

"Good," he said, and that was that.

After I'd hung up, I waited in the box for a couple of minutes, then crossed the road and let myself into the house. Mum was in the kitchen, Dad was in the garden. I went upstairs and lay on my bed, stared at the ceiling and listened to the familiar sounds of the world. There was comfort there, and pleasure and familiarity, and I let myself float in it while I could. I felt held and loved and wanted, and thought that my visit to the yew tree had given me a greater power. "Yes," I said to the ceiling, and I let the single word bounce back at me like a ball and settle on my forehead.

An hour later I was waiting on the bridge. The river was weak and slow, and the trees were high. Wood pigeons were making their sounds and, in a field above the valley, sheep were making theirs. A light breeze was twirling through the leaves, and the sun was strong, but the sense of malevolence the old witch had left at the place was there, and gave the air a chill. I tried to find a pocket of warmth, a place where the sun broke through and couldn't fail, but there was none. So I waited behind a tree, hid myself there and watched.

I watched a magpie, a single chattering bird that hopped from branch to branch to branch and back again like the evil shadow of its own image. Mum always told me to salute the magpie, but I wondered; are the old superstitions simply reflections of our fears, and do we make the superstitions real by acknowledging our fears? Sometimes I surprised myself with the things I thought. Another magpie appeared. Joy. And then another. A girl. How did it go? And how did it end? Eight is a kiss, nine is a wish, ten is a chance never to be missed. I waited. I didn't see more than three.

Pollock arrived on time. He was alone. I stepped out from behind the tree and walked to the car, and for a moment he looked a bit surprised. Surprise faded to nonchalance. He leant across, opened the passenger door, said, "Get in," and I did as I was told. He turned the car around and drove back towards Apply Cross, down through Greenham and up to the main road. We headed towards the Blackdowns, and when he'd found a quiet spot beside a dry stream, he pulled in and let the car settle. As it clicked and cooled, he turned to me and said, "You're a lucky man, Elliot."

"Am I?"

"Yes. Very."

"I don't feel lucky. And my girlfriend's in intensive care. They don't know if she'll live."

He put his hand on my shoulder. "She'll be OK."

"How do you know that?"

"Faith, Elliot, faith. Have some. It's easy. There's plenty to go around. And all types. Hard, soft, chewy, melt-in-the-mouth…"

I didn't know what he was talking about. I shrugged.

"Believe me," he said, and he reached around to the back seat and picked up a folder. He opened it, took out a sheet of paper and said, "OK. We have a plan."

"Do you?"

"Yes. And you're part of it."

"Great."

"I'm only going to tell you what you need to know: there'll be things that go on that I won't tell you about, but that's because it'll be safer that way."

"Just tell me what I have to do."

"Good lad."

Apparently it was a simple plan, and Pollock said it had hands and feet and legs and was ready to stroll down the street with a flag – whatever that meant. I had no idea, but I didn't say anything. Dickens was going to find out that I was selling the smoke to a man from Bristol, and I was so desperate that I was ready to take any price just to get rid of it. As long as I got enough to buy some peace and quiet I'd be happy. The man from Bristol was "someone you've already met".

"Who?"

"Inspector Smith."

"The bloke who came with you last time?"

"You're not stupid, are you?"

"I don't know. You'd have to ask my friends about that."

At half-past ten on the day after tomorrow, I was to drive the smoke to a transport café on the A38, between Taunton and Wellington, park and wait. I knew the place. I'd been there before. They did good breakfasts. Two sausages, two rashers, hash browns, tomatoes, heaps of beans and mushrooms and as much toast as you could eat. Ketchup in squeezy plastic bottles the shape of tomatoes and tea in heavy mugs, all served on sticky formica tables. But I wasn't to be tempted. I was to sit tight and still and stare at my fingernails and the torn posters of foreign places that hung on the wall. A canal in Venice. The Taj Mahal. The Eiffel Tower. I was to listen to the bad music from the crackly speaker over the counter, and smell the old oil as it wafted from the kitchen. Inspector Smith would meet me. He'd be dressed like a big-time dealer, and have a bag of pretend money. There'd be other people there, but I wouldn't know it. I'd be in the dark. Dickens would meet me too, but he wouldn't recognize Smith or be expecting anything unexpected. "He'll have a couple of heavies with him, but you're not to worry. We'll have you covered."

"You sure about that?"

"Cast iron, Elliot, cast iron."

"And then what?"

"We'll take the bastard down."

"You sure about that too?"

"Oh yes."

"And if you don't?"

"Faith, Elliot."

"But if you don't?"

"Elliot. This has been worked out. Every detail. Nothing's going to go wrong."

"Nothing?"

"Guaranteed. We're not taking any chances. We can't afford to. A lot of people have been waiting a long time for this."

I stared at Pollock. He stared back at me. I don't know who he thought I was or who I reminded him of, but he reminded me of someone I'd seen in a film. I don't know who that someone was or what film it was or where I saw it, but his face was lined, and there were tiny spots on his forehead. His lips were thin, and his eyes were honest and big, and I think he liked me. Maybe I was naive or maybe I was just stupid, but at that time I had no choice. I was trapped in the dark, and the dark folded its wings over my face. I had to believe him. I had to nod when he told me the plan, and as he drove away from the quiet spot and rolled back towards Ashbrittle, I watched the road, and the road became a still and peaceful place where wishes could lie down and dream.

Wishes lie down and dream? Now there was an idea, and when I thought about dreams, I wished I could go back to the time when my dreams were simple and quiet, and the worst they could do was leave me with a dry mouth. When I got home, I sat on the bench beneath the kitchen window and watched the sky and the swallows and swifts, the passing birds of the English season. They filled themselves with flies, they cut the sky to ribbons and wounds and left it crying, and as they sang they left me with my head in my hands and my bad leg throbbing. And what did I do? I sat and waited, and when Dad got in from work I fetched him a beer and opened it and watched him drink and wipe his face of his clean and innocent sweat. And when Grace came back from college, she sat next to me and hugged me and I thanked her for being my sister. "I'm lucky," I said, and I almost meant it.

"You bet," she said, and she kissed me on the end of my nose like you'd kiss a pet rabbit, or the back of an envelope before you post it to someone you really love.

"Grace?" I said.

"What?"

"You're not going anywhere, are you?"

"No," she said. "Why?"

"I wanted to check."

She looked at me as if I was mad. "What are you talking about? Are you mad?"

"No."

"Sometimes I wonder."

"And I do too," I said.

"I'm not going anywhere," she said. "And when I'm dead I'm going to haunt you."

"What if I die first?"

"Then I'll haunt you in your grave. I'll dig down and stand in front of you and make weird moaning sounds until you wake up."

"Thanks," I said.

"Oh, it'll be my pleasure," she said, and the way she looked at me made me think that she was telling the truth, more of a truth that anything I'd heard all day. And when Mum got back, she ran to me and hugged me and put her hand on the top of my head and I tasted earth in my mouth. "Come on," she said. "I'll make your favourite." So Grace and Dad and I followed her into the house, and we sat at the table while she fired up the oven, fetched sausages from the fridge and mixed up a bowl of thick batter.

20

In the morning, while the cat played with a ball of wool and the village cockerels chased their hens into the shade, Mum said she'd thought of something, and if I had the gifts she had, and a talent for the old charms, then it was a thing that would work for me. She told me it had done for her mother and her grandmother and her great-grandmother back then, and who knew how many mothers before them.

"So what do I do?"

"First," she said, "you have to have faith. You take your faith and swallow it, and then you pick an apple."

"An apple?"

"Yes. And you take a bite from it while thinking of the one thing you most want to happen in the world. It's got to be from our garden," she said, "and the thing you think of mustn't have anything to do with something you want to happen to you. Think about someone else."

"And then what?"

"You bury the piece you've bitten off outside her house."

"Her house? Who's she?"

She squinted at me, shook her head and said, "Oh please Pet. This isn't a game."

"And?"

"You keep the rest in your pocket."

"What if I haven't got a pocket?"

"You've got to take this seriously, Pet. If you don't, it won't work."

What could I do but do as I was told? I went to the apple tree, picked an apple, polished it on my shirt and thought about Sam. I thought about her brain and how it sat inside her skull, the blood vessels and sponge bits and the nerves. And I imagined the apple as her brain, and when I bit a piece out of it I imagined it as the damaged piece of her brain with the memories swilling, the thoughts gone and the ideas dead. And as I carried the bitten piece up the road to her cottage, I asked the thing that gives Mum her power or insight or whatever it is to look down on Sam and do whatever it could.

There was a little curve of earth in front of her cottage, and I could duck down beneath the window and do my burying without being seen by anyone, so that's what I did. I closed my eyes, concentrated my thoughts, brought them together in a little ball, made the ball even smaller and then dropped that ball into my heart. I let it settle, stood up, opened my eyes, tucked the rest of the apple into my shirt pocket and, as I did, one of the hippy boys came out of the side gate that lead to the other cottages. I think it was Don, but it could have been Danny. I didn't know what to expect, and as he walked towards me I took a step back. "Hi…" he said. "You OK?"

I didn't know what to say. "You heard about Sam?"

"The hospital phoned."

"I'm sorry," I said.

"Don't be. It wasn't your fault, was it?"

I shook my head.

"We're going to see her later. Sounds like you had a lucky escape…"

I shrugged. "I feel terrible."

He reached out and put his hand on my shoulder. "Fate, Elliot." He looked up at the sky. "It's a powerful thing. We can't change it."

"No," I said. "I don't suppose we can."

"And Sam's a strong woman."

"I know."

"She'll pull through."

We stood and stared at each other, and although I wanted to say something else, I didn't know what. I think he was thinking the same. "Look," he said. "Call in any time, you know that. Sam said nothing but good things about you. She's got a real thing for you, you know?"

"Thanks."

"No," he said. "Thank you." And he squeezed my shoulder and crossed the road to the garden. I watched him stroll down the path to the place where Sam and I had pulled the onions, and then I turned and walked home.

Mum was waiting for me in the kitchen. When I walked in, she said, "See if what you just did doesn't help," and then told me to go and see Dad. "He's out the back, working on your bike."

Dad's got a talent for wheels, metal and mechanicals. I've seen him mend a water pump with a matchstick and candle wax, and once he fixed a lawnmower with a paper clip and the bottom of a broken light bulb. The only reason our fridge has worked for twenty years is because he knows more about condensers than the repairman, and the reason Grace's hair drier could blow a dog into the next parish is because he turbocharged it one drunk Friday. He stared at my bike, said, "I'll have this going for you," and after an hour and twenty minutes with a screwdriver, an adjustable spanner and a roll of wire, he stood back, cleaned his hands with an oily cloth, tossed it over his shoulder and said, "It might be as good as new."

"You're a genius."

"Don't say that until you've tried it."

I took it for a spin around the green, and it made a few odd noises it hadn't made before, but there was no shake in the handlebars, the wheels were true and the lights worked. So I told him I'd take it for a proper ride, and before he or Mum could tell me to stay where I was and not be so stupid, I'd gunned it away from the village towards Taunton and Sam.

I rode fast and on the straights I overtook without thinking. Get back on the horse. Give fear the finger. Stare at the sun. Haul the walrus up the beach. Catch a fly in your mouth. All these things. And take those things, put them in a box, seal the box and send them to hell. It was almost easy.

She was still in intensive care, and the machines were still beeping. I was given a gown to wear, and the nurse said that this time I should try to talk to her properly. "Don't just mumble. Talk to her. Pretend you're having a conversation. She won't answer, but fill in the gaps yourself."

"It's hard."

"It's harder for her."

So I sat with her, watched the machines blink, listened to them beep, and I looked at her face. The tubes in her mouth and nose made little bubbling noises. Her eyes were closed and her lips were cracked, and the bandage on her head was clean and white. I felt as though my blood was pouring away like water down a drain. I held her hand, squeezed it, leant towards her and said, "Hello Sam. It's me. Elliot."

"I'm sorry. So sorry…"

"I never meant you to get caught up in all this."

"It's a mess, but it's going to get better."

"And you're going to get better too."

"And when you do, I think we should go away together."

"Would you like that?"

"Have you ever been to Cornwall?"

"I haven't, but I'd like to go. I think we could find a nice place by the sea. Somewhere where we could watch the fishing boats come in…"

"And go for a walk along the beach."

"Buy ice creams."

"Build a sandcastle. Would you like to build a sandcastle?"

"We could fly a kite."

"Do the sort of things we did when we were kids. You know…"

"Eat fish and chips."

"Take a trip around the bay."

"Sit outside a pub and chat to the locals."

"Whatever you want to do, Sam. We could even go back to Greece."

"I mean you could go back to Greece. I haven't been there before."

"We could find the bar where you used to work. Have a drink. Eat some of that food they eat."

A nurse came and took her pulse, marked something on a chart and said, "You're doing a good job, dear."

"I feel a bit of an idiot."

"You're not."

"Talk about anything you want. Just hearing your voice is good for her."

"OK."

So I did.

"I spoke to Don. At least I think it was Don. It might have been Danny. Or maybe it was Dave…"

"Anyway. They're coming in to see you later."

"I was afraid he was going to have a go at me, but he was very kind. Very gentle. He said I could call in any time, but I don't think I will. Not until you're there."

"It wouldn't be the same without you."

I squeezed her hand again, and watched as the machines made their squiggly blue lines. I looked towards the nurse. She gave me a thumbs up.

"My Dad fixed up the bike."

"It's as good as new."

"But it's making a few odd noises."

"So I've been riding carefully."

"I'm not going to crash again…"

"And my mum taught me a charm. She made me take a bite from an apple…"

"And bury it outside your cottage."

"She said that if I had her talent…"

"That it would work for me."

I touched my shirt pocket, felt the apple in there and said, "And there's something else I have to do…"

Beeeeeeeee… and Sam twitched. I say she twitched, but maybe it was a spasm. Her mouth opened and she made a sound like a cat trapped in a piano. A second later three nurses burst into the room. One started pushing buttons while another pulled the bedclothes back and the third rolled a trolley from a corner to the bedside. "Sorry," she said, "you'll have to go…" And I was gone.

I stood behind the glass and watched as the nurses worked. They were fast, and they didn't panic, but whatever they were doing was important and serious and careful. There was a machine on the trolley, but before I had the chance to see them use it, one of the nurses released a blind that came down and covered the window. I stared at the blind for a minute, then turned and walked away from the ward.

I found a drinks machine. I bought a cup of coffee and stood by a window. As I drank, nurses and doctors and cleaners and porters wandered by, lost in their work and lost in the day. I felt trapped and useless. Given a stolen present I couldn't play with. I wanted to go to bed, pull the blankets to my face and sleep. I wanted the dark, and I wanted to feel safe again.

Take me back to the past, I thought, and give me the chance to see the flight of my own life again. Let me swim in my own choices, not the choices other people make and push at me. Let me go.

An hour later I went back to intensive care. Sam's machines were beeping regularly again, and the nurses had left her bedside. One of them told me they thought she'd suffered a brain haemorrhage, but now it looked as if she'd had a small seizure. I was going to ask them what this meant, but when I opened my mouth to speak, the words I wanted to say collapsed inside me, and I felt the touch of something that rhymed with all my grief.

"Should I stay?" I said.

The nurse said, "I think you should go home and get some sleep. You look exhausted."

"I am."

"Then go."

"OK."

"We'll be looking after her," she said.

The sun shone through the hospital windows, flowers wilted on window sills, patients waited in their dressing gowns. And as I walked down the corridor to the exit, I saw Sam's parents walking towards me: her mother was being supported by her father, who was carrying an old teddy bear under his arm. It was a faded white bear, missing one eye and with a sad arm dangling down, and as I got closer to them I almost stopped and spoke to them and told them who I was, but then I thought again. They looked worse than the first time I'd seen them, lost in fear and agony, hardly able to walk straight. So I put my head down and walked on like the coward I was, slipped out into the sunshine and ducked around the side of the hospital to my bike. Before I rode away, I thought of the sound Sam had made, the little cat scream. I felt in my pocket for the bit apple, took it out, looked at its browned flesh and tossed it into a bush. Then I was away before I had a second chance to think about what I'd done, out of the car park and back on the road.

21

Sleep? It was impossible. Home? I didn't want to go home, so I went to see Spike. His friend had gone out for the day. We sat in plastic picnic chairs in the back garden, put our feet on a pile of logs and drank coffee. When I told him about being chased by the car and Sam in a coma and me in hospital and mending motorbikes with wire and biting pieces out of apples, he said he didn't believe me, so I showed him my leg and told him that he was welcome to come to Taunton and stand with his face pressed against the glass of the intensive-care ward. "If you've got the balls," I said. He put his hands up, and saying, "OK. You win," lit a cigarette and sat back. "You win, I lose, everything's fucked."

"It doesn't have to be."

"Well it is."

"And it's got nothing to do with winning."

"If you say so."

"I do."

"Well. Whatever…"

I think Spike had gone beyond fear, and was now depressed. Depressed in the sort of way that could lead to a doctor's surgery and a bottle of pills, and days in bed in a darkened room. He said he wished he could go back to work at the blackcurrant farm. "But I got the sack," he said. "I'll be lucky to get another job anywhere. Everything's fucked."

"You need to get a grip."

"Thanks."

"All you need to do is keep your head down for a couple more days. I'm getting you out of this mess."

He took a long drag on his cigarette, slurped his coffee and said, "It's a nightmare."

"Tell me about it. Second thoughts – don't. Don't say another thing."

"I've got nothing to say anyway."

And that was how we left it. I did think about suggesting that when it was all over we could go away somewhere, take the van to Cornwall or something, pitch a tent in a campsite and spend a few days drinking, but I didn't think he'd listen. All he wanted to do was make himself small, disappear into a hole, something like that. So when I'd finished my coffee I stood up and said, "Things to do, nightmares to sort. I'll see you in a day or two."

"Whatever," he said.

"Spike…" I started, but then I shook my head. There was nothing more to say. "I'll let myself out." And I left him sitting in the garden with his face turned towards a hedge.

I suppose I'd always thought that one day Spike would be reduced to this, to staring at a hedge, admitting that everything was fucked, all plans gone, ambition dissolved. When I say I'd always thought this would happen, I should say that I might have thought it, but I never imagined it would actually come true. Spike had always been a wild schemer who never got round to putting his ideas into action, at least not until he saw that smoke in the hoop house. It was typical that the first scheme he ever got off the ground dropped him in it. "Typical," I said to myself as I climbed on the bike and pointed it away from Wivey.

I rode around for a couple of hours, and when I got bored I went home and had a cup of tea. When Mum asked me about Sam, I just nodded and told her that she was the same. I didn't tell her about throwing the apple away or seeing Spike, but I did say that I wouldn't be in that night. "I'm going for a few beers," I said, "so I'll stay with some mates."

"Mates?" she said. "Which mates?"

"Mates," I said.

She knew I was lying, but I didn't tell her which mates or which pub. I gave her a hug, left the bike by the back door and walked away.

I stopped at Heniton Hill, above the place where Spike had found the hoop house and the smoke, strolled to the top and sat down. The ground was hard and stony, and my head was buzzing. To the north, the Brendons climbed to Exmoor, and to the east the land dropped towards the Somerset levels, the Poldens and the Mendips. The fields were yellow and brown, the hedges lank, the wind nothing. High birds dipped, distant cows nudged the dust, the sun was prince and king. I smelt wool in the air, and meat, and I tasted metal. Everything was dry and fainting, blown into a fly's mouth, chewed, thrown out again and left to turn to a crust. But when I turned, when I turned and focused and looked towards the purple crease of Dartmoor, something was changing. A fight was in the air. I didn't notice it straight away, but when I did, I had to blink at the sight, remind myself that what I was seeing was real and blink again.

Clouds. Clouds were gathering in a thin line over the moor. There weren't many, but they were real. And as the sun began to sink behind them, they turned to the look and colour of slashed wounds, red in the middle, pink at the sides, soft, weeping and livid. It would take time, but rain was coming. The clouds would build and climb and form themselves into thunderheads, and when they reached the height they needed they'd split and break, and the world would drink. Cows would run into sheep, sheep would prance, dogs would laugh, Ros and Dave and Don and Danny and their other friends would run into their garden and dance naked, and the rivers would sigh.

I watched the clouds for an hour. There was comfort in watching, comfort in the sight of the stream of rooks as they headed for their roosts, solace in the land as it gathered itself for the night. And as I walked away, I stopped at the rows of beech trees that grow on the hill, and ran my fingers over their trunks. I felt their strength and calm, and carried that calm away with me, held it tight and walked to Mr Evans's farm to collect Spike's van.

Night was falling fast. I walked quickly, and kept to the shadows and dips, and once, as a car appeared in the lane, I ducked out of its headlights and crouched behind a ruined churn stand. When I reached Stawley Mill, I stopped by the river to catch my breath and listen to the stars in their coursing. I heard them spin and flare, turn and light the way for their

213

planets. The moon was still bright enough to see by, and the air was warm and close.

The ghost of a headless dog sometimes roams the lanes around Stawley Mill, lost and blind and hungry. It's looking for the thing it's lost, trying to remember what it was like to have eyes and ears and a mouth, following the sound of a disembodied bark that echoes through the trees of the wooded valleys and combes. Sometimes it waits in a hedge and jumps out at walkers, other times it wanders up and down the lane, marking gate posts with its scent, leaving drops of blood on the ground. There are people who say that if you see it you will be dead within the week, maddened to death by the sight of its gaping neck and the smell of its wounds. And others say that the person who finds its head and returns it to the dog will gain the power to conjure silver from rain. I wasn't going to tempt fate or whatever power the animal wields, and I wasn't going to make myself its victim. As I headed up towards the farm I hurried on, kept my head down and walked in the middle of the road.

I crossed the bottom field below the farm, kept an eye out for Mr Evans, followed the line of the hedges to the sunken lane that led to the kale field, and stopped every fifty yards to listen for noise. I heard nothing, saw no one, kept low, and when I reached the barn I checked the stick of straw was still stuck behind the bolt, slipped the door open and ducked inside.

The smell of smoke filled the place, and the splinters of moonlight that shone through cracks in the walls illuminated the old trailer, the harrows and the van. I pulled the tarp off its roof, opened the back and looked inside. Everything was exactly as we'd left it. The smoke was still in its sacks, and the sacks were stacked in their rows. I went back to the doors, hauled them open and rolled the trailer out. I folded and rolled the tarp and put it in a corner. Then I let the van's handbrake off, took the steering wheel and put my back into pushing.

It took twenty minutes, but by the time I'd finished I had the van parked in the field, the trailer back in the barn and the harrows and other bits of machinery arranged exactly as they had been before. I closed the doors, wiped my hands on a ball of hay, climbed into the van, put the key in the ignition and took a deep breath. It started first time. I listened to the engine, let it idle for a moment, then accelerated, dropped out of the field, drove through the gate and down into the sunken lane. The high hedges shaded the moon, so I turned the headlights on and drove as carefully and quietly as the van would allow. Just before the bend that led to the front yard, I turned off the lights, floored the accelerator and shot past my caravan and the house. As I passed the front door, the porch light came on, and as I dropped into the track that led down to the road, I looked in my mirrors. Mr Evans appeared, and he was carrying his gun. He waved towards me, and then raised his arm. He put the gun to his shoulder. I heard a double crack, but then I was round the corner, the headlights were on again and I was skidding through the sharp left onto the road. Fifty yards, a sharp right, down the hill towards Stawley church and then back towards the mill and the lane of the headless dog. Up the hill towards Appley, fast as the van would go, over the cross, down to Greenham and onto the main road. I pulled in before the junction, stopped and sat in the dark with my hands on the steering wheel and listened to my heart beating like a bastard. It beat and thudded, and my forehead was covered in sweat. I wiped myself dry and waited five minutes. No one came out of the night, and no cars passed. The lights that lit the junction cast an orange light that gave the place a lost, lonely atmosphere. The ghosts of accidents, the scream of tyres, the broken bodies and the cry of pain. Nothing. Silence and quiet and lines of tarmac against the hedges. Still. I waited another five minutes, then turned onto the road and drove towards Taunton.

Driving with the smoke wasn't easy, and the further I drove the more difficult it got. It was strong stuff, sweet and warm, and after a few miles it was getting deep inside my head, boring holes through my brain and into my neck, down to my heart and my lungs and my liver and all the other parts. Down and down and further down. Colouring me. Filling me. Twitching at me. Twitch, twitch, twitch. I opened the windows, let the fresh air in, but the smoke wouldn't let me go. Bad smoke. Leave me alone. Let me do what I have to do. Stop that. Keep your hands to yourself. Leave it. But it didn't listen. It rustled. The sacks rustled. My brain rustled, grabbed an edge of paranoia and told me to slow down.

Slow down.

Slow.

Stop that.

Stop now.

Forget.

Stop.

But it didn't stop. It got worse. The fumes concentrated themselves, filled my head, burst out, broke back in and nailed themselves to my nose. The road twisted and changed. All the familiar places gave themselves new names. Pubs I had drunk in, garages I had filled up in, houses I wished I could live in, fields. A corner I had stood and thumbed a lift from. A roundabout I had slowed for. And all the way the glow of the sodium lights, beaming and shining and throwing short shadows on the road and verge.

The smoke sang to me. Songs. Psalms. Opera. German stuff. The slamming creep. The sudden lights of a car. The sudden lights of another car. A lorry. Two lorries. A bend in the road that used to be more of a bend. The cider place with wagons parked on the grass. The hill towards the Stonegallows pub and the old wonderings of what happened at that place before the pub was built and named.

The pub sign was a picture of a stone gallows. Solid and tall and built to hang two men at the same time, it cast a cloud over the clear night, spit spirits at the van, cries of grief and pain and end and loss. I flicked the windscreen wipers on. I don't know why. I leant my head out of the window. I took a deep breath. Dropped a gear. Thought I saw a crowd of ghostly, baying faces lap around the van, felt my paranoia swell, smelt blood, tasted iron, stone, rope, light, tangerines, wool, smoke, wood, socks. I smelt these things all the way to the hospital, found a dark corner in the car park, fell out of the van, rolled over and lay on a patch of grass with my eyes wide open.

I'd smoked smoke and I'd eaten smoke, but I'd never been drenched and drowned in the stuff. I was turning with the world as the stars sang and spun over me. The grass twitched and clicked with movement and life, and when I turned my face towards the sounds, the sounds fingered my ears and whispered back at me. They were talking about their lives and my life, and said things I didn't think they knew about me. And when I turned my face back to the sky, the stars told me that although the world was dark, the light was always ready to break through. It had a great power, the power to spark a revolution.

Revolution? Power? Whispers? I couldn't do this. I couldn't let nonsense fuck with my head. I had things to do. People to visit. I stood up, leant against the van and stared at the hospital. The windows shone. I could see nurses. A doctor. The ends of beds. Bright lights. They were too bright. I fell over.

As I lay in the grass again, I heard a new sound. Running water. I waited for five minutes, stood up again and took a deep breath. Fresh air. A cure.

The sound of water was coming from a fountain. I knelt at its side and dropped my head in. Cool. I pulled my head out, dropped it in again, pulled it out again, let the water dribble down the inside of my shirt to my waist. I looked back at the hospital. It was still shining. I was shining. I was shining hard like the stars and the ground and the water on my face and the smoke in my head and the van in the car park and the grass on the verge. I went over to the grass on the verge, lay down and closed my eyes. I didn't plan to sleep, but I did, and my dreams were bright and wild and long, and when I woke up birds were singing in my ears.

22

Nine o'clock. I went to the hospital canteen and bought a cup of coffee and a bacon sandwich. As I waited at the till, I caught sight of myself in a mirror. I was a mess. My eyes were bloodshot, and my hair had a twig in it. I had grass on my shirt and mud smeared my cheeks. The woman behind the counter looked at me suspiciously, and when I said, "I had a rough night," she said, "Haven't we all?"

I didn't know about that but I didn't say anything else. I found a table in a corner where I was hidden from the nurses, doctors and other visitors. The coffee was strong and sweet, the bacon was salty and the lights were too bright. I ate slowly, and when I'd finished I found a toilet. I washed my face and hands and flattened my hair, then walked down to intensive care and sat with Sam for a while.

Her condition hadn't changed. She was still plugged into the beeping machines, and as I held her hand and talked, her face gave nothing away. She could have been floating beneath the surface of a still lake, her skin paled by the dull water, her pain nibbled by fish. I watched her chest as she breathed, and I think I saw her eyeballs move beneath their lids, but I might have been mistaken. The teddy bear her parents had brought was propped at the bottom of the bed, staring blankly at her. When I left I squeezed her hand and said, "I'm going to sort everything out this morning, and when I come back all I'm going to do is help you get better." And as I walked away, I told the nurse I'd be back in the afternoon.

"You look like you need some sleep," she said.

"I do."

"Then get some."

"I'll try."

The transport café was twenty minutes from the hospital. I drove with all the windows open and my face leaning towards the fresh air, so by the time I'd reached the place, my head was almost clear. It was 10:15. There were a couple of lorries and a van in the car park, but otherwise it was empty. I sat with my hands on the steering wheel and stared at a hedge. A wren came hunting for insects, a little fat dart of terror and temper. High above me, two buzzards were soaring in widening circles, their primaries wide and their eyes bright for food. I heard the wren sing, and I heard the buzzards cry, and as the minutes ticked by, I felt my heart tighten. My palms sweated. The world ground its teeth. A sudden breeze picked up some dust and blew it at the van, then died down again. The clouds I had seen from Heniton Hill had been burnt and blown away. The temperature took a sudden leap, and suddenly it was very hot.

At twenty-past, a white Transit pulled into the car park. It slowed and pulled in opposite me, and I saw Pollock sitting in the passenger seat. He was wearing sunglasses, two days' worth of a ginger beard and a woollen hat pulled down tight. Sweat was pouring off his face. I didn't recognize the driver. Pollock saw me and put a finger to his lips. I looked away. I was patient. I kept my hands on the steering wheel. I listened to the breeze and the birds, watched clouds drift, smelt the scent of petrol and diesel. At half-past, another van arrived, drove slowly towards me and stopped. Inspector Smith was driving. He was wearing a black cap and sunglasses. He rolled his window down, looked at me and said, "Good morning, Elliot."

"Hello."

He pushed the glasses down his nose, winked, then pushed them back up. "You OK?"

"I will be."

"Of course you will." He smiled, a smile that lashed at his face like a little whip and quickly disappeared. "You've got something for me?"

"Might do."

"Want to show me?"

"OK."

I got out of my van, and he got out of his, and we walked to the back of mine. As I opened the doors, he whispered, "Act cool."

"Sure…"

"And everything'll go to plan."

"OK," I said, and he peered into the van, sniffed, whistled through his teeth and said, "That's a lot of smoke."

"It is," I said, and he winked again. Smith was confident and strong, and this made my heart slow its pace. I felt OK. I felt safe. "A lot of good smoke," I said, and he stepped back, straightened up and turned to walk back to the front of the van. As he did, I saw something swinging towards him. I ducked down, heard a crack, looked under the chassis and he was lying flat on the ground. Blood was pouring from his head and pooling in the dust. Someone in shiny black shoes stood over him. One of the shoes poked Smith's side, then started walking around the van towards me. I stood up, turned around and Dickens said, "Elliot. We meet at last. At long fucking last." His eyes were wide and glazed, his mad fucking mouth twitch was going like a train, and he was holding a baseball bat. He tapped its fat end in the palm of his hand.

I looked over my shoulder. I looked at the white Transit. I looked back at Dickens. Dickens looked at the white Transit. He smiled at it and smiled at me. "I'm sorry," he said. "Did you think you were going to get out of this?"

"Well…"

"Think that someone was going to come running?"

I looked towards the Transit again and, as I did, two men came running from the café. They were carrying black canvas bags, and as they ran they pulled guns from the bags and pointed them at the Transit. Its back doors flew open and two more men jumped out. As soon as they saw the guns, they froze and put their hands up. Suddenly Pollock was there too, and we were all standing in the middle of the car park – men with guns, men with their hands in the air, Dickens laughing and me thinking that now was the time to piss myself.

Pollock was the first to say something. "This is fucking mad, Dickens. You any idea what's going to happen when this is over? When they catch you?"

Dickens took a step towards Pollock and said, "Catch me? Even if they could, do you think I'd care?" His eyes were blinking, his mouth was out of control, he looked like lobsters were fighting in his brain. And if anyone was in any doubt, if men with guns or men with hands in the air or bleeding men were in any doubt, here was complete madness in a man. "The thing is," he said, "it's not about the smoke any more. Not that it ever really was. No." He laughed at something. "No. It's not about that at all…"

"Then what is it about?" said Pollock. "Apart from the other things we've got you on. The smack you picked up in Bridgwater last month. The speed that's waiting for you at Avonmouth…"

"Well!" said Dickens. "Let me count the ways. Let me stick a dog up your arse and count the fucking ways. The way I'm going to teach you and everyone else who fucks with me." And he pulled out a gun and shot one of the men from the Transit in the foot, and the man fell over, screaming.

"One," he said, "and counting."

"Dickens!" Pollock took a step forwards. Dickens pointed his gun at Pollock's head.

"You want to be number two? Please say you want to be number two…"

"This is mad."

"Mad? Oh yes, it is, isn't it? Teaching people a lesson is quite crazy. Or should it be sending people a message? You know, I just don't know any more. I'm feeling a little confused." He turned towards me and grinned, and now I looked down the barrel of the gun. I surprised myself. I wasn't scared. Instead, as I looked at that hole I thought about the very smooth way the metal folded around the barrel and the little ridges around the trigger guard. I watched the man's finger and I saw a bead of sweat run down his cheek and disappear under his chin. Time stretched. A second was a minute. "You…" he said, his mouth moving slowly as he tongued the words, "are coming with us. You're going to be the lesson everyone else is going to learn." He dropped the gun to his side and wiped some spit from his lips. He pointed at a red van on the far side of the car park. "That's your ride." And he took my arm and started to walk me away. As he did, one of his heavies went over to Pollock's van, pulled out a knife and stuck it in the tyres. The other went to Spike's van and started the engine. He pulled away, and the last thing I saw before I was thrown into the back of Dickens' van was Pollock, the shot man and the other man standing in the middle of the car park, scared faces pushed against the windows of the café, the huge blue sky and the sound of the buzzards' cries as they circled higher and higher, almost out of sight now, almost gone.

23

When it comes to words, Mum picks them carefully. She never swears, never says any of the words for God and, most of all, most particularly, she never says the word "hare". If she sees one, she'll call it old turpin, the cat of the wood, the stag of the cabbages, the sitter on its form, the fellow in the dew and any one of a hundred other names, but she'll never call it hare. It's bad luck or it's good luck, or it's whatever luck you want to choose – and if you don't believe in luck, then you have that choice too. I don't know why Mum has this thing about the word, but I know that in the old days women like her could escape the ducking stool by turning into hares and heading for the woods, so maybe that's the reason behind that secret.

I've seen hares boxing in the spring, up on their hind legs, a jill fending off a jack who's coming on too strong at the wrong time. And I've seen hares in my dreams, curious animals who want to take me to their hollows and run rings around my head.

I dreamt of hares as I lay in the back of Dickens's van. I'd smacked my head on the floor, and as I swam in and out of consciousness, a talking hare came to me and asked if I wanted to come with him to a place where dew ponds formed and trees dripped silver. I told him I wanted to stay where I was and rest. He was an easygoing animal, and wasn't going to force me to do anything I didn't want to do, so we sat together on a hillock and watched a horse nuzzle a gate post. Dew ponds, silver in trees, nuzzling horses – I know there are people who interpret dreams, but I'm with Mum when she says that a dream is simply your mind going to a party. A dream doesn't foretell the future, it doesn't indicate hidden loves or fears. Like clouds that shape themselves into the look of animals prancing or people talking, dreams mean nothing but the pictures they show you.

I don't know how long I was out for, but when the dream hare gave up with me and I woke up, we were still moving. I was lying on the floor in the back of the van. My head was throbbing and my mouth was dry. I thought about moaning, but I kept quiet. My hands were knotted behind my back, and my ankles were tied. One of the heavies was driving, and Dickens was sitting in the passenger seat. I didn't move. I opened my eyes for long enough to see what I saw, then closed them and listened.

Dickens was talking crazy, words tumbling out like rocks and stones rattling in a tin box, rambling about how they thought they'd heard the last of him, but they hadn't, and the next time they heard from him they'd have to rewrite the book, and when they'd finished doing that they'd have to rewrite it again and remake the film, and when they'd done that they'd have to build a fucking statue in his fucking honour. The more he spoke, the crazier he sounded, and the more spit flew at the windscreen. The words he used reminded me of things I remembered from school and the Bible, words like redemption, tribulation, plague and wrath, so by the time I felt the van slowing down and we were pulling into a garage, my mind was curdled with pain and terror. As we jolted towards the pumps, I opened my eyes and lifted my head and moaned. Dickens turned and looked at me. "Fuck me…" he said, and he hit me on the top of my head with an Atlas.

"Ow…" I said.

The heavy stopped the van.

"Ahhh…" I said.

"What?" said Dickens.

"Naaa…"

"What the fuck's your problem? Apart from the bleedin' obvious…"

"Piss…" I said. "Need a piss…"

"Yeah," said the heavy. "We all need one of those…"

I tried to sit up. "Can I?"

"Piss in your pants, fuckwit," said Dickens.

"He isn't pissing in my van," said the heavy.

"He'll piss where I say."

"But not in my fucking van."

"You wouldn't have this fucking van if it wasn't for me."

"And you wouldn't have your smoke back if it wasn't for me. And you can do what you fucking like, but the last thing dead boy's going to do is piss in my fucking van."

Dickens looked at the heavy, and the heavy looked at Dickens, and something passed between them. I didn't see it pass, but I felt it, like electricity.

"OK. Fill up and then take him to the fucking bog."

The heavy stepped out of the van, walked to the pump and started to fill up. Dickens pulled a penknife out of his pocket, clicked the blade out, started to clean under his fingernails and

228

said, "You know what? I don't think I've ever looked forward to something so much." His head twitched. "Ever. I simply cannot wait."

"What you talking about?"

"Oh you know, Elliot. The pleasure of pain. The pleasure of pain..." He clicked the knife shut and dropped it into a pocket. "I get goose bumps just thinking about it. It's a real night-before-Christmas feeling."

"I don't know what you mean."

"Oh but you will, Elliot, you surely will."

The heavy finished filling up, banged on the van roof, opened the back doors and grabbed my ankles. He undid the rope, pulled me so I could sit up, and said, "You try anything, even look the wrong fucking way and I'll break your arms." He clicked his fingers. "Got it?"

"Got it," I said, and he reached around me, undid my hands and I stood up. As I did, I heard Spike's van. I recognized the sound, and it was sounding rough and revving too high. Then I saw it. It was heading towards the pumps, but it was going very fast. Too fast. As it got closer, I saw the driver. His head was lolling against the door, his face was stoned white, a weird grin covered his face, and his shirt was streaked with sick. I knew exactly how he felt. I'd felt exactly what he felt. He was wanting water, but he didn't know how much. He was hitting the green wall, and it was high and wide and very green. And as an innocent old person jumped out of the way and yelled something I didn't catch, he sat up for a moment and tried to brake.

"Shit!" said the heavy.

Too late. The van caught a kerb, slewed sideways, bounced back and clipped a waste-paper bin. Dickens appeared. He shouted "What the fuck!" The heavy left me and started running towards the van. The waste-paper bin flew into the air, bounced down, spilt its rubbish and rolled away. The van caught the kerb again, and I heard a bang as one of its tyres punctured. It smashed into a lamp post, spun around, and I saw the driver slam his head on the steering wheel, whiplash back and put his hands to his eyes. Dickens and the heavy were fifty yards away and running, and now I turned. I turned, put my head down and ran.

I headed for a clump of trees and bushes that grew from a little hill beyond the petrol station. I dived into the undergrowth, rolled over and watched as Spike's van slewed up a grassy bank and came to a steamy halt with its front wheels spinning over a gully. The driver's door opened, and the driver appeared. He was laughing hysterically, waving at Dickens, shouting stuff I couldn't hear. A couple of people came running from the shop. I heard a siren. Dickens stopped, turned, looked towards his van and swore. I kept my head down and inched backwards. The heavy had his arms around the other bloke, who was still laughing and yelling. Dickens stood still for a minute, then slowly started to walk towards his van. He tried to look as if he hadn't noticed the mayhem, or didn't care. When he reached the van, he climbed into the driver's seat and slowly pulled away from the pumps. The heavy shouted after him, but Dickens didn't stop. He stared ahead. His face was calm and clear, and as he pulled away and onto the road, I rolled down the little hill and watched him drive slowly back the way we'd come.

The sirens came closer, and I watched as a police car pulled onto the forecourt. The heavy tried to get away, but a random person stepped out of a car, ran towards him, rugby-tackled him and sent him tumbling into the side of a picnic bench. As he fell, I heard a nasty crack, like a branch snapping. He yelled with pain, grabbed his leg and the random person gave him a kick. He stopped yelling and went very still. The other heavy lay on the floor, now laughing hysterically, rolling backwards and forwards. His howling filled the air. A policeman stood over him, sat on him, handcuffed him and tried to pick him up. At this moment, he threw up again, a great heaving gush of vomit that sprayed in an arc. The policeman jumped sideways, shouted, "Fucking shit!" and tripped over. A moment later a fire engine appeared, flew up the slip road, took the bend at a rip and slewed onto the forecourt. It stopped with a squeal and smoking tyres, and as the firemen jumped out and ran to pull out hoses and crank their equipment, I stood up, walked away and started to stroll down the road.

I didn't turn to look back at the mayhem. I looked straight ahead. I forced the sound of the sirens from my head. I refused to let anything stop me. I took steady, deliberate steps. My wrists and my ankles were bruised and sore, and my head was throbbing and bloodied, but I ignored the pain. I ignored everything but my steps. And my steps were steady and measured, and free.

After a mile or so, I came to a gate and a stile and a footpath that led through a field, so I left the road and followed my nose. The sun was high, and the shadows were short. I had no idea where I was, but when I reached a place where I could scan the horizon, I saw the clustered houses of a village. Behind me, the road I'd travelled snaked to the east, and to the north the sea shone like a distant eye. Cars glinted, a few high clouds blew, birds sang. I was a stranger here, and I felt it. If someone saw me they would have taken me for a tramp or a ghost, a lost soul at the edge of their sight. I didn't want to be anyone's ghost, and I didn't want anyone to go running for the police. So I found a sheltered place beneath a hedge, and lay down to rest and catch my breath. I was shaking, and I could feel adrenaline racing through my muscles. I closed my eyes and let some peace come down and fold around me, and I dozed for a while. I say a while, but it might have been longer. When I woke up, I heard the sound of chewing and snuffling. Half a dozen heifers were standing over me. I sat up and they scattered. I stood up and they turned tail. I stayed where I was for a few minutes, scanned the horizon and the fields and hedges, and when I saw someone strolling along a lane below me, I ducked down and froze. But whoever it was, he wasn't interested in me – he was just a farmer, or someone out with his dog. So I started walking again, and within the hour I was on the edge of the village. It was called Wedmore, a quiet place with pretty stone houses, a sleepy air and a dog napping in the middle of the road. A woman with a basket of shopping said, "Good afternoon."

I asked her the time.

"Half-past three," she said.

"Thanks," I said.

I had a few quid in my pocket, so I went to a shop and bought a pie and a drink, and sat down by a bus stop. The sun was hot, and the pie was tasty, and when a bus came along I bought a ticket to Wells and sat at the back and watched the world pass in its safe way. And for a while the trouble of the smoke and Dickens faded away, and I could have been just a quiet man travelling through the country afternoon with a whistle on my lips and the sun at my back.

24

Wells is a small city with a big cathedral and lots of tourists to get lost with. I wandered the streets for half an hour, found a telephone box, called Taunton police station and asked to speak to Pollock. I heard clicks, four rings of a phone and a voice I didn't recognize cleared his throat and said, "DI Pollock's desk."

"Is he there?"

"No."

"Know when he'll be back?"

"No. Who's this?"

"Never mind," I said, and I hung up.

I stood in the box for a couple of minutes, stared at the street, and then I called home. Dad answered and said, "Elliot! We've been worried. Mother's had to go to bed. She's not well."

"What?" I'd never heard of her going to bed in the middle of the day. "What's the matter with her?"

"She had a bit of a turn."

"What do you mean?"

"The doctor thinks she's been overdoing things. And so do I."

"Oh God."

"So he told her to get some rest. She was talking about you being in trouble. Are you in trouble?"

"I was," I said, "but I'm getting out of it. Can I talk to her?"

"Best not, son. I think she's asleep. Where are you?"

"Wells."

234

"What the hell are you doing there?"

"I had to see some people. But I'm on my way home now…"

"OK. Well, call when you get back."

"I will," I said, and after I'd asked Dad to kiss Mum for me, I hung up and went to catch another bus. This took me away from Wells, through Glastonbury and Street towards Taunton. I dozed for a while, and when I woke up we were driving across the Somerset levels. Fields of willow, flocks of lapwings, drying fences and empty ditches. Little cottages beside the rivers, orchards and herds of cows, barking dogs and gasping sheep. Wide skies, flat land, reflecting fields. Even on still days the air carries the threat of wind, and on dry days rain etches its touch on the land.

When I was working for the tree surgeon, we did a job in the garden of a house at a village on the levels called Burrowbridge. The ruins of a church stand on top of a hill there, and a swollen, muddy drain of a river runs past the place where we worked. The river was the reason we were there: the roots of the three trees we worked on were growing into the bank, and the weight of the trees was pulling the bank into the river. It was our job to lop the branches, take the trunks down to stumps, drill the stumps and pour poison into the holes. "That'll sort the buggers," said my boss, and he knew what he was talking about.

I wasn't sure. I didn't like the idea of killing perfectly good trees, and I especially didn't like the idea of pouring poison into holes, but the council had said we had to, and if we didn't someone else would, so there we were with chainsaws in our hands and harnesses around our waists.

235

It was my job to climb while my boss waited on the ground and shouted instructions. When I reached the top of the first tree, I tied myself off and looked around. I think the looking around was the best thing about that job, and the view I enjoyed from that tree was wide and stretched for miles in every direction. Mirrored plates of water, lines of pollard willow, fields of withy, curls of smoke from chimneys, little groups of sheep grazing. I started sawing, dropping the branches carefully, watching the springy ones in case they snapped back, lowering myself to the next. The boss carried the cuttings to the back of the lorry, piled them high, shouted up that I should move to the right, and laughed when I said I needed a break.

"I'll give you a fucking break!" he yelled.

He was a good bloke really, and always let me take some logs home for nothing.

As I stepped off my first perch to the one below, I took one last look around and thought that I would be the last person in the world to ever enjoy that view, so I gave myself a couple of minutes. And as I stared down at the river and the whirls and eddies on its surface, I thought that maybe I'd found a secret. Maybe I should treat everything as a last time and everything as a privilege, everything as if I was the only person in the world. I didn't need to shout about it, but I did need to remember that I was a lucky man, someone who was given a present every day. And I remembered how my boss shouted at me to stop day-dreaming and get on with the job, which is what I did that day in Burrowbridge.

The bus passed through Burrowbridge, down a long straight road and past the site where King Alfred burned the cakes and was scolded by a peasant woman. We slowed down to avoid a pair of stray sheep. They stared up at me, and I stared back, and then they skipped away, leapt a fence and disappeared into a ditch. A couple of minutes later, we stopped to pick up a woman and her dog, and they sat opposite me. The dog had different-coloured eyes. One of them was light blue and the other was brown, and it had yellow teeth. I reached out to pat it, but the woman said, "I wouldn't do that."

"OK," I said, and I sat back and watched as the flat lands rose up to meet the higher ground, and the bus rolled on through villages and little groups of houses, signs for Bed & Breakfast and free-range eggs, broken tractors in fields, and lay-bys where parked cars with steamed-up windows rocked against the afternoon.

When we reached Taunton I got off at a stop by the river bridge, walked up towards the High Street, found a telephone box, called Pollock again, and this time he answered. "What the fuck happened?" I said.

"He was ready for us."

"He was going to kill me."

"I'm sorry…"

"Sorry? You're sorry? Did you hear what I said? He was going to kill me!"

"What can I say?" He sounded like a man who'd been stood against a wall and given a bollocking.

"Have you been given a bollocking?"

"Yes."

"Good," I said, and I said it again. "Good."

"Elliot…"

"He chucked me in the back of a van like a bag of spuds. They had knives. The man's a fucking psycho!"

"Tell me about it."

"I just did. And I want to know…"

"What?"

"Why all this fucking madness over a few bags of smoke? I'm tired of it. Cos that's all it is. A few bags of smoke. Why can't he let it go?"

"I told you. He's into all sorts, and he needs to make an example of you and your mate. You're a warning to other people, Elliot."

"That makes a lot of sense."

"So where are you now?"

"Here."

"Where's here?"

"Taunton."

"You gave Dickens the slip?"

"Yes. Somewhere on the road to Bristol…" and I started to tell him what had happened.

"I know," he said. "We got the van and his heavies, but no sign of him."

"Of course not. I saw him leave."

"We found the van in Bridgwater."

"So what? You want a fucking medal?"

"Look, Elliot."

"Look what?"

"We'll get him."

"You'd better. He's a scary bastard, and he knows where I live."

"We've got people at his house."

"But he's not going to go back there, is he?"

"I doubt it."

"So you got any other leads?"

"One or two."

"He's going to be after me."

"I know. You want someone to come and meet you? Give you a bit of protection?"

I laughed. "Protection? After what happened this morning? I don't think so. From now on, I'm going to look after myself."

"That's not a good idea, Elliot."

"And you've got a better one?" I said, and before he could say anything else I hung up, left the telephone box and spat on the pavement.

I was angry now, angry and fierce, like a fish with a hook in its eye. A bush on fire. The bird with a vole in its beak. I walked fast, head down, mad as hell. I crossed roads without looking, barged past old women with shopping trolleys, kicked at stones I saw in the gutter. Panic, fear, trouble – they'd gone. Rage was my brother now, and I carried him with me to the hospital. When I passed a pub, I stopped for a moment and stared at the door, smelt the stale beer and fags, and thought about having a drink. I don't like whisky, but I thought that whisky would be a good thing to have, something to play with my fury and push it into the open. Fire in a glass. Burn me. I pushed the door open, stepped inside, stopped, stared at the three staring faces that turned to look at me and went to the bar.

The barman was fat, bald and sweaty. He looked at me, licked his lips and said, "Yes?"

I looked at the pumps. "Half of bitter," I said, "and a Bells."

"Double?"

"Why not."

He pulled the beer, slammed it on a mat, turned to the optics, drew the whisky, slammed it next to the beer, and I fingered the cash into his hand. While he fetched my change, I took a slug of the beer, then went to sit at a table in the corner.

It was a grim pub. Sticky carpets, sticky tables, full ashtrays, a broken juke box and an old dog lying by the bar. I finished the beer and took a sip of the whisky, and as the drink hit the back of my throat, I gagged. Pollock's words came back to me, the ones about looking after myself not being a good idea. And as I took another sip and my throat got used to the burn, I sat back and thought that he was as wrong as he could be. All I could be was myself, the man who took his mother's gift and made it his own, the man who found a hung man creaking from a tree, the man who lived in a caravan and dreamt of hares, who watched a man take a pitchfork in his thigh and walk away. Someone with a friend and a girlfriend, a sister, a mother and a father, and a job.

I was wrong about the whisky. It didn't push my fury into the open. It took it to one side, stroked its cheek, whispered in its ear and told it to be quiet. It sang a little tune to it, the sort of thing you'd hear on the classical radio, and then it went quiet for a moment. And when I drained the last of it, held it in my mouth and let it swill, I think I tasted the sea, mist, salt and tears. And as I stood up and said goodbye to the barman and left the pub, I felt something like relief, or release.

The hospital was ten minutes down the road, but I did it in twenty. Slow, steady, letting the whisky drift, the anger fade, the thoughts dim. And when I got to the hospital, a nurse met me outside the ward. Something had happened to Sam. She didn't understand how, but it had happened anyway. She sat me down in a corridor and said, "She came out of her coma this morning."

"She's awake?"

"Yes."

"And how is she?"

"It's difficult to say. We'll know more in a few more hours."

"Can I see her?"

"Of course. She's been asking for you."

So I followed the nurse and sat by Sam's bed and held her hand. She was asleep and cradling her teddy bear, but after half an hour she stirred and moved her head and opened her eyes. When she saw me, she stared at me as if she didn't know who I was or where I'd come from, but then recognition spread across her face and she said, "Elliot?"

"Hi," I said.

"I'm in hospital."

"I know you are."

"I've been asleep."

"I know. For a couple of days. I came to see you. And your mum and dad were here too. The nurse made me talk to you…"

"What did you say?"

"A load of bollocks."

She smiled and said, "I had a long dream."

"What was it about?"

"Dogs."

"Dogs?"

"Yes."

"Was it a nice dream?"

"Yes," she said. "It made me feel better."

"What happened with the dogs?"

"They were my friends. They fed me biscuits and showed me how to dance a dog dance."

I squeezed her hand. "You're going to get better and better all the time."

"I know," she said, and we talked until she fell asleep again – the bakery in Ashbrittle, whether dogs were better than cats, our favourite films, our favourite colours, our favourite ways of spending a Sunday afternoon. When I left, I took a bus to Wellington, called Dad and asked him to pick me up from outside the town hall. I drank a quick pint in a pub and, as I sat and the evening came down, the day caught up with me and left me staring blankly at a wall. There was nothing else I could do, nothing but watch and wait and lose myself in the beer and the chatter of the people who had nothing to talk about but easy hours.

25

Mum was still in bed. She looked like she'd lost half a stone. Her cheeks were sunk, her eyes were dull and her hair was lank and dirty. When she saw me she let out a deep, long sigh, and managed a little smile. "Pet…" she said, and she patted the covers. "I thought you were dying."

I sat on the bed, took her hand and said, "I was never going to die. Not even once."

She reached up and touched my head. I had a lump there and crusted blood in my hair. "What happened?"

"I got hit."

"By Spike?"

"No. Someone threw me into the back of a van."

"Why?"

"Because he didn't like me very much."

"And why didn't someone you don't even know like you very much? I don't understand. It doesn't make any sense. You're a good boy…"

"It's a long story."

"Of course it is."

"Can I tell you another day?"

She stared at me. It was a long, hard stare. "You'd better," she said. "I can't go on like this. Half knowing, half not knowing anything at all. It's making me ill. You all think I'm strong, but I'm not. I can see things, I can understand things, but that's as far as it goes. The rest of the time I'm like you…"

"I will," I said, and I went downstairs to make her a cup of tea.

I spent the night in my old room, and in the morning I got up early and walked down to the farm. The relief was milking. I asked her if she was having any trouble. "Quietest herd I work with," she said, and she tapped one of the cows on its flank and pulled the handle to release it into the yard. "We keep them happy," I said, and I left her to her work. I went round to the front, knocked on the farmhouse door, and when Mr Evans came to the door I said, "I'm back."

"Are you now?" he said.

"You want me to do some work?"

"You want to do some work?"

"Yes."

"You've sorted out your problems? Told that Spike to get lost?"

"Sort of."

He stared at me. I think he was looking for something in my eyes, some clue or meaning. "All right then. Take a hook down to the sidling fields and get rid of the thistles."

So I did. It was hot, long work, but it was good to be back doing the things I like to do. A simple job in the sunshine, the herd watching me from a hedge, the sound of a barking dog floating from a neighbour's farm. The chatter of birds, the soaring buzzards, the smell of the dry land.

The thistles were covered in seed heads. As I cut them down, the seeds broke into the air, drifted like snow and eddied in their way. I remember Mum telling me that there were signs in the way seeds floated – something to do with a poor harvest, something to do with a drought in the parish – but I couldn't remember exactly what, and it didn't bother me. I let the plants lie where I'd hooked them, and by the time I'd got to the bottom of the field, I had my shirt off and was covered in sweat. I had a bottle of water with me. I unscrewed it and took a long, deep gulp. The water tasted of release and promise, honesty and innocence. There was nothing wrong with the water at all. I closed my eyes and tipped some over my head and rubbed it into my hair. The dust failed. I beat the dust. I stretched and yawned. I was close to the place where I'd found the hung man, so when I'd finished drinking and washing, I propped the bottle in a hedge, jumped over the fence and walked down to the place.

Apart from a small knot of blue-and-white tape tied around a branch, and the places where the undergrowth had been flattened by heavy boots, there was no sign that anything unusual had happened here. No sign of violence or blood or fear. But as I stood beneath the branch where the man had died, I felt a cold finger touch my face, a finger that stroked a line towards the icy chambers of a dead heart. It drew a pattern on my skin, a circle and a star, and it drained the strength from my muscles. The yew in the churchyard at Ashbrittle had touched me in this sort of way, but never with such a dark shadow. The yew's memories were diluted by the years and people. The yew's memories were almost benign now, and weak, but this memory was fresh and strong. I stepped back, the finger dropped away, and a voice whispered something in my ear. I couldn't say I understood what

245

words it said, but I understood their sense. And their sense was this: keep away from this place. It will infect you. It will take your soul and give it to the birds, and the birds will carry it to their nests and feed on it. I shuddered and took another step back. The voice faded. I turned and, as I did, a rook blew out of the wood and flew up and over the sidling fields.

In the old days, the way a single rook flew would tell you something. If it headed left, something in your past was going to come back to haunt you. Something you did, something someone else did, something a dog did in its yard – it didn't matter. If the rook headed right, the future was about to flash at you and bite hard. If it flew straight up, death was around the corner. If it flew straight and landed in a tree, life was going to carry on as it always had done, and maybe get better one day. But whatever it did, if you watched a single rook for more than a minute, trouble would be your bride, and your bride would leave her posy on the altar.

I picked up my bottle, took another swig, felt the water run down my throat and went back to the thistles. By the time I'd finished, I'd cleared the field and was ready for lunch. I went back to the caravan, made myself a sandwich, ate it at the table and watched the sky. A single cloud was drifting from the west, house martins were swooping, and the trail made by a high aeroplane split and floated. For a moment, the day was at peace and all the bones of the earth were quiet. I heard a dog barking. It was about a mile away. It barked for about five minutes, and when it stopped and the quiet came down again, I closed my eyes and dozed for half an hour.

26

The relief came to do the evening milking, so I went home to see Mum. She was up and about, said she felt better, didn't understand what had come over her and was making chicken soup. As she stirred the broth, she told me that when she was younger she used to think she was being followed by a white cat with black paws and a black tip to its tail. "Not all the time, mind, but when I was worried about something it used to be there, always just round the corner. I think it was looking after me." She spooned some soup to her mouth, took a taste, nodded, added a pinch of salt and said, "Have you ever seen anything like that?"

"Never," I said. "Do you still see it?"

"No. It disappeared when I was about your age."

"So what did it mean?"

"I don't think it meant anything. It was just there. You know, Pet, most of the time I don't think things are meant to mean anything. We're born, we do what we have to do, we die. That's all. Every now and again you have a bit of sadness, then you get a bit of joy, but most of the time you just have to make the best of what you've been given. The gifts you've been given. You understand what I mean?"

"I'm beginning to."

"Good," she said. She tasted the soup again and nodded. "Are you staying tonight?"

"No. I'm going back to the farm. I think I'll be milking in the morning."

"You are a good boy," she said, "just easily led," and when she smiled I could see her sickness running away from her face, chased to the top of her head and flowing away like smoke blown through a hole in a door.

I left her grinding pepper into the soup, rode back to the farm and, as the night fell, Spike arrived on a moped he'd borrowed from the bloke he was living with. It was a knackered insect of a thing, with a broken light and holes in its saddle. One of the mudguards was hanging off its bracket, and it sounded like a fart in a firework factory. He parked it behind the caravan and knocked on the door. He looked thin and pale. Maybe I should have been angry, and for a moment I thought about telling him to get lost, but he had this pleading look in his eyes, like a sick dog sheltering under a hedge. "Can I come in?" he said.

"OK."

He sat at the table, and I fetched some beers. I opened mine and took a swig, but he just stared at the bottle, rubbed the label and sniffed. I'd never seen him like this, so lost and worried and shelled. I told him about the mess at the transport café, the guns and knives, and when he asked if he'd ever see his van again I said, "I shouldn't think so. Last time I saw it, it was smashed into a lamp post."

"And the smoke?"

"You have to ask?"

"Yes."

"Gone, Spike. It'll be in some police lock-up."

"So that's it then," he said.

"What did you expect?"

He shook his head, looked at the floor, scratched the top of his head and mumbled, "I think I'm going to go away."

"Where?"

"Anywhere. Maybe Wales. I could get work up there."

"You probably could," I said, "but you'd be running away. And you've never run away from anything."

"I don't care. I'm just so tired of this."

"You're tired of it?"

"Yes." He opened his beer, closed his eyes and took a swig. "How you do think I feel?"

"I don't know."

So I told him, and showed him the bump on my head. "They were going to kill me," I said.

"Shit."

"It was. And all for some smoke."

"I'm definitely going to Wales…" he said, and he took another swig on his beer, stared out of the window and sucked his teeth. "Definitely. I've been a fucking idiot. I can't stay here." I was about to agree with him when Mr Evans knocked on the door. I opened up, and he said, "You got a minute?"

"What's the problem?"

"Mr Roberts just called." Mr Roberts ran the neighbouring farm. "Two cows got through the top fence. He's got them in his yard."

"You want me to fetch them back?"

"Please."

"OK," I said, and as I said the word, I felt something odd move in my blood. It was something I suppose I'd been expecting for twenty-one years, something that crept in like a spider might creep into a bed, slowly and carefully, a knowing look in its dozen eyes, legs feeling the way and twitching at the air. A witched animal, a gentle thing, a frightening beast, a nip in its mouth and a plan in its brains. And as it moved and my blood swilled, I felt light and ready. I stood up, gave Spike another bottle, told him to sit tight and walked into the twilight with a stick and a torch.

Mr Roberts's farm was down the lane, over the river bridge at the bottom of the valley and up the other side. As I walked, I swished at the hedges with my stick, and the first stars peeped out. An owl hooted. Something like a fox or a badger scurried away. The owl hooted again. A car revved up the road from Stawley mill.

I reached a gateway where I could stand and look up at Mr Evans's farm. Lights were on, and I saw the outline of Spike's head in the window of my caravan. He reached up and pulled the curtain. Headlights swung against the night. I walked on.

Another owl called to the first. Mum had said something to me about owls and their calls, but I couldn't remember exactly what it was. Probably something to do with ancient knowledge and doom, but maybe not. Whatever. I walked on. I heard the car again, closer now, still revving. Then it stopped, and I didn't hear it any more.

I stopped at the river bridge for a moment, and watched the water as it trickled over the rocks. A gang of rooks shouted from the trees. The air smelt of burning leaves.

I walked up the track towards Mr Roberts's farm, and when I reached the gate, his dog started to bark. It was a big collie with ragged ears, tied on a long leash to a ring in the wall. I went up to the back door, knocked and waited. He answered the door in a string vest, braces hanging down from his trousers, a pipe in his mouth. He was a small man and had very clean teeth. "Elliot. I've been expecting you. They're in the yard."

He pulled on his boots, and I followed him to the yard. The farm was neat and tidy. Everything was in its place. Hand tools were propped in a neat row, and a small Massey Ferguson was parked beyond the parlour. The cows were standing in a corner of the yard. He'd given them some hay in a net that hung from the wall. "They're quiet," he said.

"Always have been," I said.

He held the gate open, and I tapped them with my stick, followed them out and shook the man's hand. "Thanks again," I said, and he said, "You'll come over and mend the fence in the morning?"

"Of course."

"I put some galvanized over the hole, but it won't hold."

"Don't worry, Mr Roberts. I'll do it." And then I ran to catch up with the cows and drive them down the lane and back to the herd.

They were slow beasts, and as we walked I put a hand to their backs and patted them along. The rooks were still shouting and

the owl called again, and as we crossed the bridge the smell
of burning leaves was still strong. I said, "Come on," as we
started to climb the hill, and a second later I heard a crack. I
say it was a crack, and that is what it was, even though I knew
it was a shot. Not loud, but it was clear. For a moment I didn't
think the sound meant anything. People shoot day or night for
all sorts of reasons. But then I heard another shot, a different
calibre this time, a rifle. I tapped the two cows with my stick,
yelled, "Ho!" at them, and as they started trotting I ran.

The herd were lying in the sidling fields. I came to a gate
where I could let the cows in, pushed it open and shooed them
along. I followed, swung the gate back on its latch and ran.
When I reached a place where I could see the farm, I saw a
pair of headlights turning and swinging down the track, and
heard another shot. I didn't stop running, and when I reached
the fence around the front yard I jumped it, slipped, pulled
myself up and ran on. Mr Evans was standing at the top of
the track with his rifle in his hands. He turned when he saw
me, shouldered the gun and yelled, "Elliot!" His fury was back,
this time bigger and wilder than ever.

"What's going on!"

"You're asking me?"

"Yes."

'Well, I think I winged him!"

"Who?"

"The bastard who put a shot through the caravan. Him!" He
pointed towards the headlights. They disappeared, appeared
once more and then they were gone.

"Who was he?"

"I don't know. I didn't see his face."

"Where's Spike?"

"Spike?"

"Yes."

"I don't know," he said, and I ran to the caravan.

One of the windows was shattered. I opened the door and stepped inside. There was glass on the floor, and the air was thick with drifts of blue smoke. I said, "Spike?" and walked towards the place where he'd been sitting. An empty bottle of beer was sitting on the table and a spliff was steaming in the ashtray. He was lying on the floor, his right hand tucked under his head. I bent down, reached out and shook his shoulder. He groaned, opened his eyes, looked up at me, licked his lips and said, "What the fuck happened?"

"Someone tried to shoot you."

He blinked. I blinked back at him and waved my hands at the smoke. The smoke waved back at me like a ghost.

"With a gun?" he said.

"No, Spike. With a fucking bow and arrow."

"What?"

"With a gun! Through the window!" I pointed at the glass. The floor crunched.

"Fuck."

"He thought you were me."

He sat up. "He thought I was you? Why did he think that? And who the fuck was he?"

"You have to ask?"

He thought about that for a moment, let the thought sink, then shook his head.

"Are you hit?"

He looked down at his stomach, reached up and felt his chest, and touched his face. He had a fresh graze on his forehead, but it was nothing. "No," he said. "I think I'm OK."

I sat down next to him. "You sure?"

"Yes," he said as Mr Evans appeared in the door. He stepped up and into the caravan, looked down at Spike and shook his head. "You two!" he yelled. "Are you ever going to learn?"

I didn't know what to say.

There was a mad, red boiling behind his eyes, "Well?" he screamed. Spit flew from his mouth. "Are you?"

I shook my head.

"Is that a no?"

"I don't know."

He pointed at Spike and said, "You…" He took a deep, wheezy breath. For a moment I thought he was going to have a heart attack. Then I didn't. And he didn't. He was too strong. "You've got ten minutes to get off my land." And then he turned to me. "And you… you've got an hour."

27

Spike didn't need ten minutes. He was out of my caravan before Mr Evans had crossed the front yard. "That's it," he said. "I'm out of here." He grabbed his moped, pushed it off its stand, freewheeled across the yard, jump-started it, and rode down the lane without looking back. "Where are you going?" I yelled, but my words were grabbed by nothing and lost in the dark. I didn't even see them leave – they were just gone. I was left standing by the hole in the caravan window, the vague smell of smoke still in the air, and the sound of a distant dog barking at the night. "Spike!"

Nothing.

"Come back!"

Like he would. He didn't stop.

Mr Evans stood on his doorstep, cradled his gun, clicked his tongue against the roof of his mouth and said, "Good riddance to bad rubbish."

"He was my friend," I said. "He might be an idiot, but he's not bad. Not really."

"And that's what you think, is it?"

"Yes."

"And after all this, all this nonsense, you think your opinion is worth anything?"

"I do."

He shook his head. "If I hadn't put a bullet through the back of that bastard's car, I'd be calling the police. And I'd make sure they threw the bloody book at you."

"So why don't you?"

"Why don't I what?"

"Call the fucking police?"

He looked at me as if I'd hit him. "You…" he hissed. "And I thought you were a good lad. I thought I could trust you. I thought I could rely on you. I thought…"

"But…"

"Don't 'but' me, Elliot. Never do that…" He looked at his watch. He tapped his watch. "I make it fifty-five minutes," he said, and then he turned around, disappeared into the farmhouse and slammed the door behind him.

I stared at the door. It needed a coat of paint. One day, I could have painted that door. I would have taken a pot of gloss and a brush and spent an afternoon giving it a good lick. But now it was too late. The time had slipped away. The time was an eel on a mirror, and all I had left was an empty trap.

It didn't take long to collect up my stuff and pack it into a bag, and when I'd finished, I took one final look around the caravan. The bed Sam and I had shared was crumpled and dead, the little table where I'd eaten lunch was broken. The ✳ spliff Spike had been smoking was burnt to its roach. I picked it up, licked my fingers, squeezed its tip and flicked it out of the shattered window. Then I picked up my bag, carried it to my bike and tied it to the pillion. The light from Mr Evans's television was flickering across the yard, and for a moment I

✳ rubbish. It would have gone out !!! ...

256

saw his shadow move against the wall of his front room. His face appeared at the window, his hands cupped around his eyes. I know he saw me, and maybe he wanted to say one last thing to me, but he didn't look in my direction. He turned away, and I was left to climb onto my bike without a goodbye or a thank you or even a nod. What I deserved, I suppose, but as I rode away I thought that was it. I couldn't hold down a job for longer than a few months. Mr Evans's farm had joined the list of failures. I was a lost fuck in a fuckery of stupidity. And that thought stayed in my head like the rest of the things that swilled in there. The regrets and loss and leaving, and the thought that Sam was still lying in her bed, her head lost like a boat that had dropped a snapped mooring. The rope trailing in the water, the current taking it slowly at first, then getting quicker, the little waves cresting around the hull, the wind pushing it one way and then another. And as I rode through Stawley and took the turning to the mill and the hill to Ashbrittle, I cursed that wind and shouted her name. I shouted and I cried and I shouted again, and took the bridge by the mill too fast. I almost came off, but I caught the skid in time, slowed, stopped, dropped the bike on the verge, leant against the bridge and stared at the water.

The river was low and black, a drain in the night, and as I stared at it my thoughts turned from Sam to Dickens. If Mr Evans had winged him, if the man was out there with a hole in his shoulder and blood in his lap, where was he? And how was he?

What does a wounded animal do? Where does he hide? What are his instincts? What are the questions he asks himself, and how do the answers come? Do they come by air or are they picked from the trees? Are the trees tall or are they small? Is the air sulphured or is it clear? Is the hole the wounded animal finds a deep hole or a simple hollow? Do his eyes see straight? Does his nose smell danger, or does it fool itself into thinking danger is a false thing? Does he curl in a ball or wait to pounce? So many questions, but I didn't know the answers. I didn't want to know the answers. They were too dim, too faint and grey.

I looked up at the tops of the trees that grew along the river bank and sniffed the air. I whispered my mother's name and called for my Gran's spirit. I didn't expect to hear anything, didn't expect an answer, but as I stood there, I heard a noise.

When I say it was a noise, I'd say it was less than that. I'd say it was a faint rustle, the sound of leaves rubbing against a breeze, the moon diving into its own reflection and swimming towards an edge of the light. And as I turned towards that diving, it stopped, waited and took a breath.

I focused on a place where the river had carved a hollow into the bank, and as I did, I felt a cold draught in the air. It came like the loving dust of someone blowing on your cheek, and then it was fading and gone. And a moment later I saw something slink across the hollow, disappear behind a fallen branch and appear again. At first I thought it was shadow, then I thought it was solid, then a shadow again. I took a step. I looked at my feet. I took another step. And as I did, I smelt something so rank and bad that I almost gagged. Rotten, putrid, dead – you choose the word, but it wouldn't have been strong enough. It caught the back of my throat like coal smoke on a heavy day. I coughed. The shape froze. I froze. The night took a deep and heaving breath and held the smell tight to its chest.

I don't know how long I watched the shadow until it shifted again, but when it did, it moved fast, away from the hollow and out of sight. It rustled through the wood, came closer, and although it was difficult to imagine how, the smell came stronger. Now it was almost solid, as if I could reach for my penknife, take it out, click it open, cut a slice from the air and put it in my pocket. And a moment later, a few yards ahead of me, I heard a dull thump and saw something moving in the verge, something low and squat and dark. I suppose I'd been expecting to see Dickens, a hole in his shoulder and his face twisted in sweat and pain, but as the shape moved down the lane, I realized I was looking at a dog. But not a dog. This was the bad dog. And the people who talked about it were right. It was the dog with no head. No bark. No smell. No sight. And as it stumbled towards me, I found myself frozen. I tried to move, but I was rooted. My legs wouldn't budge, and my arms were cold and weighted. I forced myself to whisper "Go…" but I could not. I tried to turn my head to look at my bike, but I was stuck. And as the dog loped towards me, I shut my eyes and refused the sight, told myself it wasn't possible, wasn't happening, and I was alone in the night. But when I opened them again the dog was still coming to me, and I saw that one of its back legs was lame. It walked with a dragging limp, veered towards the ditch that ran along the side of the lane, and lowered its neck as if the head that wasn't there was smelling for something. And as it did this, I was overcome with a feeling of deep, inconsolable sadness. This feeling came from nowhere, and for a moment I felt blinded and lost. I reached out to hold on to something. I staggered. I found a branch. I wrapped my hand around it. It was hot. The branch was hot. The sadness deepened and swelled, staggered through my veins and leant against the chambers of my heart. I closed my eyes against it, screwed them tight, listened to my breathing and waited.

And as I waited, a tunnel appeared before me, a dark mouth in the lane. I was drawn into it, and it folded around me like a blanket folds around a weeping child. I began to move along its length, and the spidery feeling I'd felt earlier came back. It stroked me and rubbed my face, and its haired legs wrapped themselves around my face. And as this happened, I saw scenes from my life and scenes from the lives of people I knew. I wasn't afraid or surprised, and I wasn't astonished. I just felt expected and ready. For here I was at school with a cheese sandwich in my hand, and here I was standing by a stream with a fishing rod. There was Dad, his head under the bonnet of a knackered van, there was Mum staring at a flight of crows. Grace, her arms covered in flour, Spike coming up behind me and pushing me and my fishing rod into the river. Spike, laughing and falling off a log and banging his head so it bled. The man from the pig farm showing me his gun, the view from the top of a tree on the Somerset levels. And beyond these scenes, feelings. Feelings of longing and trouble, feelings that I was arriving somewhere, at a place where I was expected. A place I recognized from a dream or something my mother had told me. It was sweet and calm, and then it was bitter. It was quiet and then it was too loud, and it tasted of salt. It took my senses and swirled them, and the scenes of the people swirled, and I heard the sound of bells ringing from far away. And I saw a light, came to the end of the tunnel, and I was standing at the place where I'd begun.

I stood for a moment, and when the strength came back to my legs, I opened my eyes, let go of the branch, took a step back and another to the side. The dog was still in the lane, and I watched as it moved past me. I heard its paws padding, saw its tail hanging down, watched its broken leg drag along. The feeling of sadness was fading quickly, but the smell was burning now, fierce and hot.

Something – the dregs of the sadness, the need for touch? – made me want to reach out and stroke its matted coat. But as this thought came, so the dog reached the end of the ditch and turned the corner and left my sight, and I was left standing where I was, alone and silent in the long dark of the night.

I waited for a while, but the dog didn't return. I didn't want it to come back, but I did want it to come back, and this confusion made my head ache. And then all I could do was turn, walk back to my bike and ride home.

Mum was sitting in the kitchen. She couldn't have known I was coming, but she knew what had happened. I dumped my bag on the floor, sat at the kitchen table and leant my head in my hands. Should I tell her about the dog and the tunnel? Did she know already? Had she ever seen the dog? And what about the tunnel? Was this the thing you had to experience before you passed through the gate to the place where signs and portents

261

are more than the simple things they appear to be? I looked up at her. She was staring at me. I opened my mouth. She put a finger to her lips and shook her head. I nodded and said, "I got the boot."

"Of course you did," she said. "I've been expecting it."

"I know you have," I said.

I didn't tell her that Dickens had tried to shoot Spike or that he thought Spike was me, but I did say, "It was messy."

She stood up, put the kettle on and said, "I think we need a cup of tea."

"I think I need something stronger." And as I took a beer from the fridge, Dad appeared from the garden. He was carrying a cabbage. He put it on the draining board, noticed my bag on the floor and said, "Does that mean what I think it means?"

I nodded.

"Elliot... Elliot..." he said.

"Want one?" I held up a bottle of beer.

"I think I do."

So we sat around the kitchen table, and I tried to tell them that I hadn't wanted this to happen, that Mr Evans thought I was a good worker, but Spike was my friend and what could I do?

"You should have dumped him years ago. He was always a bad one."

"But he's my friend."

"I know. But sometimes you have to put yourself first..."

"And sometimes you have to stand by your friends."

They couldn't deny that, and I sat back, took a long pull on my beer and opened my mouth to tell them about the bad dog, but stopped before anything came out. They'd listened to enough for one night, and I didn't want them to think I was losing it. So I finished my beer, picked up my bag and went upstairs. As I lay down on my bed and stared at the ceiling and listened to Mum and Dad tidy up the kitchen, I closed my eyes and let the day fade into the dark. The house clicked, the cat padded across the landing outside my room, the bed squeaked. And as the world crept to its own sleep, I heard my blood rush and fade, and the quiet came down like leaves.

28

I remember what happened next. My memory is clear. I could look into it and see through the swirls and eddies to the bottom. I could see fish swimming in my mind and smoke flowing in the current of my thoughts. Yes, this is exactly how it felt, the smoke snagging a thought and curling its way around, choking it and leaving me speechless.

The day after I left the farm and Spike left for wherever he was going, I phoned Pollock. I told him what had happened, and he told me I should have called him earlier. I told him that calling him earlier wouldn't have made any difference, and everything he'd done so far had been shit, so what good would calling him earlier have done? I think he understood what I was saying, but it was difficult to tell. He sounded beaten, and when I asked him if he knew where Dickens was, he said, "We found his car in Bristol. Hole in the back window and blood on the front seat, but he was gone."

"Well done, Sherlock," I said. "Another result."

"I wouldn't worry," he said.

"And why the fuck shouldn't I worry? I'm shitting myself."

"He's gone."

"Yes," I said. "You already told me that. But where?"

"Spain."

"Spain? What are you talking about?"

264

"He had friends over there, and we know he had a couple of false passports." He made a wheezing sound, as if he'd just been punctured.

"You're sure he's in Spain?"

"99% sure," he said.

"So there's a 1% chance that he's going to turn up tonight and stab me in the neck with a fucking pitchfork."

"I think you can rest easy, Elliot. We're watching the ports, the airports, anywhere he might try to use to get out of the country."

"But you said you're 99% sure he's already left the country."

"Sure. But we think…"

"I think," I said, "it's what he thinks that counts. And as far as I can tell, what you think hasn't been your strong point. But then what has been?"

"Look," he said, and he took a deep, weary breath. I heard it leave his body and drift away. It was a breath that gave up on him. "You've got my number. If you see him, even if you think you've seen him, call me."

"Don't worry," I said. "I will." And I stared at the phone for a moment, wondered if I should say anything else, turned back on myself, put the receiver down and went to make a pot of tea.

I made lots of pots of tea. I got very good at making pots of tea. I'd warm the pot, pour freshly boiled water on the leaves, and leave it to brew for four and a half minutes. Fresh milk, clean cups, sugar if you wanted it. Easy when you know how. And when I wasn't making pots of tea or staring at the ceiling or talking to the cat, I rode into Taunton and sat with Sam in the hospital, and I watched as she took pain and turned it into something good. Sometimes Ros was there, sometimes Dave, Don and Danny were there too, and we'd sit on plastic chairs and talk about the vegetable garden, if it was ever going to rain again, the heath fires that were burning Exmoor black, and the cost of brown rice. But mostly it was me, a bowl of fruit and my dirty face, and my nonsense talk about making pots of tea or nothing in particular.

Two weeks after she'd woken from her coma, she was walking again. Her first steps were from her bed to the door and back again, but by the end of the following week she was walking to the bathroom, and the doctors said she could move from intensive care. The day she was moved I met her parents for the first time. I was nervous and expected them to shout at me, but before I could say something her mother took me to one side and said, "Samantha told us what happened. We want you to know that we don't blame you for anything. In fact, we're very pleased to meet you. She says you've been very attentive."

I didn't know what to say apart from "Thank you".

Her father looked at me over the top of his glasses. He reminded me of a teacher I used to have at school, and I'm not sure if he agreed with the things his wife had said, but he didn't say anything to me. He nodded and said he had to go and check the parking ticket on his car and, as he left, her mother said, "Don't mind him, Elliot. He's always a bit off with new people. He'll come round to you one day."

Sam was given her own room with a view of a garden and hills and trees, and a couple of days after she'd moved in she asked for a pad of paper and some crayons, and started doing pictures of landscapes. Fields full of sheep. Trees without leaves. Waves rolling onto a beach. Farmhouses on hills. She did one of a herd of cows grazing in a water meadow and gave it to me. "I'll put it on the wall," I said, and when I got home that's what I did.

I taped it to the wall over my bed. I looked at it and saw myself standing in my boots in the middle of the meadow, and I saw birds crying and dipping over my head. I heard music, piano music, slow and careful music, played by someone who knew exactly what they were doing. Dipping through the sad notes, leaning towards the sound. Waiting like a groom at a plain altar.

And when I wasn't sitting with Sam or staring at her picture, Dad made me go with him to work. Once I tried to tell him that I was too tired, but he told me that I had no choice, that I wasn't to sit and brood, so what could I do? I behaved like a good son, and did as I was told. One day I went to one of his jobs in Bathealton, a big old house with a derelict tennis court, a ruined greenhouse and an overgrown walled vegetable garden. The place was owned by a pair of sisters who'd inherited it from their father. They were old-style women who wore jodhpurs, tweed coats and scarves on their heads. One of them had been something important in the War, and the other was a sculptor. They fought a constant battle to keep their world intact, and after they'd said hello to me and shown Dad what they wanted him to do that day – "We'd like you to dig some potatoes and tidy up the ground. And after that, maybe trim the hedges along the drive…" – I sat on a box in a shady corner and watched him work.

I don't think I'd ever watched him work before, not for hours at a time anyway. He was methodical and slow, and as he dug the spuds, he handled them like eggs, carefully rubbing the earth off their skins and placing them in a basket. He looked like he was part of the garden, a man in his world. A couple of times he stood up to stretch and feel his back, then went back to the job. He didn't ask me if I wanted to help him, and I think if I'd offered he would have told me to stay where I was. Kind and weathered, I know he was worried about me, but I think he used his work to take that worry and turn it into something good. His power and magic wasn't like Mum's, but it was still real, still offered and given. And when he stopped and poured two cups of tea from his thermos, he said, "When I was your age, things were different. I never had your sort of trouble."

"I don't know anyone who's had my sort of trouble."

"Nor do I."

The tea was weak and tasted of tin, and as I drank he took a deep breath, and I waited for him to say something else, but then he shook his head and the words didn't come out.

"Dad?"

"Yes son?"

"I'm sorry."

"We know," he said. "And you don't have to say anything else. Just promise me one thing."

"What's that?"

"That the next time you see trouble coming, you'll walk away from it."

"I'll do more than promise," I said. "I swear it."

"A promise is enough," he said, and he smiled, patted my shoulder, leant his back against the warm wall of the garden, closed his eyes and let the sun shine on his face.

29

Spike sent me a postcard. It arrived in the morning of a late August day. He didn't tell me where he was staying, but the picture was of a Welsh mountain, and the postmark read "Porthmadog". He wrote:

EL. I TOLD YOU THAT I WOUD COME TO WALES AND HER I AM. BET YOU DIDNT BELIEVE ME BUT I GOT A JOB IN A FOREST AND CUTTING TREES WITH A CHAINSAW. ITS FUCKED. I COME BACK FOR SOME STUFF NEXT MUNTH AND SEE YOU THEN. SPIKE.

I imagined him sitting in a room somewhere, licking the end of a pencil, staring at the back of the card, staring out of the window and then staring at the card again. Wondering if he would ever see Somerset again, or if Wales would be home for the rest of his life. I missed him, missed his stupid laugh and the way his hair stuck up like a mistake. And, if I took myself to one side and had a quiet whisper in my own ear, I missed the idea that he could be round the corner, ready to lead me into trouble or adventure or just a simple mess.

I read the card again. "I come back for some stuff next munth…" But what stuff did he have left? A comb he'd left at his sister's place? A baccy tin on a shelf somewhere? A hat on a hook at the blackberry farm? I didn't know. I turned the card over and looked at the picture. There were sheep on the side of the mountain. They looked cold, wet and hungry. How long before Spike decided it would be a good idea to steal them and sell them to a butcher from Birmingham? A couple of weeks? I didn't want to think about it.

I tucked the card into the corner of the mirror that hung by my bedroom door and went downstairs. Dad and I were going to work in a garden on the road to Staple Cross. He'd decided that I'd done enough sitting on boxes and walls, and it was time for me to start working again. And maybe, if I had any sense about me, I could learn something about gardening and work with him every day. "Maybe," I said. "That's what I said," he said.

So we made some sandwiches, filled a thermos, climbed into the pick-up and drove out of the village, up the lane towards Heniton Hill, past the place where Spike had found the smoke, and along Burrow Lane. The pick-up was in a worse state than ever, and as we drove, the suspension made a noise that sounded like cats fighting a steel bird.

The garden was on a ridge above the place where the mad Professor had lived, and we went to work in a huge shrubbery. I didn't know what the bushes were called, but they were leafy, wiry and covered in papery flowers. The old dear who owned the place wanted us to weed the bed, clear out some dead wood and trim the edges. Which is what we did.

We'd been working for a couple of hours, whistling and humming and sometimes being quiet when Dad went to his bag, pulled out the thermos, and we sat on a wall to drink a cup of coffee. The air was heavy and close, and as it moved, it grew thick with something we hadn't felt for months. If this thing could have been a colour, it would have been purple, and if it had been a taste it would have been silver. The noise would have been the moaning chimes of bells sunk beneath the sea, but there was no noise. Not at first, anyway. Not for the first half-hour. But then, like a day dawning in a day that had already dawned, it started.

It was slow to begin with, a dark smudge above the distant western moors. A line like a child might crayon across a wall, fine at first, then smeared down and down towards the floor. It was slow and it was spreading, and then it grew and began to loom, and a whistling breeze blew through the bushes.

Dad nudged me, pointed and said, "Is that rain?"

"No," I said.

"It is," he said.

"No way," I said. "It's smoke." But I was wrong.

We'd been working for about ten minutes when the first drops came. At first they were small and fine, blown like seeds against a window. And then, as the sky darkened and the clouds bloomed, a roll of thunder barrelled across the land from the moors.

"Yes!" he said. "It's bloody rain!" And a minute later the skies opened like a cracked egg, and the world filled with water.

The drops were fat and warm, and I tipped my head back and let them fall on my face. Dad did the same, running his hands through his hair and around the back of his neck and under his chin. And as the rain fell, the land gave off a scent I hadn't smelt for months, a sweet and generous scent that filled the air. Fresh and flowered and earthy, and full of promise. Another clap of thunder rolled towards us, and as it did, birds began to sing. They sang from the trees and bushes, and they sang from the roof of the house, and the telephone wires that stretched across the garden. They didn't mind the rain, and nor did we, and although we were soaked to the skin after five minutes, we stayed outside and watched as puddles appeared in the lawn, and little streams of water began to run over the grass, through the shrubbery and into the fields beyond.

The old dear came from the house, stood on the veranda and called for us to come in, but Dad shouted, "We're enjoying it!"

She laughed, and I laughed, and Dad laughed, and she shook her head and stood and watched as more thunder rolled over from the west, and the rain settled in.

It was still raining when we drove home, and it was still raining when we sat down to eat our tea, and when it was time to visit Sam, it was still raining. I took the road slowly, and avoided the worst of the floods that had appeared around the blocked storm drains. When I arrived at the hospital, there was a vaguely crazed atmosphere in the air, as if everyone had been told good news and they had to go for a large drink. Some nurses were gathered around the entrance, smoking cigarettes and laughing, and some patients were at the windows, pointing and staring as the gutters overflowed and the clouds flew by.

Sam was one of those patients. She was sitting on the window sill as the rain poured down the glass, drinking a cup of tea and smiling at the sky. "Amazing!" she said. "I thought it would never happen."

"I know. Dad and I were working up near Staple Cross. It was so quick. The clouds came in over the moors. It was like the world was ending."

"It must have been incredible."

"It was. We got soaked, but we didn't care."

"I want to be out in it."

"You will be," I said, and I kissed her and she put her arm around my waist, and we stood and watched and listened as a squall whipped around the hospital and chucked the rain like a doll. And when a nurse came and asked her if she'd like shepherd's pie for tea, she laughed and said she wanted the biggest helping of shepherd's pie in the hospital, and a bowl of apple crumble with custard. And as I watched her laugh, and the nurse laughed and said something about diets, for the first time in months I felt trouble fade, and the clouds that lowered over Taunton lifted the clouds from my head and folded them into a parcel of smoke and whispers.

30

Landscapes print themselves on people's minds. They start slowly and push themselves in gently, and they never stop. They become part of someone, like an arm or hair or an eye or a finger. Remove some people from a landscape, and they hurt as much as if you'd cut off their nose. Take the same people back to their landscape after they've been away for a while, and they fall in love and heal themselves of trouble and pain. I worked this out for myself after reading too many copies of the *National Geographic* magazine and watching too many documentaries on the telly. The landscape could be a Mongolian steppe, a housing estate in Leicester, an Arizona desert, an African jungle, a Cambodian jungle or the skyline of New York – it doesn't matter where it is, but the place will have the same effect. The bowled hills and river valleys of the border country in the west of England are my landscape, and when I wake up in the morning and look out at the fields and woods and hedges, I know I am looking at the frame of my heart.

On the first real day of autumn, while the wind blew from the west and the trees bent with it, the nurses took the last bandages off Sam's head. She had a scar on her brow, but they said it would heal, and by the end of the year she'd be as good as new. "She's a lucky woman," a doctor said to me. "It could have been far worse."

"It was bad enough," I said.

"That's true," he said.

She was discharged a couple of days later. I sat with her in the back of the hospital car and held her hand, and she smiled all the way back to Ashbrittle. When we reached the top of the hill, she asked the driver to stop and let us out, and we walked the rest of the way.

There was drizzle in the air, a wish of rain that drifted and spun around us, and filmed on our faces. We strolled across the village green and through the churchyard, and stopped at the yew. We stepped into its divided trunks, and stood there and put our arms around each other. The power was gentle and strong, and as we held each other, I felt it in my legs like little shocks of electricity. I stood still, and she trembled. "Feel it?" I said, and she nodded. "Yes," she whispered, "I think I do," and the tree quivered over us and fed us with its memories, its echoes and all the things it had seen.

I thought about telling her some of the old stories about the tree, of the singing children and their ribbons, of the slaughtered men and the laughing gods. But I didn't. Instead, I said, "When you were really ill, Mum taught me a charm. She thought it might help you get better."

"What was it?"

"I had to bury a piece of apple in front of your house."

"Why?"

"Because she told me to."

"And did you?"

"Of course I did." I said. "I always do as she says."

We walked on around the corner from the churchyard and stood in front of Pump Court. I pointed at the little triangle of ground. "I buried it there."

She stared at the spot and took my arm. "Thank you, Elliot." she said. "Thank you for your charm."

"I wanted to do more, but I'm not a doctor."

"You did all you could."

She went to the front door of her cottage, and I followed her inside. The others were out, and as we sat in the kitchen with a cup of tea and some biscuits, she said, "So what are we going to do now?"

"I don't know. What would you like to do?"

"I've got an idea."

"Are you going to tell me?"

"Of course."

"Go on then."

"You want to go upstairs?"

"Yes," I said, and that's what we did.

Her room was at the front of the house, with a sloping ceiling, crooked pictures on the walls and a high brass bed. There were old rugs on the floor, and the smell of something sweet in the air. She kicked her shoes off, lay on the bed, patted the covers and said, "Come on." And as I lay down beside her, she took a book from the bedside table and passed it to me. I opened it and looked at the first page. It was called *Isabel's Skin*.

"Some of it's set in Ashbrittle," she said.

"Is it?"

"Yeah. It's about that mad scientist who kidnapped a woman and did crazy stuff to her skin."

"Someone told me there was a book about that." I turned the pages. They smelt of damp, and as I turned them they sounded like leaves cracking under dry shoes. "His name was Professor Hunt."

"That's the one," she said. "Some of it reminds me of us."

"What do you mean?"

"Read it. You'll see." She reached over and touched the page I was looking at. "You could read to me. If you want."

"Read to you?"

"Yes."

"Now?"

"If you want."

I didn't know if I could, but I said, "OK," and she folded her arms, rested her head back and closed her eyes.

"Which bit?"

"Any," she said, her eyes still closed.

"OK. Shall I start at the beginning?"

"Good plan," she said, so I did.

I liked the feeling behind the words I read. They were about losing something precious and finding it again, and I wanted to tell her that they were the things I felt. The emotion and the loss, the finding and the love. One of the sentences read: "I was not lost when I found you, but I had no idea where I was." I wanted to say these words to her again, wanted to watch her as she listened, but she was asleep. So I put the book back on the table beside the bed, leant over her face and kissed the top of her head.

I lay back and I thought. I suppose I could have thought that I used to have a job working for a dairy farmer but managed to screw it up by refusing to tell my best friend to go fuck himself. Or I could have thought that birds are fat raindrops and pigs are the pink shadows of our souls, let loose in a world of trouble we have wished upon ourselves. Or I could have thought that next week I would pack a bag and walk away from Ashbrittle, and find a job in a place where no one knew me and the sun shone on people who failed. But I didn't. I kissed Sam's head again, touched the scar on her head and said, "Hello." She didn't wake up.

I sat up and looked outside. Beyond the bedroom window, the sun was bleeding though the clouds, and a blackbird was singing from a tree. He had the sweetest song, flutes in honey and water, angels in their houses, the promise of a warm evening. I looked beyond him, over the hedges and trees, and down the lane towards the village green. The world was full and ripe, a huge apple on a branch. I saw my dad come from our house. He stood in front of the pick-up and shook his head. There was something wrong with the carburettor, and he was going to try and fix it. Then I saw a dog, a scruffy thing that liked to chase leaves. It was called Rusty and only had one eye. It lived with some people who owned a cottage on the far side of the green. It barked at a pigeon, then lay down in the middle of the road. Another pigeon flew past, and a crow. A pigeon followed by a crow meant something, and it meant something important, but I couldn't remember what. So I let the moment pass, and turned over and lay back, and let the sound of Sam's dozing snuffles wash through the watery afternoon.

Peter Benson's new novel
OUT IN AUGUST 2012

David Morris lives the quiet life of a book-valuer for a London auction house, travelling every day by omnibus to his office in the Strand. When he is asked to make a trip to rural Somerset to value the library of the recently deceased Lord Buff-Orpington, the sense of trepidation he feels as he heads into the country is confirmed the moment he reaches his destination, the dark and impoverished village of Ashbrittle. These feelings turn to dread when he meets the enigmatic Professor Richard Hunt and catches a glimpse of a screaming woman he keeps prisoner in his house.

Peter Benson's new novel is a slick gothic tale in the English tradition, a murder mystery, a reflection on the works of the masters of the French Enlightenment and a tour of Edwardian England. More than this, it is a work of atmosphere and unease which creates a world of inhuman anxiety and suspense.

978-1-84688-206-7 • 250 pp. • £14.99

Also available by Peter Benson

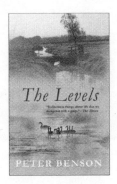

Winner of the Encore Award, a trenchant critique of modern civilization, describing how one family's tropical heaven becomes hell.

978-1-84688-192-3
176 pp. • £7.99

Winner of the *Guardian* Fiction Prize, a lyrical portrait of the landscape of the Somerset Levels and a touching evocation of first love.

978-1-84688-191-6
176 pp. • £7.99

Weaving in the dramatic events portrayed by the Bayeux Tapestry, an absorbing novel which brings to life a fascinating period of English history.

978-1-84688-194-7
172 pp. • £7.99

Winner of the Somerset Maugham Award, a novel exploring the evolution of an unlikely relationship, in a beautiful countryside setting.

978-1-84688-193-0
176 pp. • £7.99

The gripping tale of a quiet and solitary private detective whose uneventful life world spirals into a circle of chaos and death.

978-1-84688-196-1
230 pp. • £7.99

A compelling tale of surfing and coming of age, and an intense examination of a young man's struggle to establish his identity.

978-1-84688-195-4
224 pp. • £7.99

A beguiling and poignant novel about the fulfilment of dreams, the affirmation of life and finding love in unexpected places.

978-1-84688-197-8
202 pp. • £7.99